CANDLELIGHT
Supreme

"I HOPE YOU DON'T ENTERTAIN ANY HOPES OF MY BEING YOUR LOVER," PAN MURMURED.

Silver studied the look she gave him. Gutsy little brat! "That is disappointing, because that was my intention. You must know that I desire you, that I want you. Why else would I invite you up here and take care of you?"

"An everlasting font of human compassion?"

"I've been known to give to charity, but at this point I'm thinking more along the lines of striking a bargain with you, a business proposition, if you like."

"Which is?" Pan asked icily.

"That we live together . . . here, at my apartment. If after four weeks we don't suit each other, we split, with you getting a cash settlement and introductions to top people who could give you a job modeling. If we do suit, then we become lovers for as long as we choose."

CANDLELIGHT SUPREMES

SILVER LOVE

Hayton Monteith

A CANDLELIGHT SUPREME

Published by
Dell Publishing Co., Inc.
1 Dag Hammarskjold Plaza
New York, New York 10017

Dell ® TM 681510, Dell Publishing Co., Inc.

Candlelight Supreme is a trademark
of Dell Publishing Co., Inc.

Candlelight Ecstasy Romance®, 1,203,540, is a registered trademark of Dell Publishing Co., Inc.

ISBN: 0-440-17899-1

Printed in the United States of America

March 1987

10 9 8 7 6 5 4 3 2 1

WFH

To Our Readers:

We are pleased and excited by your overwhelmingly positive response to our Candlelight Supremes. Unlike all the other series, the Supremes are filled with more passion, adventure, and intrigue, and are obviously the stories you like best.

In months to come we will continue to publish books by many of your favorite authors as well as the very finest work from new authors of romantic fiction. As always, we are striving to present unique, absorbing love stories —the very best love has to offer.

Breathtaking and unforgettable, Supremes follow in the great romantic tradition you've come to expect *only* from Candlelight Romances.

Your suggestions and comments are always welcome. Please let us hear from you.

Sincerely,

The Editors
Candlelight Romances
1 Dag Hammarskjold Plaza
New York, New York 10017

SILVER LOVE

CHAPTER ONE

Sterling Galen III, nicknamed Silver by his father to avoid the confusion that can occur with more than one person in a family bearing the same name, had come into the cafeteria for a cup of coffee only because it was in the same building as his doctor's office.

Silver had stayed for three cups because he had become fascinated with the antics of a most unusual young woman. In fact, he had been watching her since she came into the restaurant, as she looked over the food, sat at first one table, then another, then finally approached the food again.

Despite being on the too-slender side, she was quite beautiful, with the most lovely coloring. Silver didn't think he'd ever seen anyone with just that shade of deep red hair who had the violet eyes that this creature had. The eyes should have been green or the hair should have been brunette. The red hair–violet eyes combination was outrageous, out of sync . . . and stunning. Her hands were graceful, her mouth piquant and inviting, the lower lip full and kissable, the upper one a tender curve. He felt a stirring of desire, as he always did at seeing a very attractive woman, and continued to watch her antics.

Silver had been wrestling his own bête noir after having seen the doctor and been told that it would be another three months before his face would be ready for another repairing operation. Automatically his fingers touched the puckering tissue on the right side of his face. The smooth roughness was a familiar sensation.

The accident that had burned and scarred him had occurred over two years ago, and he'd learned to live with the surprised, sometimes horrified, often compassionate and curious gazes of passersby. He'd also been left with a limp from the multiple breaks in his right leg, but this, too, had improved each day, so that he had done without his crutches, then discarded his cane. According to his physicians, the limp would disappear altogether.

Silver barely noticed the face in his mirror, mostly because of the good prognosis put forth by the experts who'd tended him and told him that he would be back to normal very soon.

All his life he'd been Silver, the boy with everything—looks, money, power and the ability to do what he liked best . . . be a professional race car driver.

He'd enjoyed it all—the groupies, the parties, the fast lane, the high life of racing—almost as much as the driving, and when it ended he had been surprised that he hadn't missed the hoopla as much as he thought he would.

There had been a social void for a while of his own choosing, but soon he had begun to see some old friends, dine with women, who seemed eager for his company and not bothered by his scarred face.

At first Silver came into Manhattan every day from a home he owned on Long Island, to work at the corporate headquarters of Galen Enterprises. It was the parent corporation that housed the engineering and business center of Galen Motors and Galen Electronics. Shortly after Silver had become the CEO of Galen Enterprises upon his father's retirement, he had moved permanently into the apartment that was attached to his office on the penthouse level of the Galen Building.

It had surprised Silver how rapidly the work absorbed his interests and how, though there were times when he missed racing, satisfied he was with his life.

Still there had been times when he was down, like now, just after visiting the plastic surgeon who was treating him. The end result was going to be a rebuilt face, tissue and bones, which would make him look very nearly like himself, but in the meantime he had to be patient, and that wasn't Silver's strong suit. He was a man of action, used to doing things, not just talking about the nebulous future, as the doctors were able to do with impunity.

His irritated musings were interrupted when he noticed the very slender young woman getting onto the beverage line. She took a large foam container and filled it with boiling water, then put napkins and a soup spoon on her tray. Then she looked around until she found a table that suited her, in a corner, before slipping a plate with two rolls and four pats of butter onto her tray.

Balancing carefully, she made her way to the table and seated herself, unfolding a paper napkin and placing it in her lap and putting another under her chin.

Lazily Silver watched as she shook ketchup into the cup, stirred it, put two pats of butter on top, then shook pepper liberally over her concoction.

He could feel the smile drifting across his face as she leaned over and sipped the very full cup, her eyebrows raising, her mouth twisting. No one could say she wasn't innovative. Humor rose in him like a tide, and he had to struggle not to laugh out loud.

Gamely the shapely female drank her mixture, interspersing it with bites of roll and butter and sips of ice water. More than once she paused to shiver and dab at her mouth with a napkin. Mystery lady was reaching for the second of the rolls sitting on her plate when an attendant in the Automat-type restaurant came up to her and snatched the plate away.

Silver couldn't tell what the worker was saying, but he could tell that an argument was ensuing. Though it was in low tones, he was pretty sure the girl had just been told she wasn't allowed to take the rolls unless she ordered an entrée.

The attendant became red-faced and began gesticulating and pointing over his shoulder. All at once he stalked away, a purposeful look on his face.

The young woman stood at once and looked around her, grabbed her coat and purse and darted through the maze of tables to a corridor leading to the rest rooms.

Silver smiled ruefully to himself, shaking his head, more than a little disappointed that the tableau had ended.

He threw some money on the table and rose to his feet, deciding to visit the men's room before he left the restaurant. After all, he had drunk three coffees while he watched the slender girl's performance.

He was standing in front of the urinal when he happened to catch a movement in the mirror in front of him. Silver focused on the third cubicle but saw no feet. Then a head appeared over the door.

"Pardon me. I don't mean to intrude. In fact, I don't usually come into men's rooms." The head disappeared.

Silver felt like laughing as he rezipped his trousers. "No? I imagine that's a comfort to quite a few people. Are you coming out of there?"

"Are you through?"

"Yes, ma'am."

The cubicle door opened, and the wraithlike girl with the violet eyes and red hair uncoiled herself from her vantage point on the toilet seat. She came out to stand next to him at the sink and wash her hands in imitation of what he was doing. "I think the manager wants to speak to me, and I don't have money to pay for the rolls. I didn't think he'd look for me in here, but he might have sent a waitress to look for me in the ladies' room."

"Astute of you." Silver noticed she glanced once at his face in frank and clinical scrutiny, then seemed to forget about it. He heard the door begin to open behind him and crossed the room to push it shut again. "Be right out. Cleaning in here." He noticed the knitted cap sticking out of the pocket of the girl's coat. "Put that on and we'll get out of here." He couldn't help but notice the shaky sigh of relief that escaped her.

"Hey, mac, what's the holdup? I gotta use the head." The querulous voice reached them from the other side of the door.

"Let's go." Silver took her arm, pulled the hat down low on her forehead and pushed past the waiting man.

"We can't go out the front door. They'll see us," she told him, bracing herself to meet the angry restaurant manager. Silver, who was a great deal stronger than he looked, pulled her along beside him down the corridor to the main part of the restaurant.

As though he had all the time in the world, he helped her on with her coat and directed her toward the door to the street. "Wait in the vestibule; I'll be right with you." Silver stared down at her. "Don't run off."

"I've no pressing engagement." She stared back at him.

Silver still kept an eye on her as he paid for the rolls and informed the manager that he wanted to hear no

13

more about the incident. The man looked at the twenty-dollar bill and nodded, mollified.

Silver rejoined her, and they stepped through the door to the street. He noticed she began shivering. "Why don't you wear a warmer coat? This is New York at the end of February. Spring doesn't come until April, if then."

She glared up at him. "This is my only coat. If you intend to lecture me, I'll be on my way."

"No. Come with me." Whistling, he hailed a taxi and bundled her into it, noting how she huddled down into her coat at the sudden warmth. "Galen Building, Park Avenue."

"That will be a long walk for me," the girl mumbled into her coat.

"What's your name?"

"Pan Belmont."

"Pan? Good Lord, I might have known you'd be from Greek mythology. In disguise?" Silver laughed.

"Very amusing. *Pan* is a shortening of Patricia and Ann."

"And I'm Sterling Galen III and have been called Silver since I was a boy."

"How colorful," Pan began flatly. Then recognition flashed across her face. "You're the race driver who crashed a couple of years ago. I thought you were dead."

"Comforting."

"You did have an awful crash, and I guess I never read any more about it." Pan turned on the seat to face him. "When I was in college I studied nursing for a while and I worked as an aide in a burn center. From what little I know, I'd say you're on the mend."

Silver felt a jolt at her noncommittal tone. He was used to sympathy and encouragement, not cool indifference. Pan annoyed him. "I am, but not as fast as I'd like."

"Don't spit at destiny, Mr. Galen. It has a habit of spitting back. And after all, you can see the light at the end of the tunnel." When the car pulled over to the curb, Pan looked out the window at the tall glass-and-steel structure that had the appearance of a modern pyramid and glistened in the sunlight. "I think we've arrived at the Emerald City, Silver Man." She looked back at him. "Thanks for paying my bill at the restaurant." Pan put out her hand.

"We won't say good-bye yet." Despite his irritation with her, she intrigued him. "I might have a job for you."

"What?"

It pleased Silver that he had shaken her from that aloof aplomb of hers and hooked her interest. "Yes. We'll go up to my office and talk about it." He urged her out of the cab.

Pan tried to free herself from the grip on her elbow but she couldn't as he hustled her across the sidewalk and through the huge glass doors with *Galen* scrolled in gold across them. "If this is a white slavery deal you have cooking, count me out. I'm into modeling, not mattress aerobics."

"Thank you. I needed that." Silver felt like telling her to get lost, but he couldn't deny the tingling awareness he'd felt since meeting up with her.

The doorman nodded to the boss, barely concealing his curiosity about the woman he had in tow. The boss usually had a spectacular creature on his arm, even with the mess his face was after the crash at Indy. His tastes had never run to street urchins.

Silver went right to his private elevator, which sped them up to the penthouse office and adjoining apartment that he used.

"Nice," Pan commented when she stepped into the

15

cherry-paneled office with the floor-to-ceiling windows that gave a magnificent panoramic view of the city.

"Thank you." Silver went to the phone, ordering food and drinks sent to his office, then taking directives and messages from his secretary. "Fine, Olive. I'll do that. See if you can switch and cancel the rest of my day. No, I'm fine. I just have some personal business to handle. Yes, I'll be here for the next hour or so. Thank you."

Pan didn't watch him as he talked. Instead she prowled the office, looking at the original paintings on the walls, knowing that the Sargent and the Monet would cost the earth on the open market. She put her thoughts on shut-down, not considering her future or past, letting her mind dwell only on what was in front of her eyes: the dust rising around the cowboy as he slouched in his saddle in the Sargent, the soul-wrenching kaleidoscope of colors in the Monet.

"You have an interest in art?" Silver studied the back of her head, the red hair crackling around her head, the curliness of it heavy and tousled. His hands itched to touch it.

"Who wouldn't like Sargent and Monet . . . and I do like the mélange of moods created by the two works, one so real, the other so surreal. Marvelous effect. You had a wonderful decorator."

"Thank you." Again she'd nicked him with that sharp tongue, assuming that it was a decorator and not he who'd chosen the masterpieces. "Shall we sit down?" Silver indicated the twin couches covered in blue silk that sat at right angles to the fireplace.

Pan was a little taken aback when he sat down next to her, but just then someone knocked at the door and brought in a trolley laden with food, with another attendant carrying a silver coffee service and another a tray of wine. In minutes the glass coffee table between the couches was laden with food: salads, soups, tiny sandwiches, fruit.

Pan salivated, not even noticing when the three attendants withdrew, watching as Silver offered her soup in a fine china bowl.

"No doubt this won't replace the lovely tomato soup you were making at the restaurant, but you might try it. It's clam chowder."

Pan nodded. "Necessity is the mother of invention, and I needed to eat." She spooned the hot soup into her mouth, making low, satisfied sounds in her throat. Finishing two bowls whetted her appetite for the fruit, and she peeled a banana, offering some to Silver. It shook her a little when he took a bite, but she finished the rest. Then she tackled the apples and cheese and drank a large glass of milk.

At last she sat back on the couch, sighing. "That was so delicious." Pan turned to face him as he sat next to her on the couch. "But I hope you don't entertain any hopes of me being your lover. No deal."

Silver studied the chin-up look she gave him, her eyes not wavering. Gutsy little brat! "That is disappointing, because that was my intention." It pleased him when her color faded a trifle, but that was the only manifestation of faltering. "You're sure you wouldn't like to forget the preliminaries and go right to bed?"

"I'm sure." Her voice was steady. Why in blazes had she come to his office with him? And more to the point, why did his eyes look like hot lava at the moment? He was acting as though she had insulted him, instead of the reverse!

Despite the facial scarring, Pan would have bet her nonexistent next paycheck that he didn't have trouble attracting females. The damned silver stud probably had a stable of women. He was a hot, sensuous article and he knew it. Her eyes roved from the windblown style of his wavy black hair, over his very expensive Savile Row business suit, down to his Gucci shoes. He was a prime piece of male goods and he damn well knew it!

Silver watched her eyes and how her thoughts changed their color from violet to lavender and then to the deep emotion of purple. They fascinated him, just like the rest of her. "I don't go in for rape, lady, or any other kind of violence unless I'm threatened."

"I should hope not, because if you tried to force me I'd do my damnedest to emasculate you with a drop-kick," Pan told him in the same colorless tone.

"We've certainly cleared the air on that point. Forewarned is forearmed."

"True."

"Am I dealing with a black belt?"

"I trained at a police academy for a time. I learned a few things." No need to tell him that when they told her there would be a regulation FBI check, she'd washed herself out of trying for the security job.

"You seem to be a Jill of all trades—model, cop, soup maker . . ." Silver enjoyed jabbing at her. She was so cool, so assured.

But Silver was growing more intrigued by the moment, and that irked him almost as much as her attitude did. Instead of his interest waning, it became more and more piqued. "So I guess we're clear on the point of rape. We both despise it." He lifted his hand from the back of the couch and touched the tips of the tousled red locks. "Your hair is incredible."

"Too thick . . . and curly. It has a mind of its own." Pan was glad of the change of topic. She had the feeling if he probed too much, asked too many provocative questions, she would tell him too much. The man was actually magnetic. Pan had the feeling that her blood had begun to run backward in her veins in response to him; that if he chose he could pull any information he wanted from her by magnetic osmosis.

"No. It's perfect." Silver touched her nape with gentle fingers and felt the slight flinch, quickly controlled. He removed his hand from her skin. "As long as we're being blunt about how we feel and what we want, I think we should talk more about this, delve a little deeper."

Had he read her mind? "Were we doing that?"

"Oh, I think so." Silver's smile twisted, seeing her eyes turn a frosty lavender as though to shut him out, pull back from him. "You must know that I desire you, that I want you. Why else would I invite you up here and take care of you?"

"An everlasting fount of human compassion?" Pan arched one brow, her voice matching his in caustic silkiness.

"I've been known to give to charity, but at this point I'm thinking more along the lines of striking a bargain with you—a business proposition, if you like."

"Which is?" Pan asked icily, feeling as though her teeth would never unclench. Somehow she managed to keep her voice level.

"That we live together . . . here, at my apartment. If after four weeks we don't suit each other, we split, with you getting a cash settlement and introductions to top people who could give you a job modeling. If we do suit, we become lovers for as long as we choose."

She blinked, feeling a wrenching qualm. "Does this bargain include my right of refusal to any and all sexual advances until I'm ready, if ever, during the four-week trial period?"

"It does."

"How much?" Pan felt caught between an abyss and salvation, knowing the gamble she was taking, but realizing that she had little choice but to take the desperate leap.

"Meaning the settlement, of course. Let's say fifty thousand."

"Make it a hundred and you have a deal." Pan rushed her words, bracing herself for a scathing denunciation but determined to hold the line.

"Fifty sounds fair enough to me."

"A hundred sounds better." Pan held her breath.

"Seventy-five and it's a deal."

"Done." Pan exhaled.

Silver put out his hand.

Pan was about to put her hand in his when she drew back.

"What's wrong? Have you thought of a codicil to our agreement?"

"Four weeks, you said?" She didn't miss his deep sarcasm, the unamused glitter in his navy blue eyes.

"Right."

"Done."

Silver had to school his features to prevent the frisson of sensation that went through him when she clasped his hand. Her bones were fragile, the skin soft, but the grip was firm. A very charming, wily sprite come to earth! "Today would suit you? For moving in here, I mean?" He noticed her barely perceptible indrawn breath.

"Yes, but what you see is what you get. My landlord is keeping the rest of my clothes until I pay him my back rent."

Silver turned and pressed a button on the console. "Ladder, get in here."

A tall man entered the room, his spare body bowed slightly, as though he had always compensated for his great height by stooping. Silver rose to his feet, greeting him with a smile.

Pan knew that Silver must be six feet three or four, and the man called Ladder towered over him.

Ladder nodded when introduced to Pan as Ladder Bateman, and nodded again when Silver gave him instructions and Pan gave him her address. "I'll take care of it. Any of the furnishings yours?"

"Just the clothing, the portfolio and the box of dishes on the kitchen table. Would you be careful of those things?"

"Yup. See you later."

When the door closed behind Bateman, Pan felt a chill of cold perspiration under her arms, but she gritted her teeth. She was doing the right thing for . . . both of them. "He's an unusual man."

"Yes. We met in Vietnam at a battalion aid station and we've been friends since. His title is special assistant to the CEO."

"Impressive," Pan muttered, her mind racing with the ramifications of her actions that she'd brought on herself all in the space of an hour. Developing insanity should have taken longer than that.

"Would you like to see where you'll be living?"

Pan jumped to her feet, nodding. She was suddenly very restless. "Fine."

"Just a moment. I have a call to make, then we'll explore." Silver leaned forward and pushed one of the buttons on the table console. "Olive, get me Charine on the phone, please." He watched Pan as she began prowling the room again, pretty sure she was struggling to keep her equanimity, though her facade was cool and controlled. She neither questioned who he was calling nor evinced curiosity in anything else. For the moment he had the sensation that she'd melted away from him, that she was rising from the floor to the ceiling, aloof from all else.

The buzzer sounded, and he picked up the phone. "How are you, Charine? Yes. Of course, you're a very sharp lady. Size seven or eight, I'd say. Tall. Five nine and a half . . ."

"Five feet ten." Pan faced him when he repeated the numbers over the phone, noting the warmth in his voice as he talked a little longer before breaking the connection. "I've heard of Charine. She's a top American designer."

"Of French origin, but yes, she's been in this country for many years. As I understand it, she was a pin girl for the great Coco Chanel."

"You know her well." It wasn't a question.

"Yes. Shall we look at the apartment?"

"Yes. And you know your women's sizes well, too. I do wear a size seven."

"You should wear a nine, at least, for your height."

Pan shrugged. "Models should be slender. Besides, I'm up a size from what I was."

"You wore a size five!" Silver tried to mask his surprise as he looked her over from head to foot. "You must have been emaciated."

"Changing your mind?"

Again her chin came up and she faced him, legs slightly apart, hands hanging loosely at her sides, her expression calm, waiting. Silver was both fascinated and repelled by her peculiar sangfroid. It was as though she

22

had practiced and rehearsed the trip to the guillotine and, through her experiences, her fatalism had been honed to a fine edge.

"No. Are you?"

"A bargain is a bargain."

"So they tell me." Silver took her arm and steered her across the large office to a recessed doorway in a library wall, the books that framed it revealing the catholic tastes of the owner, ranging from Twain to Goethe, Racine to Shakespeare.

Pan didn't look at the room they entered but rather up at her host. "Would you mind if I borrowed from your library now and then?"

"You're welcome to read anything you choose, whenever you choose." He lifted his eyes from hers, irritated by the slight breathlessness he felt. The sensation of dangling from Pan's string like a puppet was singularly unpalatable. Silver wanted this relationship but he wanted it on his terms, and he was determined that the stirrings of desire would not blind the commonsense outlook that he was determined to maintain where she was concerned. His feelings for her were running higher and faster by the moment, but he would keep a tight rein on that too. "By the way, you look like a fledgling girl, despite your coolness and presence of mind."

"I'm twenty-four and I'm not a virgin . . . and I did notice your palpable relief."

"Sharp lady, aren't you?"

"Sometimes." Pan let her gaze drift around the apartment, her pleasure in the huge dining room, living room combined with stone fireplace in between and kitchen separated by a bar increasing as her gaze lit upon the warmth of cherry paneling offset by the turquoise drapes and twin couches on either side of the fire. "It's very spacious, and I like the balcony off the bedroom."

"So do I. The one upstairs is mine. Your room is over here." Silver led her to double doors on the far wall, throwing them open so that she could see into the silver-and-pink interior. He was proud of the second bedroom, not just because of its spaciousness, its huge round bed with silver spread and throw pillows, but because of the huge silver bathroom with hot tub, sauna, steam room and exercise center. The furniture was silvered oak, and one wall was a huge closet and storage area. Though slightly smaller than his bedroom, it was almost the twin in amenities.

It jolted him when Pan began to chuckle. His head whipped her way as her mirth increased, turning to laughter. "You don't like it?" Silver faced her, stiff-lipped.

Pan shook her head, her body quivering with amusement. "Oh, it's so funny. You're a comedian. Right?" She faced him, tears sliding down her face, her breath coming raggedly as she laughed harder.

"I hadn't thought so." Her amusement penetrated his irritation. He was caught between wanting to join her and desiring to wring her neck. "Don't choke on your mirth."

"This room is a howl." Her voice dropped several decibels. "Silver Galen in his Silver Seduction Room. Lord, I love it. Definitely the title of a Victorian novel . . . or better yet, you could call it the Silver Harem. Mind boggling."

Her laughter crawled over his skin like a goose-bumping caress. Although she annoyed the hell out of him, his desire for her had increased, not lessened. No woman he'd ever brought into the room had reacted in such a

24

way, but as he looked around it, seeing it with her eyes, he could feel his lips twitch. "I have always liked the color scheme in here."

"So do I, but you must admit you've overdrawn the sensual aspects when you have a room designed after your name." Pan dabbed at her eyes with a wrinkled tissue she'd pulled from the pocket of her jacket.

Silver stared at her. "I like the hues, and I gave the decorator a list of the color schemes I liked. She came up with this, and I'm very comfortable with it."

Pan shot him a quick look. "And you're very irked with me that I didn't swoon over your Passion Pit. Right?"

"You don't pull any punches, lady." For a moment he thought he saw a flash of pain in her eyes. Then that chin came up even further. He saw the fragile bones of her hands distend as she clenched them and the slight sway of her body as though she'd braced herself for a blow. Silver glanced around the room again before his eyes came back to her. "A body blow to my ego, yes, but I have to tell you that I'm glad you're straightforward. If we decide to share this room we'll have it redone, Pan."

"We will?" Pan hadn't expected that. "Actually I like the color scheme," she finished weakly.

"So do I." Impulsively he leaned down and kissed her nose, noticing how her eyes widened, though she was as still as a statue. "I can see that you'll keep me on my toes."

"Do my best," Pan said breathlessly, a tingling running from her head to her toes. She would have said that it must have come from skipping meals, except that she'd just dined sumptuously.

"Now we'll look at my room." Silver slipped an arm around her waist after they left the room and returned to

25

the great room to ascend the open stairway to the second level of the apartment. It struck him that if he chose he could have counted her ribs with his fingers, though her waist didn't seem all that slender.

The upstairs room was in beige and cream, accented with rose and black pillows and bedspread. There was a sitting room open to the bedroom, with a television, couch and chairs and a large expanse of windows.

"How do you like this one?"

Pan's smile trembled over her face. "It's very nice. Thank you for showing it to me . . . and I did like the other one. It's just that I have this absurd sense of humor." She took a deep breath. "I shouldn't have said—"

Silver pressed his forefinger against her lips. "Don't say that. If something is to build between us, we should be open with each other."

"But not blunt," Pan finished, her lips moving against his finger.

"That feels very good."

"You're easily pleased."

Silver shook his head. "No. I'm not. And that's something you'll find out about me. Are you easily pleased?"

"About some things I am. I don't care what kind of pasta you give me. I love it all. I don't care what type of beef you give me. I dislike all kinds. Does that help any?"

"Not really. You seem to be open, but in truth you're a very enigmatic woman. Aren't you?"

"Maybe."

Silver watched the impish smile flit across her features and he bent to kiss her, as surprised as she was by his action.

When she didn't push him away, the kiss deepened and he slanted his mouth across hers, but when he would have thrust his tongue between her lips, she jerked her head back, though her body remained in place. "I don't think that's for nodding acquaintances, do you?"

Silver clasped her loosely at the waist. "Oh, I don't know. It's rather friendly, I think."

"You're very sardonic, as though you sat among the clouds in judgment on the rest of us." Her voice changed again, this time to a rough Cockney. "You're a right proper member of the gentry, ain't ya, guv." Pan could feel Silver's fingers dig into her flesh, even though his face remained expressionless.

"Very good. Did you ever do repertory in London?"

"Dublin."

Silver stared at her. "Nothing you say is believable, yet I think you're telling the truth . . . most of the time. Are you?"

"Most of the time, yes." Pan had no intention of revealing anything of the real reason she had entertained his proposition, and since he would have no way of divining her secret, she could be candid with him most of the time.

"You have dabbled in a great many types of work, haven't you?"

"Yes." It had been on the tip of her tongue to tell him that when you're on the run, you take what you can get until you have to run again, but she bit back the words. Telling him very little about herself would ensure that she had a place to stay for a month. When she leveled with him, he would be only too glad to get rid of her, but by then she would have seventy-five thousand dollars, enough money to take care of her for some time to come.

"Recalling Dublin?"

"What?" Pan blinked her eyes. "When you're reminded of something you tend to think about it," she replied obliquely.

Silver studied her closely. She hadn't lied to him, but her answer hadn't been straightforward either. What was she hiding? Pan Belmont had gotten under his skin. Antenna he'd thought dead, or at least bent, were now quivering in an awareness of her. He wanted to delve, dig, discover everything about her. No detail would be too small. "Would you like to rest for a while? I have a meeting this afternoon and I'll be busy until about six or after."

"I would like to shower, but I'll wait until my clothes—"

The buzzer at the door leading to his office interrupted her.

"Maybe you won't have to worry about a change of clothes, if that's who I think it is." Silver released her and turned away, taking the stairs to the first level of the apartment two at a time, feeling a sense of anticipation when he opened the door. "Olive; good. These are some of the things from Charine's?" Silver saw the flash of disapproval in her eyes, quickly masked, before she nodded.

"The rest should be along later today, or tomorrow."

"Thank you." Silver closed the door again, forgetting his secretary almost immediately as he turned, boxes piled in his arms, to stare up at Pan, who had come out of his bedroom and was leaning on her arms on the balcony railing and looking down at him. "These are for you. Come down and look at them." He didn't wait for her to respond before striding across the room to the foot of the stairs, balancing the packages easily.

Pan watched him as she descended, not speaking until she was eye level with him, one step from the bottom. "Clothing wasn't part of the deal."

Silver stared at her, noting the slight tightening of her

28

lips, the wary look of her eyes, the way her chin had raised two degrees. "Balking at a few bits of material?"

"Not at a few bits of material. Charine's is not exactly a factory outlet, is it?"

"No, it isn't, but this is no big deal either."

Pan inhaled, aware that she could have made a stronger argument but not willing to make the effort. For the first time in many weeks she didn't foresee tough times ahead, and it felt so good not to be in the grip of that particular tension. Her eyes strayed to the large boxes with gold scrolling on the lids.

Silver saw the direction of her gaze and smiled, moving back so that she could precede him into her bedroom. He followed her, his eyes on the rhythmic sway of her hips, her graceful stride.

He quickly removed the covers, exposing to her gaze gauzy underthings, dresses, blouses and pencil-slim tailored slacks of finest jacquard and silk worsted. "What do you think?"

"I hope you aren't going to deduct this from my money. I'll end up with bus fare."

"Nasty little money grubber," Silver said silkily.

"Needs must when the devil drives," Pan said absently, fingering the airy fabrics, lifting the dresses in front of herself.

"Another little saying so common in England and Ireland?"

"What? Oh yes. Clichés can be useful." She pulled out a set of pink sweats in finest cotton. "Sweats? From Charine's? My goodness, that's a surprise."

Silver's breath caught in his throat at the soft, delighted laugh that issued from between her lips. "This must be what you're going to choose to wear this afternoon."

29

"Yes. And then I'm going to do some work on my résumé and portfolio. You did say that you would introduce me to the right people in the modeling world?" Pan had no intention of telling him that she'd modeled for Valentina in Rome and the House of Rouleau in Paris. Since she was not going to use her background as a cachet into modeling, there was no sense bringing it up at all.

Silver nodded, feeling no small irritation that she was already referring to the time they'd part as though it were a sure thing, as though the month trial was not a consideration.

Pan saw how his eyes narrowed, already able to discern the signs of anger in him, though his face was expressionless. She grinned at him saucily. "Hedging my bets."

"Good idea," Silver told her, feeling an answering smile tug at his lips. "It doesn't clash with your hair at all."

"What? Oh, the pink color. No, I don't know why but pink is a good color for me, even some hues of red and orange. Red hair is strange. It reacts differently on almost everyone." Pan had the macabre feeling that she'd left the planet, conversing about such mundane things as hues and color tones with the man who had just propositioned her with a most generous stipend.

"I'll see you later. Ladder will bring your things to you from the elevator that opens into the foyer." Silver took her arm and led her out to the hall and along to the living room again, pointing to double doors in the far wall. "That's just for us, and there's an entrance to the street so that you can have the added safety of the doorman. We have security on twenty-four hours a day."

"I feel like the president's dog."

"If it's any consolation, you don't look like a canine at all." Silver kissed the nape of her neck, his lips lingering there. "See you later, Red."

"Don't call me that." Pan had to fight against the squeak that suddenly was in her voice. She tried to still the trembling of her hands as she clasped them in front of her.

Silver laughed out loud, striding across the large living room. "Sue me." It wouldn't be a smooth relationship, but it was going to be a damned diverting one. He hadn't felt such a zest for the future in many, many moons. He paused at the door leading to his office and turned to look up at her. She was still standing where he'd left her, in the doorway of the hall leading to her bedroom. "See ya, Red." He slammed the door behind him.

"Don't call me that," Pan repeated in a whisper, her eyes glued to the closed door. She had the absurd notion that she'd just signed her own commitment into Silver Galen's harem.

In the sudden silence of the apartment she looked around her. What had she done? Saved her neck? Or cut her throat? All at once she threw back her head and laughed out loud. Not only had she gone where angels fear to tread, she'd jumped in with both feet.

Silver lost his temper more than once at the meeting. He was like his father that way; he didn't suffer fools gladly, and it had caused many sighs and grimaces in the firm when the staff discovered that the easygoing heir to Galen's was just as tough an infighter as the Old Man. "Hemmings, you tell them that if they renege on this deal, I'll come after them, and not only won't they have a deal left, they won't have a company either. Got that?"

31

"All right, Silver, I'll tell them, but we'll have to get our legals in on this."

"Then do it. Now what's next on the agenda?" He shot out his wrist, his face twisting in irritation when he saw the time.

More than one of the staff shot speaking looks at one another. Maybe the rumors were true. If Silver had brought a woman to live with him in the apartment that very day, that could account for his impatience. He'd had a host of women before and after the accident, but he generally had set them up in other apartments, not the one in the Galen Building. He could be seen at all the trendy places in Manhattan, with gorgeous women on his arm.

Finally the meeting broke up and the men were ushered from the conference room.

"Is the place on fire, Ladder? We were just given the bum's rush."

"Ask the boss." Bateman shrugged noncommittally. If he thought the actions of the CEO strange, he wasn't about to gossip about him.

Silver went through to his office from the conference room, pressing the buzzer on his desk console while loosening his tie.

When Ladder came into the room, he looked up at him as he yanked the tie from his collar and threw it onto the desk. "Well? Did you get her things?"

"Yup. Didn't have much, but a few of the dishes are good. Some of it's Belleek and Haviland . . . and a very full portfolio for a fledgling model."

Silver pondered this information, then smiled at the man who was closer to him than anyone. "You're waiting for an opening to tell me that I'm a fool. Save your breath. I won't listen. What do you think of her?"

Ladder tilted his head sideways. "She's an original, I think. She could be deadly or angelic or both."

Silver threw back his head and laughed. "That's the way I see her too." It made his fingertips tingle just to think of Pan.

"Just make sure you don't wake up one morning with your letter opener between your shoulderblades." Ladder's laconic observation elicited another laugh from Silver. "I mean it. I know you like to live dangerously, but it seems to me you haven't covered your ass as well as you could with this one." Ladder didn't miss the reckless glint in Silver's eyes. "What do you know about her?"

"Not to worry. I feel alive with her. That's good enough for me. She intrigues me enough to pique my interest, to sting alive a part of me that's been dormant."

Ladder heard the satiny determination in his friend's voice. "And I say you're no hibernatin' critter that needs to be booted awake come spring. And what's more, she's not the Good Witch of the North, so watch your step." Ladder saw the flash of irritation in his friend's eyes and smiled. "Go to someone else if you want toadying. You won't get it from me."

"I'd be satisfied with a little respect now and then," Silver shot back.

"Oh, I think I can give you a . . . little respect." Ladder grinned when he saw the reluctant smile on Silver's face.

"Damned impertinent bastard."

"So you keep telling me." Ladder reached into a covered crystal dish and took out some candies and popped them into his mouth. "Damn. I like those pink ones. Nice and spicy." He chewed slowly, savoring the sweets. "Taking the lady out to dinner tonight?"

"Not unless she insists. I would like to dine quietly at

33

home and talk to her. There's so much I don't know about her."

"Enough to fill an encyclopedia, maybe? Put a detective on her."

"Damn you, Ladder, get out of here."

Ladder chuckled, reaching for more candy before he turned and ambled across the room and out the door.

Silver checked his messages, put a few cryptic words into his dictating machine, then rose to his feet stretching, a yawn widening his mouth.

He slowed his movements purposefully. Silver didn't want to give her the idea he was rushing to her side, even though that was just what he was doing. Laughing ruefully, he opened the door to his apartment with the key, and locked it behind him. Pan Belmont had a strange effect on him, and he was not sure he was comfortable with the feeling.

"Pan?" The silence of the apartment made his skin shiver with apprehension. He tossed his jacket at a chair, striding across the living room to the hall leading to her bedroom. If she'd gone, he had no way to find her . . . even a detective would have a time tracing her down, but he would get one.

At the doorway to her room he stopped suddenly.

Pan was stretched out on the bed with the bedspread over her, a towel wrapped around her hair, as though she'd intended only a short rest but had fallen into a deep sleep.

Silver approached the bed, staring down at her. He was tempted to check her respiration at first because she was breathing so deeply and so slowly.

Sitting down on the edge of the bed, he watched her. She looked about thirteen, her face softened in sleep and very vulnerable.

34

Her eyelashes fascinated him. They were dark, with red-gold tips. Her brows were the same deep hue, not the red that would have matched her hair. What a chameleon she was, taking on all colors of her environment.

Pan groaned and turned over, stretching the silken sheet away from her and finally pushing it all the way off her body.

Silver couldn't have turned away even if he'd wanted to . . . and, of course, he didn't.

Pan Belmont was beautiful even if thin. Her skin was the translucent milkiness that is only given to certain red-heads. Her breasts were pink tipped and uptilted, and the lovely space at the junction of her body was covered with a generous triangle of red-gold curls.

Silver had to still his hand not to run his fingers through it, press his mouth there. Not all the adjurations to himself changed how he felt; he couldn't tear his eyes away. Her legs were long and shapely, with slender ankles and calves. Her shoulders were broad for her size, and slightly sloping. Her neck was long, supporting her well-shaped head.

His eyes ran down her legs to her toes, which were lightly painted with a pinkish lacquer, the feet slim, with high arches.

Sighing deeply, he lifted the silken sheet and pulled it up high on her form, shutting away the exquisite vision from his eyes.

"No!" Her voice was strong but laced with fear, even though she was still sound asleep. "You don't frighten me. No."

Silver saw her body tremble, the silken covering slipping low again as she began to thrash in her sleep. To his surprise, her face began to perspire, her lips and chin quivering with agitation. Her head tossed back and forth on the pillow as she became more distraught. With no plan in mind, Silver slipped between the sheets, lifting her into his arms, feeling the damp chill of her skin.

Pan whimpered once, then, like a child seeking the solace and warmth of a parent, she turned and burrowed into him, her hands clutching at him, clinging.

"It's all right, darling, I'll take care of you." Still holding her to his body with one hand, Silver managed to shrug off his clothes piece by piece, leaning back from her so that he could kick them to the floor. Slight alarmed moans issued from her throat at the separation. Silver felt compassion stab through him as he gathered her close to him again.

"Shhh. Go back to sleep, darling. It's all right. I have you." Silver pressed his face into her fragrant hair, the clean, healthy odor of her body a surprising jolt to his libido. "You're safe now."

Pan groaned into his neck, her hands stealing around his middle, nails dragging against his skin and making the breath catch in his throat. Then she seemed to slide into a deeper sleep, her respiration slowing, her lips parting slightly, her body limp.

Silver didn't know how long he had been holding her before his own eyelids began to droop.

Sleep took him like a velvet whirlwind, his grip tightening on her as though he had to ensure that she remain where she was—in his arms.

CHAPTER TWO

When Pan opened her eyes all was darkness, and she had no idea where she was. From the experience of moving often from place to place she'd learned not to panic at the lost feeling but to take the time to orient herself in the blackness, though the square patches of moonlight on the ceiling were not enough to identify her surroundings for her.

Taking deep breaths, she tried to move, but she couldn't budge. A weight on her middle trapped her where she was. She reached down and touched what she sensed was a hirsute male thigh, and for a flash in time she thought she was back with Sydney again. No, he was dead. Pan could recall that. She'd been alone for almost two months, and their plans to marry and have a new life had all died with him.

It was Silver Galen who was beside her! She should run, escape! But where would she go? Pan relaxed, squeezed her eyes shut—and all at once Sydney's face was there.

Pan lost interest in where she was and who was breathing stentorously next to her as she recalled Sydney Blakeney, her English fiancé, who'd studied at the University of London before coming to America and apprenticing himself to an accounting firm.

37

Pan had met him when she was a temporary office girl at the accounting company, and they had begun dating. She hadn't been in love with Sydney, but he had been unfailingly kind to her, and when after four months of dating he'd asked her to move in with him, she had, explaining to him first that she didn't love him but that she cared for him. Pan had informed him that she was positive she could never love anyone, not with the great pulsating emotion talked about in romance novels. "I find that sort of chicanery intolerable," she'd lashed out angrily.

Sydney had held her, chuckling in her ear. "Well, then, it's my job to change your mind about romance, lady. I'll prove to you how great it is, and you'll forget the bad moments."

Pan had allowed herself to be soothed, and soon he'd had her laughing, but she hadn't really changed her opinion of love. To her it was a perversion to trap the unwary. And she was determined never to let it happen to her.

Sydney hadn't cared about her strong opinions on romance. He'd loved her and been very open about his feelings. Each day of the six months they'd lived together Pan's feelings for him had grown and blossomed, and when he'd asked her to marry him, she'd said yes. It was then that she'd sat him down and told him every facet of her past life. But far from putting him off, he'd told her he loved her even more.

"I don't care about the past, Pan. The present is what counts and it's ours. We'll build our own future. Your past is as dead to me as it is to you. I don't have any family, and I love kids. We'll get married and build our own dynasty."

Pan had laughed, feeling safe for the first time in many months. "Yes. I'd like to have children."

38

So they'd begun organizing their lives and working hard and planning happily. Just three weeks before their wedding day Sydney had been hit by a cab that skidded on a street in Manhattan, climbed the curb and killed one pedestrian. A freak accident that shouldn't have happened!

Pan had been poleaxed, her grief magnified by the added knowledge that she had lost the first bright sparkle in her life since her short, happy childhood with her father and mother and the brief time of contentment she'd had with her uncle. The loss, plus the strain of her pregnancy, had brought on a flulike illness that weakened her considerably, making her unable to work. The small jobs she had melted away, and she was left without funds.

Sydney hadn't worked long enough to accrue benefits in his company. He had been poorly insured, so the little money that came to Pan went right to paying their outstanding bills.

In the succeeding weeks Pan had had a difficult time finding steady work after her stint as temporary help was over. Her rent payments fell behind, and her landlord threatened her with the eviction that had subsequently taken place, with her belongings left behind as collateral.

And now! Lord, she had opened a Pandora's box. She had just contracted to live with a—a bon vivant to the max. Black humor assailed her as her groping fingers found the hard-muscled arm that manacled her to the bed.

"Darling, you have a wonderful feathery touch," said a voice in Pan's ear. "But you are arousing me, which is not what you planned, I'm sure."

"You've got that right," Pan muttered, her hand freezing in place, the rest of her body becoming stiff as a

39

board. She heard a rustling sound in the dark. Then the light went on over the bed.

"Hello, Silver. What are you doing here? I thought we'd agreed that we would make the decision on sleeping together when the month ended. Right?"

"That's roughly the understanding." Silver made no move to leave her.

"I suppose it's evening." She looked away from the glittering eyes and sardonic smile and grimaced at her watch. It didn't have an illuminated dial, in fact, it didn't even tell the correct time anymore, but she was loath to part with it even if she couldn't afford to have it repaired. As it was, her belongings were dwindling more and more.

"It's just after eight o'clock. Would you like to dress and go out on the town, or shall we dine here?"

"Ah, what would you like?"

"I want to please you, so choose."

"Well, if you must know, I'm dying for a grilled cheese with sliced tomatoes on rye toast, with a crisp apple and a huge glass of cold, cold milk."

Silver laughed out loud, his head thrown back, his teeth gleaming in the lamplight. Pan thought he had a wonderfully strong throat. "You have very few cavities."

Silver's mouth closed with a snap at her conversational tone. "Thank you, I think. Do you have a great many cavities?"

"Actually, no. I have very good teeth. Would you like to see?"

"I'll take your word for it . . . but maybe at the end of the month I'll want to examine them, just for the record."

"To finalize the sale, so to speak."

"So to speak." He pushed back the cover, which she yanked back over herself again, then rose to his feet, clad

40

in briefs that hugged his body. He turned to face her, smiling wickedly when he saw that her eyes had gone to his very aroused body. "As you can see, you interest me greatly . . . and I'm going to make every effort in the next few weeks to convince you to join me in my bed as I joined you in yours." He saw the questioning wariness in her eyes. "You're wondering why I came to bed with you?"

"Since the bargain was somewhat different, yes, I was wondering."

"I came in here to see how you were when I came back from my office. You were having a nightmare . . ." For the first time he saw her discomfited, her eyes sliding away from his. "Do you want to tell me what causes you to cry out in your sleep?"

"No."

"All right." He turned away from the bed, bending to pick up his things. "I'll get things started for our meal. See you in the kitchen."

He was gone before Pan could say anything, but for long minutes she stared at the closed door, then looked around her, blinking her eyes. It was as though with his departure the atmosphere stopped crackling with electricity, and the earth, which had been tipped on its axis, settled back into place with a thump.

No way would she tell him about her past. He wasn't Sydney!

For the first few minutes after her shower Pan toyed with the idea of not wearing any of the new clothes that Silver had had delivered from Charine's, but the moment she touched the filmy underthings, her resolve melted.

Spraying herself with the small amount of Chanel perfume she had left in her purse vial, she donned the clothing, sighing at the comfort of the pink sweats and pink

41

walking shoes that matched them. "I don't look like a beauty queen, but what the hell," she muttered at her mirror image.

Twisting her flyaway red hair into a coil on top of her head and using the barest touch of pink lipstick readied her for her first dinner with Silver Galen. Taking a breath, she left the room and walked along the hall out to the center of the living room, looking up the stairs. Would he be up there or in the kitchen, as he had said?

What would dinner really be like? Caviar on French craquelines? Toast points with shrimp and lobster bits?

Pan's tummy turned over at the thought of rich food. She needed plain things. She had morning sickness at all times of the day. Pressing her hand over her middle, she wondered when she would begin to feel a kinship with the embryo growing within her. Being pregnant with Sydney's baby had been a good happening in her life, but she wasn't used to it yet. It was as though it were occurring to someone else. Still she was determined to be healthy and to keep the baby the same way.

Wandering through the large apartment, her rubber-soled shoes sinking into the luxurious carpet and making no sound, her eyes touched on the many very expensive objets d'art scattered around the room.

Following the sounds from what she assumed must be the kitchen, she walked through an open door to a black-and-steel paradise of modern cookery.

Silver had his back to her as he stood stirring something in an iron pan on the stove, a huge bowl of freshly torn spinach at his elbow. She must have made a sound, because he turned to face her, a large hot mitt over one hand. "Good Lord, I'll be arrested." He noticed her eyes widen slightly when he threw back his head and laughed.

Then he saw her pull back. He shook his head. "Don't mind me."

"I don't."

Silver noted the coldness of her tone and how that chin of hers was jutting out again. "I'm not laughing at you, darling. The joke is on me. How can you look twelve years old in that outfit and still look sexy as hell?"

"Do I?" Pan started laughing too. "Well, you look very silly in an apron that says *Save the cooks of the world. Kiss me.* And you also have something smoking behind you."

"Christ, the salad dressing." Silver didn't speak to her after that. All at once he held the hot mixture over the bowl of spinach and drizzled it over the the whole thing. "Sit down. This is best eaten at once. Your grilled cheese is done, and I have your apple at your plate. Is that a big enough glass of cold, cold milk?"

"Heavens, I said a glass, not a quart." Pan felt inordinately pleased that he'd made all the things she wanted, and though she argued with herself that it didn't mean anything, not really, she couldn't smother the small joy of being catered to by Silver Galen.

"Ummm, spinach salad with—almonds—and mandarin oranges—and mushrooms and real bacon as crisp as anything." Pan looked up at him admiringly. "I've never had this with a hot dressing, but it's wonderful."

"Thank you." Silver felt that he was swelling to twice his size because she had praised him. It delighted him to see her munch her grilled cheese and apple and drink the milk, leaving a white mustache on her mouth. "You're hungry."

"Yes, but a great many people in our country are much hungrier than I," she told him simply, crunching on the crisp apple.

43

"I thought we'd have ice cream sundaes and coffee for dessert. What do you think?"

"Ice cream, yes. Not coffee. I'll stick with milk." She didn't tell him that coffee had begun to give her terrible indigestion so she avoided it.

They dined in companionable silence, content to listen to the soft music coming from the stereo system.

"Now we have dessert, a specialty of mine." Silver grinned at her when they carried their soiled plates to the kitchen.

"Oh?" Pan smiled back. "This I have to see."

Silver was tickled with the way she hung over his shoulder while he made the sundaes.

"And don't forget the crushed pineapple and chopped walnuts," Pan urged him after he brought the dishes of assorted toppings from the refrigerator. "Who does this for you?"

"You mean puts all the flavorings and toppings in the little dishes? Well, my housekeeper does that. Usually once a week is sundae dessert after dinner."

Pan cupped her chin on her hand, leaning forward on the center island, not taking her eyes from the slowly building mounds of sweets. "It's so pretty. You must have been doing this for a long time."

"You could say that. I used to be a soda jerk when I was in high school. It was a Greek ice cream shop and the high school hangout. Their ice cream was wonderful. Mrs. Tillson, my housekeeper, searched for a long time before she found the type I craved in a little Italian shop a few blocks from where she shops." Silver added a cherry to the top of each sundae, then carried them to the kitchen table.

Pan stared at hers, then looked up at Silver. "I hate to eat it. It's so beautiful."

It shook him how much her smile affected him. She was a wood nymph who was entrancing him more and more. He had the eerie sensation that she was rekindling his emotions so that his reactions were doing turnabouts and cartwheels. His life had always been orderly, and even with the chaotic pain and horror of the accident and its agonizing aftermath, he had never once lost control. Even when he'd backed away from family and friends for a while to get himself back on keel, he never lost his incentive for full recovery or his determination to be as much of a success in business as he had been as a race car driver. He'd had to abandon racing because of the accident that had marred his face and left him with a slight limp, so he was determined to be a success in every other way.

Now, along came a reed of a girl—no, woman—into his life. Pan was twenty-four years old, twelve years his junior, and with no more than nudging words she was beginning to eat away at his armor, invade his nerve ends like an insidious microbe; and he didn't have a clue where she was coming from or where she was going. Silver had the feeling that he was hanging by a rope from a cliff. He could either climb back up again or he could let go and fall into the cloudy abyss whose depths were hidden from him. What disturbed him most was that he was so inclined to let go!

"Your smile is twisted again, as though you were looking at the world while sucking lemons . . . or something." Pan put her head to one side and studied him. "Have I annoyed you?"

"I don't know. Maybe. You've certainly gotten to me, and I'm trying to handle that." Silver put his spoon into his ice cream and tasted it, trying to change the subject.

"Has nothing ever intrigued you before you met me?

Goodness, I don't know whether to be flattered or run for my life. Are you telling me that no ravishing creature has taken you by storm before?"

"Now who's being caustic, devil?" Silver smiled at her, wiping his mouth with the cloth napkin. "Women have always interested me, and a time or two it was pretty important to me. How about you?"

Pan stared at him for a moment and answered seriously. "I lost someone who meant a great deal to me. No other person meant so much."

"And do you have a family?"

"I'm an orphan." Pan told the lie with the ease of long usage. "There's no one."

"I have a good-size family. A brother and a sister, nieces and nephews, cousins—"

"By the dozens," Pan finished, relieved that he hadn't pressed her about her family. She had no intention of telling him anything about the Drexels.

"Yes, but I intend to spare you the typhoon of a family get-together until we've lived together for a while."

Pan paused with a spoon of whipped cream, fruit and nuts almost to her mouth. "You sound as though our life together is a fait accompli."

Silver shrugged. "Not really. I just like to plan ahead."

"From my experience it's better not to project too far. Minute-to-minute, hour-to-hour, day-to-day getting along is the most fruitful way to make it on this galaxy."

"Are you from another world?"

"Maybe. Who knows?"

Silver noticed that her features had tightened, the veil seeming to drop over her expression again. "You are so singularly unfettered in life—it shouldn't bother you to ponder the future."

46

"Oh, I have an anchor or two. They just aren't burdensome."

Silver sat back, pushing his empty dish to one side, studying her in tingling awareness, anticipation fanning his long dormant instincts. Pan touched him, bringing him back to the fast-paced, vibrating life he'd once known and embraced. The change in him, the withdrawal from such a life, had been so gradual he hadn't even known there was a metamorphosis . . . until now.

"Why don't you rest tomorrow, and the next day we'll talk to some people I know about a modeling job for you. What do you say, Pan?"

"Well . . ." Pan hedged, feeling her way. He seemed to be reassessing her, changing things. That could be bad. "I could perhaps do office work if you weren't able to get modeling jobs for me. I'm not fussy and I can handle a word processor."

Pan projected ahead to a few weeks from now and how she would look. Already her waistline was changing. Perhaps even before the four weeks were up she would have to explain to Silver Galen about her changing figure. She faced the prospect with the same fatalism she had adopted in her life since the many upheavals and revelations of a few years ago that had sundered her very existence and almost driven her mad. There was no one or nothing on the planet, now or ever, that she would give her trust to now that Sydney was gone.

"Oh?" Silver studied her. Another hidden compartment in her life. "Well, let's talk to the modeling connections first and see how that works out; then we'll look at the business side." God knows she was beautiful enough and slender enough to get the most demanding modeling assignment.

"If you say so."

47

Silver noticed how she pushed away the half-eaten ice cream sundae. Something in the conversation they'd just had had made her lose her appetite. "Let's listen to some music, shall we?"

Pan nodded in agreement, but first began to clear the table, carrying things to the sink, where she rinsed them. "We'll put them in the dishwasher rather than wash them by hand." Silver didn't try to dissuade her from her chores, having the feeling that the mundane actions somehow soothed her and that she would have resisted him anyway. She was an anomaly in his life, both simple and complex, straightforward and devious. Pan was going to drive him crazy!

Later when they were sitting close together on the couch but not touching, the sounds of Rachmaninoff wafting around the room like a pulsating cloud, Pan fell asleep.

One moment Silver was watching her through half-closed lids as her eyes roved the room in detached relaxation. The next moment she was sliding toward him, her breathing deep and regular. He pulled her into the circle of his arm, frowning down at her. She seemed to require a great deal of sleep. It flashed across his mind that she could be ill, and he wondered how she would react if he insisted that she see his physician.

Lifting her easily into his arms, he marveled again at how light she was. Carrying her from the living room and down the hall leading to her bedroom, he placed her on the bed, then slowly began to undress her.

His body soon responded to what he was doing, and though his feelings toward her at the moment were of compassion and caring, his libido intruded forcefully. "Damn!" His irritated laugh was low, but Pan still moved in her sleep, muttering in protest. Not wanting to create more havoc for himself by dressing her in one of the filmy nighties that Charine had sent, he placed her, unclothed, between the silky sheets, bringing them up to her neck.

For a long moment he looked down at her, studying the face that was so childlike in sleep, noting the blue shadows under her eyes, the restless movements of her fingers as she clutched the hem of the sheet.

His reaction to her surprised him even more when he pulled a chair over to the bed and sat down, watching her. He was not only curious about her, but he felt tied to her somehow, and this realization made him uneasy.

His life had been pretty cut and dried. He'd been protected by wealth, denied little. It had never been his nature to feel protective about anyone, since the rest of his family and his circle of friends had been as much cared for as he had. The Galens had always given generously to charity. They sponsored a soup kitchen in New York, and he and his siblings had worked many hours there, at the insistence of their parents. The Galen Trust had purchased an old hotel, refurbished it and leased it to tenants on the poverty level for small sums of money. They maintained it as carefully as they did the high-monetary-return properties they owned.

Yet it wasn't until Silver's stint in the Peace Corps, after he'd been graduated from college, teaching farming techniques in Ethiopia, that he'd come to realize the consummate agony of persons raised in the yoke of poverty.

When he returned from Africa he convinced his family that continually sending money, farm implements and manpower was the only way to make a mark with the poor in the drought-burdened area. The Galen Trust had begun a reclamation plan on ten square miles of arid African soil.

49

With the same recklessness and high hopes of the young he'd gone to Vietnam to save that country. His disillusionment had been awesome and complete when he'd only seen misery, degradation, useless killing and poverty.

Silver had become politically active in the struggle against war and poverty after that, but somehow the core, the nucleus of the man himself, had managed to remain aloof, apart, alone.

With all that had happened in his life, Silver had never felt the flaming desire to protect anyone that Pan was eliciting from him at that moment and that had been growing from the time he'd seen her trying to make tomato soup from hot water and ketchup in the restaurant.

The slip of a woman on the bed was chipping away at him, much as he was trying to put a chink in her defenses. It was a benign and sensuous war.

Midnight had come and gone before he left the bedroom and went up the stairs to his own room, first taking a cold shower that didn't seem to have an effect on his active imagination.

His hand hovered over the phone next to his bed as he dried his hair with the free hand. Relief was a phone call away. Marcia Deeds would be glad to assuage the sexual discomfort he was feeling; but somehow he couldn't call. He didn't want Marcia. Pan was the face in front of him, the tender body that should be writhing under his.

Silver swallowed a snifter of cognac, punched the pillow flat under his head and closed his eyes.

Silver was at work, or so Pan assumed when she showered and dressed in tailored gray trousers with a matching thick-ribbed cotton sweater in pink and gray plaid,

50

and went to the kitchen to eat. She'd had a bout of morning sickness, and now she was hungry.

After eating toast, oatmeal, milk and juice, she was too restless to sit around the apartment. She donned the full-length fox fur coat that Charine had sent along, the luxurious warmth making her sigh.

The key for the elevator and the apartment was on the shelf where Silver had left it. When she put it into the lock, the doors slid soundlessly open and she stepped inside and was whisked to the lobby of the Galen Building.

Pan nodded at the security man.

"Good morning, Miss Belmont. Have a good day, ma'am."

Startled at being addressed by name by the man, she just nodded and walked past him out to the sunlit, cold March day, feeling toasty warm as she looked up and down Fifth Avenue and tried to decide which way to go. As she was inhaling deep breaths of fresh air, someone stepped to her side.

"Would you like some company? I'm Ladder."

Pan looked up at the very tall man with the velvet-soft brown eyes and nodded. "I remember."

"I don't have to stay if you want to be alone. Silver doesn't want you to feel as though you're in prison."

"I don't. Please, I'd like the company, unless it would interfere with your work." Pan assumed the security man had called Silver's office and told him she'd left the building.

"I'm free."

They walked in silence, out of sync with the fast pace all around them. The two of them strolled, looked in windows, up at buildings, at the traffic.

"You're a very peaceful companion, Ladder," Pan told him after they'd walked ten blocks.

"So are you."

"Thank you." Pan felt a cramping in her middle but it soon left, so she didn't suggest they turn back.

"Would you like to purchase anything? You have carte blanche in any store," Ladder told her matter-of-factly.

"I don't need anything right now." She hugged the coat around her as a gust of March wind caught them. "This coat is so warm."

"Do you need a hat? Or boots?"

"I'm pretty warm, but I think I've had enough air. We can go once around the block and return."

When they were standing at a corner waiting for the traffic to subside, she felt another twinge in her middle and put her hand there. It felt as though something had twisted her insides, but then the sensation disappeared.

"Fifth Avenue is always bustling," Pan observed, looking up at her companion, who smiled and nodded. "You were in Vietnam with Silver."

"He found me wounded and carried me to a battalion aid station. I'm no lightweight, and he carried me a few miles."

"That's why you're friends."

"That, and the fact that he continued to visit me, help me out, bring things to me and my buddies. When it was time to come home we came together."

"And been together ever since? Even when he raced?"

"Especially then. I was his mechanic." Ladder's face closed, his mouth tightening.

"You were there when he had his accident."

"Yes."

"It must have been awful."

"It was a ball of hell rolling down the speedway." Ladder sucked in a shuddering breath. "I never thought I'd get him out."

"But you did, didn't you? I saw the scars on your hands and wrists when we first met."

Ladder shrugged. "They were nothing. I got worse in Nam, but Silver. . . ." He shook his head.

"You've never talked to him about how you felt, or anyone else either, have you?"

"Silver is all I've got. There isn't anyone else, and I just couldn't discuss it with him."

"Then why not tell me? It might smooth out your dreams." Pan felt him stop and stare at her. She paused and looked his way. "It isn't voodoo. I know all about keeping things inside so that they balloon into nightmares. The pattern is quite familiar to me."

"But you don't tell anyone about it."

"I can't. Nothing is stopping you, is there? You can't hurt Silver, can you?"

Ladder shook his head and resumed walking, his somewhat stooped body cushioning the worst of the March wind from Pan. "He was driving hard, to win, like he always did, and it looked like he was going to take the Indy. He was Mercury that day." His smile twisted. *"Mercury* was the name of the car and—"

"Is the other name for Quicksilver."

"Right."

"Go on, Ladder. I didn't mean to interrupt."

Ladder shook his head. "You didn't interrupt me." He eased around an older woman pulling a cart with all her possessions stashed in it, and two or three coats on her back.

"Excuse me for a moment, Ladder." Pan went back to the bag lady, reaching into her pocket for money and pressing it into the woman's hand. Then she strolled back to Ladder. "Pardon me. Please go on with your story." Pan noticed the softening of Ladder's look, the slight lifting of his hard mouth. She shrugged. "It's nice to be able to give someone a hand."

Ladder walked on beside her for a few silent moments, seeming to study the people passing. "Well, as I said, he was leading, driving hard but well. One of the drivers, up ahead of him but actually a lap behind him, took the curve wrong and skidded. It looked like he would be able to correct even though he skated along the wall, but somehow he lost it coming out of the turn and he caught the tail end of Silver's car, flipping it over . . . and over. Silver was still on the track and moving when he came upright again, fighting the wheel every step of the way, and he damn well almost got the Mercury free of the other vehicles, but two of them caught him again and he hit a stanchion, exploding the gas tank and catching fire. Silver could have gotten out then on his own, but he stayed with it to steer away from the reviewing stand. Sure as hell that car freewheeling into that wall would have sent a ball of flame right up the stand. Who knows how many would have been killed?" Ladder's rapid-fire commentary seemed to have him in thrall. It was as though he'd forgotten Pan's presence, his stride lengthening so that she had to hurry to stay with him.

"He drove right through the fence into the cleared area in the center, but by then his car was in flames." Ladder swallowed hard. "When I reached him, he was trying to get the canopy off but the smoke was getting to him. I ripped it off before they could get the cutting tools to it." Ladder stopped dead in the center of pedestrian traffic, people flowing around him as though he were a rock in a stream, his eyes tortured.

"And you lifted him out of there so that the medics could treat him."

Ladder's jagged sigh tore at Pan and she put her hand through his arm. "You saved him."

"But not soon enough, don't you see? If I'd gotten to him just a few seconds earlier, he wouldn't have had those terrible burns."

"He chose to spare some other people the pain of burning. If you hadn't gotten him out when you did, his lungs would have burned and he would have died. *You* saved him, and if you hadn't torn off the canopy when you did, he wouldn't be here today."

Ladder looked down at her, his sad smile twisting his face. "Thank you, little lady. It has helped to talk to you." He shook his head. "I still can't believe I spilled my guts that way."

Pan laughed out loud. "I don't suppose you'd like to stop at Rumpelmayer's for a sundae, would you?"

"Hot fudge?"

"My favorite. I salivate just thinking about it."

Crossing from Bergdorf Goodman's, the two of them rounded the corner of the Plaza Hotel and entered the famous ice cream shop. They ordered the sundaes, Ladder looking incongruous in one of the little pink chairs.

Pan ate every scrap of hers and drank a glass of milk. She was sure it was the fast way she'd eaten the ice cream that caused a cramping again when they rose to leave.

"Something wrong?" Ladder saw the crease between her eyes and the hesitant way she rose from the chair.

"No, just a stitch in my side."

He nodded and paid the check and they left, walking down the avenue again.

"Tell me about Vietnam. I know what I've read in the papers but I've had little contact with anyone who was there."

"Vietnam can't really be talked about," Ladder told her in a noncommittal voice.

"You'd rather I didn't question you about it."

"It isn't that, Pan. It's just that it was so bloody awful all the time—so stinking, rotten, terrible—that there is no way to talk about it except in four-letter words."

"No saving graces?"

"The people—both that you served with, and the civilians. The Vietnamese are good people—kind, gentle, loving. I married one."

Pan was taken aback, feeling guilty that she had probed into a part of this man that he seemed to want to keep private. "I shouldn't have asked you about Nam."

"I had to leave her behind, because I couldn't get the papers processed before I was shipped out with the hospital unit." Ladder took a deep breath. "The minute we were stateside, Silver got the wheels in motion. I was able to go back in a few months, but it was too late. She was dead; so was our child." Ladder exhaled, his face expressionless.

Pan couldn't say anything. Lord, and she thought she'd had troubles. She put her hand through Ladder's arm again as they resumed walking in silence, and they were still arm-in-arm when they crossed the foyer of the Galen Building.

"Ladder," the security man said as he came around from his station and approached them. "The boss has been asking for Miss Belmont. He's called down about ten times now." The security man grimaced his discomfort. "Hot under the collar, he is."

Ladder chuckled. "It's all right, Benny. Ring him and tell him we're on our way up."

"Right."

"Let's go, Pan." Ladder's grin stretched across his face

56

as he gestured for her to precede him into the elevator. "I guess Silver's chomping at the bit."

"And that pleases you?"

"Yes. For too long he's been aloof from things, getting more cynical by the day. I like to see him worked up now and then." He chortled. "Maybe I'll have to duck."

"If he throws a punch at me, I'll smack him back." Pan straightened from the wall, glaring at the tall man when he threw back his head and guffawed.

"Sorry, Pan. I'm not laughing at you but at the picture of you doing just that. Oops, here we go," Ladder whispered as the doors slid open into the apartment and Silver was standing there facing them, his face tight, his eyes going first to Pan, then to Ladder.

"Where the hell did you take her?"

"Rumpelmayer's." Ladder grinned, ambling by his gape-mouthed employer and along the hall leading to the offices. "Bye, Pan. I have some work to do. See you later."

"Thank you for the company, Ladder." Pan waited in the foyer next to Silver, her eyes on him as he watched his friend's departure.

"Damn him to hell, he could have called me when he knew you were going to be gone that long."

"It wasn't a car date, Dad, and I'm home under curfew," Pan said in a baby voice batting her eyes, noting how his mouth twitched.

"Damn you, Pan, I was worried."

"That's silly. I've been roving around Manhattan for— years."

Silver heard the hesitation in her voice before the word *years*. He took her arm, turning her to face him. "You have a great deal you're hiding from me, and I don't like

57

that, but I'm not going to put detectives on you to find out your background."

"Please don't."

"But I do want to ask you some questions. For instance, am I harboring a fugitive? If I am, I will continue to do so, but I would like to know if I should take any precautions to keep you undercover."

"My picture is not in the post office, nor am I a spy of any kind."

Silver smiled down at her. "But your chin just went up a notch, so I guess you do feel a little threatened by questioning."

"I will answer any question you ask me . . . unless I can't answer it."

Silver laughed. "Beautifully ambivalent." He kissed the top of her head. "I missed you badly today. I was damn well ready to toss the entire legal staff out the window and have lunch with you." He shot a quick glance at his watch. "I have a meeting in five minutes, but I want you to prepare yourself for a night on the town. Do you like dancing?"

"Love it."

"Good." He kissed her once quickly on the mouth and turned away. Just before he opened the door leading to his office he looked back at her. "I won't try to make you uncomfortable, but I'm still going to ask questions."

"And I'll answer what I can."

"Fair enough, darling. See you later."

Pan felt her heart jerk at the endearment. Silver Galen was too charming for his own good.

All at once she felt fatigued, and it delighted her that she could just go into the bedroom and take a nap. She didn't have to worry about people knocking on the door and expecting rent.

"Pardon me, miss. I didn't mean to startle you, but I thought you might like some homemade soup. I'm Mrs. Tillson, Mr. Galen's housekeeper."

"Oh yes, he told me about you. Thank you, Mrs. Tillson, but I'm not hungry, just tired. I think I'll take a nap."

The older woman frowned. "Are you feeling all right, miss? You are a little pale."

"Just tired, thank you." Pan couldn't wait until she reached the bedroom, stripping off her clothes helterskelter and climbing between the silky sheets, sleep coming at once.

When Silver entered the apartment that evening, Mrs. Tillson was waiting for him all ready to leave.

"Miss Belmont is still sleeping, sir." Mrs. Tillson's lips tightened. "She seemed very tired when she came in from her walk with Mr. Bateman. Miss didn't take any of my homemade soup, she was so tired."

"I'm sure she'll have some tomorrow. You have a nice evening and a good day tomorrow."

"If you think you'll need me then, sir, I can put off my day. I don't usually take a night and a day together anyway."

"Don't be silly, Mrs. Tillson. We have plenty of food, and you deserve the time with your sister. Enjoy, and give her my best."

"I will, sir. She's so grateful for what you've done for her Paul, sir."

"Mrs. Tillson, you tell her to forget that. As long as the boy is getting along in school, my concerns are met. Make sure you tell him about studying so that he'll be ready for college."

"I will, sir, and thank you."

When his housekeeper left by the back elevator, Silver went through to Pan's bedroom, not bothering to turn on a light but letting the hall illumination guide him.

His housekeeper's words went around and around in his head as he sat on the bed and looked at Pan's partially shadowed face. Was she worried about something? Or ill? Would that be the reason she was so often tired?

Even as he watched her, she began the thrashing around she'd done the other night.

Again Silver soothed her by climbing into bed with her and holding her, his body reacting in the same overtly sensual fashion.

Pan opened her eyes and knew almost at once that she was being held and that it was Silver who was holding her. She turned her head and looked up at him in the dimness of the room, able to tell by his breathing that he was awake. "I can barely see you. What time is it?"

"A little after seven." Silver looked at the illuminated dial of his watch. "Would you like to stay home tonight instead of going out?"

"No, actually I think that it would be fun to go dancing, but I'd like to shower and shampoo first. Would that make it too late?"

"Not at all. I'll shower, too, and make some reservations. Any choices on the food?"

"No. I like everything. You choose."

This time when Silver rose from the bed he was clothed, but Pan noticed that his body was aroused.

"Yes, darling, I'm afraid you have that effect on me."

"Try cold showers."

"Nasty brat."

Pan was still laughing when he left, shutting the door behind him.

She sang in the shower, feeling rested and hungry and

eager for an evening out with no worries, able to blot out the near and far past in the enjoyment of dancing.

Silver would be a delightful companion: urbane, witty, knowledgeable about many things. Pan would enjoy herself, but she had begun to be uneasy about her feelings for him. She hadn't been able to maintain the sangfroid she had managed in the beginning. He was able to titillate her sense of humor as no one had been able to do, not even Sydney.

For all that Ladder had told her about Silver, she found that she hungered to know more. What had he looked like as a boy? Had he been tall then, or short and chunky? He must have been sports-minded even then. And clearly it took great shrewdness and business acumen to handle the complex of Galen businesses. When did he develop those traits?

When he went to college, was he shy or outgoing? *Shy* didn't seem to fit Silver Galen, but then people changed so much in the years between childhood and manhood.

By the time she had toweled herself dry and was doing the same to her hair, she had thought of many questions that she wanted to ask him. The only barrier to doing just that would be that Silver would think he was free to ask questions back.

Choosing a dress from the ones Charine had sent was a fun chore. She had thought when she first felt the rich fabrics that she would be repelled by the memories that would assail her, but she just found that it was enjoyable.

Pan finally settled on a pink satin suit with gray velvet lapels. The skirt was a bit tight, but she didn't think it would be too bad.

She twisted her hair on top of her head and wore small gold button earrings as her only jewelry. The three-inch-heeled slings in gray suede were comfortable but they felt strange, since she hadn't worn heels for a long time. Sydney had been the same height as she, so she'd worn flats most of the time.

Sydney! It shocked Pan when she had to concentrate very hard to bring his image into focus in her mind. Silver's face seemed to have ballooned in her brain. Pan shook her head, not even trying to question her reaction.

When she was ready she turned slowly in front of the ornate free-standing mirror. Inhaling with pleasure at wearing such lovely clothes, she was aware that she had never looked better, even if the makeup didn't entirely cover the fact that she was too pale.

Feeling festive had become alien to her, but she felt that way now and looked forward to the evening. Snatching up her evening purse, she almost ran from the room. When she crossed the living room she looked up toward the balcony and Silver's room.

"I'm over here," he told her softly, thinking that she had a fragile loveliness that was almost ethereal. Her hair caught the lamplight, sending out small flames, the pink of her suit giving her skin a pearly glow.

Pushing away from the small corner bar where he'd been leaning as he watched her come from her room, he approached her, his arms outstretched. "You've lovely, Pan."

She watched him come toward her, both fascinated and frightened by his magnetism. "Thank you." Pan saw the amused awareness in his eyes as the strong arms went around her and he leaned toward her. Wanting to turn away wasn't enough to make it happen. That hard, sensual mouth mesmerized her.

The kiss was gentle, though Silver wanted to bury himself in her, but he restrained the demands of his libido and rubbed his lips gently on hers, his tongue tracing the outer edge. "Ready?"

"Yes." Pan felt out of breath and not quite on balance as Silver put the fur coat around her shoulders.

They were silent but close as they descended to the garage under the building and walked to a corner parking place, their footfalls echoing loudly in the stillness.

Pan stopped to look at the car whose door Silver had just opened. "It's a Ferrari?"

"A Lamborghini. Would you like to drive?"

Pan chuckled. "As though you'd let me."

Silver took her arm and led her around to the driver's seat, ushering her in and then taking his place on the passenger side. "Go."

"All right." Pan bit her lips as she carefully turned on the ignition and put the powerful vehicle in gear, jerking it a little when she reversed, then angling it around to head up the ramp to the street.

Silver sensed her trepidation and he had to smile at the way her chin tilted just a bit more as they eased out into traffic. "Turn left, then make the first right. We don't have far to go."

"Easier to take a taxi," Pan said softly as a multitude of cabs and assorted vehicles crowded around her, making their way down one narrow street.

"You're doing fine. I'm not worried."

"That makes one of us," Pan muttered, hearing his deep-throated chuckle again.

The drive to the restaurant was short, but Pan felt as though her hands were manacled to the wheel when she pulled up in front and the valet came for the car.

Silver was around the car in front of the boy, lifting her out and slipping his arm around her waist as they walked

63

into the club. "You were very good, you know. I don't let most people drive my car."

"Wise of you." Pan noted that the moment they came in the door the maître d' was there, directing them to a table; the best table, it seemed to her.

Once they were seated, Silver looked at her, his head to one side. "You're a very independent woman, I know that, but would you mind if I ordered for both of us? They have a lobster madrilene that is wonderful. Then if you like, while we wait for our dinners, we'll dance."

Pan had a moment of rebellion, but the prospect of getting out on that floor with such danceable music was too great a temptation, so she nodded. Besides, she loved lobster, any way she could get it.

Silver could dance. The music was the Latin rhythm of a tango.

"Oh." Pan grinned up at him. "You know the moves."

"So do you. Have you ever traveled in the Latin countries?"

"Yes." Pan wished she'd lied, and she was very relieved when Silver swung her out from his body, seemingly not interested in pursuing the question.

It was when they were dancing to the second tango that she felt the twinge in her middle, annoying her more than making her apprehensive.

They danced slowly then, to a swaying love ballad, and Pan closed her eyes.

"A beautiful song, isn't it?" Silver breathed into her hair, loving the fresh scent of her.

"Yes."

Silver leaned closer, his body almost tenting hers. "Pan, you are so lovely, and more and more I want you with me." He watched her as she leaned away from him, opening her mouth to speak. Then a surprised and pained look appeared on her face, the words forgotten. "Pan, darling, what is it?"

"Help me." Agony took her, and she fainted in his arms.

CHAPTER THREE

"Yes, I'm her husband. Her name is Pan Belmont. She uses her maiden name, but I will sign everything for her." Silver signed his name with a flourish, then called his own physician. "Zeb, I want the best for her. I don't care what it takes." It had been over two hours since he'd learned that Pan was pregnant and in the process of having a miscarriage. In all his life he'd never moved faster or more surely as he organized the powers that be to help the woman who'd become so important to him.

When Silver was joined by the obstetrician who had treated Pan in the emergency room, it was difficult for him to sit as the physician invited him to do. "When can I see her?"

"In a little while, Mr. Galen. My name is Petra Seanu, and I've examined your wife." Dr. Seanu inclined her head until Silver took a chair opposite her. "I'm afraid we couldn't save the fetus. I'm sorry. But nothing in my examination of the patient leads me to think that your wife could not bring another child to term."

"Thank you. Have you told her that?"

"No. She's been very groggy. I'm not sure she even knows that she's aborted." Dr. Seanu held up one hand. "She was very weak and semiconscious when brought in. I'll tell her when she's a little stronger."

"No. I'll tell her," Silver snapped, jumping to his feet. "It's my place." His voice lowered.

Dr. Seanu stared up at the man whose face looked chiseled from steel, the vivid scarring in no way taking away from the tough good looks of the individual but rather adding to the picture of a very uncompromising person. "Would you mind answering a few questions for my patient's history?"

"I've already contacted my personal physician, Zebulon Quince. He should be getting an obstetrician for my wife."

"That is your right, of course, but until another doctor has taken over I intend to do as much as I can for my patient." Dr. Seanu rose to her feet, raising her chin.

Silver laughed out loud. "You should get along with my wife, Doctor. She has the same habit of lifting her chin when thwarted."

Dr. Seanu relaxed a little, thinking that Pan Belmont had a very handsome and sensuous husband.

"I want to see her. I'll just sit with her, Doctor, not bother her."

The doctor nodded, watching him stride down the hall. She wondered if Pan Belmont knew how lucky she was having Silver Galen for a husband.

A man in a wrinkled suit approached the doctor. "Pardon me, ma'am. My name is Grice. That looked like an old friend of mine. Silver Galen? Could you tell me why he's here?"

Dr. Seanu looked over the younger man with narrowed eyes. "I'm sorry. I don't give out information about anyone in this hospital." The doctor walked away, her head in the air.

"That was Silver Galen or my name's not Bill Grice."

The young man strolled to the nurses' station, positioning himself on one side so he could see but not be noticed.

When the personnel were all gone at the same time, he moved swiftly to the rack of charts, letting his eyes rove not for name but for the room number he'd seen Silver Galen enter: 317. He yanked the chart and opened it. Pan Belmont . . . Who the hell was that? Grice's finger went down the paper swiftly. Married. Spouse: Silver Galen. "Jee-zus." Grice let the history drop back into place, looking around him like a ferret with a kill before he sprinted down the hall.

"Where the hell is a telephone? Ah, there we are." His hands shook when he dialed. Who could ever imagine that he would stumble on such a story while visiting his sick uncle? "Lou, yeah, it's Grice. Have I got a story for you! I want an exclusive on it. Yeah. Listen to this."

Pan's eyes fluttered open and she looked right into Silver's. "Baby?"

Silver leaned over and took her hand, kissing the palm. "You lost the baby . . . but the doctor says it wasn't anything you did, and that you can carry another child to term."

"Thirsty." Pan felt the tears run down her cheeks into her hair as Silver held the bent straw to her lips. "Wanted the baby."

"I know. I wish you'd told me, Pan."

Her head moved negatively on the pillow. "Couldn't. Figured I . . . would tell you . . . at the end of the . . . four weeks. Then . . . you would throw me out but . . ."

"By then you would have the money to care for the baby and yourself." Silver watched her nod, knowing that the talking had tired her. "You have no need to fear

68

that. I may be able to take you home tomorrow, and you'll have all the care and nurturing you need." He kissed the palm of her hand. "If, after a time, we want children, we'll have them."

"Haven't decided to stay with you." Pan was too tired to keep her eyes open.

"You haven't, but I have, and I intend to convince you of it."

"Tired."

"Go to sleep, darling. I'll stay right here."

"Thank you."

Silver did stay the night, after securing a cot from one of the staff and putting it next to Pan's bed. It was much too short, but since he was up every time she turned over, moved or cried out in her sleep, he didn't need a very comfortable bed.

The next day Pan was examined by Silver's physician and pronounced in good shape considering what she'd been through. After much persuasion from Silver, the doctor allowed Pan to be discharged as long as she would have private nursing at home for a few days.

In the early afternoon, with two dozen cream roses on her lap, Pan was wheeled down the corridor by Silver, toward the emergency exit where a car awaited them.

When the doors opened, the place turned into chaos. As Ladder got out from behind the wheel and came around the car, people with microphones and portable television cameras sprung at Pan and Silver, some of them shouting questions and waving hands, papers, pencils and tape recorders in their faces.

"What the bloody hell is this, Ladder?"

"Damned if I know." Ladder turned sharply when a reporter tried to push past him. "Get back or I'll shove that camera down your throat."

69

"Is it true you've been married for some time, Silver?" A mike was shoved in Galen's face.

Silver saw fear on Pan's face when someone took her picture. "Ladder, get her out of here. I'll handle the vultures. Hurry."

"Right."

The two men lifted Pan into the back of the limousine and slammed the door. Then Ladder was around the car and under the wheel, and the big car was moving away, gathering speed.

Silver, accustomed to the eccentricities of the fourth estate, faced them, smiling. He knew that if he didn't give them some statement now, they would hound both him and Pan each time they attempted to leave their building.

One of the woman reporters stared at his scarred face. No wonder he was still attractive to women. If anything, the scar added to his mystique, his aura, the magnetism of the man. Lucky Pan Belmont, whoever she was.

"Now, what is it you wish to know about my wife?"

"When did you get married?"

"Where did you meet her?"

"Is it true you lost a baby?"

The questions went on, Silver fielding them with the ease of long experience that he'd gained when he'd been a driver. Some of what he told them was true, but he had no qualms about hedging and dissembling.

"We found it easier to marry quietly rather than have a big shindig neither of us wanted."

"When your parents were questioned, they said *no comment.* Why?"

"My family understands my need for privacy."

"Will you have other children?"

"My wife and I like children very much, but that is a

70

decision for the future. Thank you, ladies and gentlemen. If you don't mind, I'd like to get home to my wife."

The press parted like the Red Sea and allowed him through, still asking him questions, but though Silver smiled and nodded he did not say any more to them before getting into the closest cab and giving the driver his address.

Pan was caught in a pain-filled euphoria. She realized, with a fatalistic sense of calm, that she had been photographed; her picture would be shown on television coast to coast. Her period of running away and hiding out would be over soon; the matter had been taken out of her hands, and she felt a strange mixture of panic and relief. She fell asleep as soon as the nurse pulled the cover up to her chin.

Unwanted dreams came at once. She saw herself on the stand, being cross-examined by the defense counsel.

"No, no, that is not the way it was," Pan shouted at the judge, who pounded his gavel and didn't seem to hear her.

The nurse heard the elevator doors open with a quiet hum and smiled at the tight-faced man who entered and whom she recognized as the husband of her patient and the owner of this sumptuous apartment. "Good evening, sir."

"Good evening. How is she?"

"Sleeping, though restless. I've changed the sheets twice." The nurse studied him for a moment, noticing that his eyes kept going to the closed door of her patient's bedroom. "Ah, sir, you wanted me to remind you about having a night nurse. I should call the exchange if one will be needed for the midnight shift."

71

"What? Oh yes. I think we'll just have the day shift. I should be able to care for—my wife at the other times." Silver focused on her. "Will you be leaving at seven?"

"Yes, sir."

"Fine. Why don't you have a cup of coffee. I'm going to sit with my wife for a while." Silver pulled his tie free of his collar, undoing the top button of his shirt.

He wanted to be with Pan. It was so good to have her under his roof again. He'd hated even the short time she'd been in the hospital. Now as he entered the darkened room he pulled up a chair and slumped down into it, staring at the curled-up figure on the bed, wondering at how small she was when she had the courage of a pride of lions—except when she'd had her picture taken outside the emergency room of the hospital.

Fear! He had seen it in her face when the photographers aimed at her. His intrepid Pan Belmont had been in the grip of terror at that point, and that had been the primary reason he'd had Ladder hustle her away from there. All day that image of her had been in the front of his brain, and it had reinforced the notion he hadn't been able to shake since their first meeting.

The dead certainty that Pan Belmont was on the run from something in her past had gone around his head like loose marbles in a metal drum all day. What in her life had given her such a fright of photographers and reporters? Was she a criminal? Silver sighed, watching her as she turned over and muttered in her sleep. Whatever it was that was eating away at her was going to be known to him, and soon, because being in the dark about her was driving him crazy.

There was no sense telling himself that what Pan did with her life didn't matter to him. She mattered to him and she was getting under his skin more every day.

Baby! Who the hell would have figured she was pregnant? It irked and annoyed him more than he cared to admit that she had freely admitted she was using him to get the money they had agreed on when they struck the bargain. Maybe he would have tossed her out the door when he found out at the end of the allotted time that she was pregnant and using him to finance it. Silver shrugged. It was ridiculous to speculate. She was going to stay here now. He would see to that.

Silver had figured the first moment she had begun to dicker with him over price that she'd had an ulterior motive, that the motive had to do with her future in some way. But a baby hadn't occurred to him. He'd thought from the start that she wanted the money to tide her over while launching a modeling career.

Yawning, he shifted his body, trying for a comfortable spot. There wasn't one on that chair. He squinted around the room. There was a chaise longue he could try, even though he was sure it would be too short.

Rising to his feet, he proceeded to disrobe, not turning on a light as he tossed his clothes toward the chaise longue. There was more than enough room for him in the king-size bed with Pan.

Quietly he slipped between the sheets, staying over on one side of the bed. Gradually his eyes closed and he relaxed. It was so much better than last night, when Pan was in the hospital.

Silver's eyes flew open when he felt nails digging into his waist. Automatically his arms came up. "Pan? What is it, darling? Are you in pain?" He looked down at her, noting how wide-eyed she looked.

"Don't leave me," she whispered to him, her voice little more than a croak, her fingers digging into him.

"I won't, darling." He lifted her body close to his, feeling the clamminess of hers.

"I have to get up, go to the bathroom," she muttered.

"I'll take you." Silver switched on the overhead light, lifting her despite her protests and carrying her to the bathroom. "There. You call me when you're ready or if you need me. Don't lock the door." He leaned down and kissed the top of her head. "And stop being embarrassed. We live together."

"Not yet," she mumbled over his harsh laugh.

Silver went back into the bedroom, noting that the sheets were soiled. He stripped the bed, taking the linens to his room where there was a chute to the laundry room. Then he took clean linen from the cupboard and remade the bed.

"You're going to run out of linen," Pan told him, leaning on the doorjamb of the bathroom.

"You should have called me." Silver scowled at her as he hurried across the room and lifted her again.

"I should be walking, you know," Pan told him when he placed her on the chaise longue while he put the finishing touches on the bed.

"Tomorrow you can do your walking. Not tonight." He leaned over her. "Would you like a hot drink or something to eat before we go back to bed?"

Pan shook her head, feeling unsure of herself all at once. She wanted him to sleep with her, hold her.

"To answer your unspoken question, I am sleeping with you from now until you're less shaky . . . and maybe even then."

Pan put her arms around his neck when he hoisted her into his arms again. "No one would ever believe that you would be sleeping—ah, well, just sleeping with a woman." She laughed weakly.

"You're right about that, but since I have no intention of putting it into the tabloids I think our secret is safe." He lowered her to the bed, pulling the sheets up to her neck. "There. Comfortable?"

"Yes." Pan picked at the hem of the sheet with her fingers. "But it must be a discomfort for you—well, what I mean is—this arrangement."

"If you're asking does my libido get in the way, yes, it does, but I imagine that many men feel a bit frustrated in such situations, don't you?"

"I suppose." Pan's voice was almost inaudible.

Silver slipped into bed beside her and took her into his arms. "I didn't say that to hurt you—about the miscarriage, I mean. I suppose I just want you to concentrate on what Dr. Seanu said about this having nothing to do with future pregnancies."

"I wanted the baby." Pan shuddered against him at the admission. "It was all of Sydney I had left, and he was so good to me."

Unsaid but stated very loudly to Silver was an admission that not many people had been good to her. "You loved him very much?" Who was this Sydney who had colored her life so deeply? Silver felt both compassion for her pain and jealousy that someone else had been the focus of her life for so long.

"Not the silly romantic love that some people talk about, but the very solid day-to-day respect that is the only emotion that counts between people."

"Are you a cynic about love, my Pan?" Silver murmured into her hair, his hand massaging her back.

"I suppose I am. Sydney used to say I was being silly, that he would change my mind, but he wasn't able to do that. He was such an optimist."

Silver felt her chuckle vibrate from her body to his,

ambivalent emotions erupting in him like a flood. He wanted to make love to her, and he wanted to make her forget Sydney. He wanted to be the one who would make her laugh in that soft warm way! Passion and jealousy— what a fool he was!

"What are you thinking, Silver?"

"Stupid things."

"Like what?"

"I'm jealous of Sydney, and that irritates me." When she smiled, he looked down at her crossly. "It isn't funny."

"Aw, have you never been jealous before?"

"Never." And he hadn't. It threw him out of stride, like sliding down the washed decks of a ship when it heeled over hard, which gave him an idea. "I'm going to take you on a cruise."

"We were talking about feelings and you jump to that. Why?"

"I'm going to make you very well, so that when I convince you to marry me—"

"Live with you, not marry you. That's not in the picture."

"I read somewhere that marriage is making a comeback. Mustn't botch up the statistics. Don't you want to be trendy?"

Pan thought he had the largest, most wonderful navy blue eyes, the lamplight emphasizing the touches of gold raying out from the pupils. "Not marriage. We haven't even decided on living together yet."

"You haven't. I have."

Pan stared up at him. "I feel warm now."

Silver kissed her nose. "Good. So do I, so please don't ask me to leave this bed."

76

"I won't." Pan inhaled shakily, her eyelids drooping. "Tired."

"Of course you're tired. And you're going to have to spend a good bit of time in bed in the next few weeks."

"Weeks? Don't be silly. I can rest for a few days, but Dr. Seanu didn't say anything about weeks."

"I want you well, on your feet and active," he told her gruffly.

"Big plans?"

"You could say that."

"All right. I'll be tiptop in no time."

Silver saw the shadow cross her face and he tightened his hold. "The doctor told me that the loss of a child in miscarriage can be just as painful physically and mentally for the mother as losing a full-term child. I'll help you get through this, darling."

Pan tucked her head under his chin. "It's funny, I didn't even feel differently after getting pregnant. But now that I've lost the baby, I feel . . ." Pan swallowed hard, fighting the tears that rose in her. "Bereft."

"I know, I know. I understand, I do."

Pan felt the tears dry as that warm clasp tightened even more. Not even with Sydney had she ever felt so safe.

There were no more words between them.

When Silver felt her body slacken and her breathing deepen he cuddled her close, letting his own eyes shut. Never had he felt so good in bed with a woman. There had never been a time when he'd wanted to sleep with a woman in his arms. Now it was so natural, so right.

Sleep came like a velvet blanket, his last thought being that he hadn't set the alarm. Hopefully he would waken in time, since he had an early meeting.

* * *

"Sir, sir, I'm sorry to waken you," Nurse Kester told Silver when he came groggily awake. "A Mr. Bateman is in the other room, sir, and he says that you must rise now. It's eight o'clock."

"Wha? Oh, Lord. Overslept. Damnit. All right, nurse, go and tell him I'm coming, but please don't waken my wife. I'd like her to sleep as long as possible. Then she can have breakfast later," Silver whispered to the woman, who nodded and moved toward the door.

When he was easing from the bed, Pan's eyes flew open. "Shhh, darling, go back to sleep."

"You're leaving me."

"Just for a little while. I have a meeting, but I'll be back after that and we'll have lunch together."

Pan looked around as though orienting herself. "All right."

"That's my girl." Silver kissed her gently on the mouth, then swung his legs to the floor.

"You'll shock the nurse if she comes back and sees you in just your briefs." Pan laughed softly.

"I don't care if she sees me swinging from a light in the nude if it makes you smile." Silver threw her a kiss and ambled toward her bathroom. "I won't use your bathroom, sweetheart. I just want to wrap a towel around myself when I go upstairs."

"I thought you didn't mind being seen by the nurse."

"I might drive her wild, and that would make you jealous."

"Baloney." Pan leaned back against the pillows, watching him until he disappeared in the bathroom, then returned with a towel wrapped toga-fashion around himself. "Pick up your clothes." Pan pointed to the things on the chaise longue and on the floor in front of it.

78

"Mrs. Tillson will get them." Silver blew her a kiss, noting her flash of irritation at his remark, then he was gone.

Ladder was in the front room, a cup of coffee in front of him, the morning paper in his hands. "You'll be late."

"Did you stall them?"

"Yup."

"Good. I'll be down as soon as I shower."

"Right."

The nurse came through from the kitchen with a tray.

Ladder uncoiled his length and approached her. "If you don't mind, ma'am, I'll take that. I'd like a word with Miss Belmont."

The nurse frowned at him. "You mean Mrs. Galen?"

"Pardon me? Ah, yes, I guess I do." Ladder noted the tight-lipped disapproval as she handed him the tray.

"Mrs. Galen must have her bath directly after her breakfast. It is imperative that she rest."

"Yes, ma'am," Ladder answered laconically, moving down the hall to the bedroom and pushing the door open with his elbow. "Good morning."

Pan looked up, smiling. "Food. Good. I'm hungry." She sat up, pulling the sheet up with her.

Ladder placed the tray on a side table, then bent to retrieve a negligee from the chaise longue. "I expect this is yours. Silver doesn't look too good in this color and he wears more ruffles." He could feel his own smile widening when she laughed, the sound trilling around the room like audio sunlight. "You'd better eat all of this. Your nurse has announced that she's coming in to give you a bath after you've eaten, so I imagine she'll be checking your tray." He chuckled when her mouth dropped open.

"Well, I'm going to take a shower. I'm not an invalid and—"

"You'll do as the nurse tells you," Silver said as he came into the room, dressed in a dark worsted silk suit with a silver and blue tie, his shirt the palest creamy blue.

"You look the image of the successful stuffed shirt," Pan told him tartly, gripping her half-empty orange juice glass as though it were a missile.

"Why, darling, are you feeling testy?" He approached the bed warily, his eyes on her throwing arm, ducking and giving her a quick kiss on the lips. "I'll be back for lunch, and you had better be in bed."

"What a provocative remark, O Sultan." Pan glared at him, setting down her glass and grasping the pillow behind her head.

"Isn't she sweet, Ladder?" Silver ducked the bed pillow that she tossed at him, reaching down deftly to steady the tray on her lap. "See you later, love."

Ladder followed his boss out the door after telling Pan that he would be back to visit her, his thoughtful gaze on Silver Galen. He stood quietly while Silver gave a host of instructions to the nurse. Then the two of them went through the door into Silver's office. "I understand you're married."

Silver gave him a sharp look. "You know damned well I'm not."

"The nurse thinks you are."

"So does the hospital. It was easier to get things done that way." Silver had one hand on top of his chair back, standing behind his desk, as he went through his mail and his agenda for the day. His motions stilled as he looked at his friend thoughtfully. "Someone at the hospital called the press about it, though. I complained to the chief of staff."

"Then you want to put out a statement denying the marriage?"

80

"No!" Silver exploded. "No," he said in a quieter voice. "Just let things go as they are. Things have a habit of taking care of themselves."

"The Commodore might feel differently when he gets wind of it."

"True." Silver gave Ladder a hard smile. "But not even my father thinks he would be successful interfering in my life."

"He'll try."

"Let him. I don't intend to explain Pan to anyone."

"Good. I don't think you could explain that whole situation." He stared at his friend. "And I sure as hell don't think you want to delve into your own motives on this."

Silver glared at his long-time friend, who stared benignly back at him. "Someday I'm going to break your nose for you."

"So you've been telling me these last dozen years and more."

"Have I? Then you've been fairly warned." Silver glared at the letter in his hand.

Ladder didn't take his eyes off his friend. "Do you love her?" Ladder didn't miss the enigmatic veil that dropped over Silver's features when he looked up again.

Silver took a deep breath, his features tightening before they fell into a mask again. "She intrigues the hell out of me."

"Cobras are intriguing."

"It isn't that type of fascination."

"You could hurt her."

"Then it's a tradeoff. She could tear me apart." As Silver walked away from the desk, the red call light on his private outside line flashed, signaling a call. Silver grimaced. "The Commodore. I'd bet anything on it. Handle it, Ladder." He strode across the office to the conference room, where he threw open the door. "Good morning, ladies and gentlemen. Sorry I'm late. Let's get right to it, shall we?"

Ladder glared at the console, then lifted the phone. "Good morning, sir. No, sir, he isn't. Yes, a conference. I don't think I'd better tell him that, sir. Ah, yes, calling him about dinnertime might be best. Yes, of course, I'll give him the message. Thank you, sir." Ladder replaced the receiver, exhaling in relief, thanking whatever fates were listening for keeping the Commodore at his home on Long Island most of the time.

Ladder followed Silver into the conference room, the sudden cacophony of voices a very familiar sound to him. He took a chair in the corner away from the conference table, a briefcase open on his lap.

"I tell you it was Trisha; she's gotten herself married. I should know my own cousin, shouldn't I?"

"Dexter, sit down and stop that infernal pacing," Maeve Drexel ordered her stepson. "Even if it is Trish, that shouldn't worry us. We've been doing very well without her in our lives, I think." Maeve shot a quick look at Alan Winston, her smile softening. Alan had been her lover since shortly after he had come to work for her husband, Henry Drexel.

"So I've been telling him." Alan smiled at Dexter, thinly veiled contempt twisting his lips. "I told you not to worry. That committal order is still valid if we want to move on it." He shrugged. "In the meantime we are running the Drexel Holding Company as it should be run."

"And doing the inferior work that made the Triangle Building collapse in Mexico City during the last earthquake." Dexter glared at the man, who had been ordering him around since he'd moved in with Dexter's step-mother. Alan Winston took every opportunity to try to make him feel less of a person than he was and Dexter resented him more every day.

"We were cleared of any wrongdoing," Alan snapped, his face mottling with angry color.

"All right, we've been all over this." Maeve Drexel glared at her stepson. He used to be much easier to manipulate. Of late he had been asserting himself in a most irritating way. "Dex, stop bringing up old news. And you, Alan, don't blow your top." Maeve strolled across the large drawing room of the mansion on the hill in San Francisco, her curvaceous figure made taller by the haute couture dresses she affected, her dark hair and dark eyes a dramatic contrast for her slightly olive skin. She had no intention of giving up this house and the way of life it provided her, even though the business and the house belonged to her husband's niece.

Maeve's husband and Dex's father, Henry Drexel, had given her a taste for the good life, and she wasn't going to let anything change that.

Not that her husband could ever have given her the cachet into such wealth when they had first married. Henry had been a rather inept man from one of the oldest families in San Francisco, who'd bumbled along in genteel poverty in the family's paper business.

It had been Julius Drexel, Henry's brother, who'd been the go-getter, first marrying Linda Belmont, then using her money to form a newspaper business that had grown into a chain that was second to none in California, with a news service in Europe and Asia.

Maeve's lips tightened when she thought of her brother-in-law and sister-in-law. They had never warmed up to her, even though Henry had worked for Julius.

Maeve had been forced to be polite to them because Julius was Henry's boss. How demeaning that she and Henry had had a lower standard of living than his own brother!

It had been a stroke of good fortune when Julius and Linda had been killed in a boating accident, leaving their only child in her husband Henry's custodial care.

Maeve's lips tightened as she recalled how her husband had changed with the death of his brother. He had no longer been amenable to her every wish. Trisha Belmont Drexel, his niece, had become the focus in his life, and it had become paramount to him to protect her interests in the newspaper business that the Drexel Holding Company controlled.

Trisha had become so close to her uncle after the death of her parents that Maeve and Dexter were almost shut out. That had angered and frightened Maeve, especially when her husband had told her in no uncertain terms that he would tolerate none of her shenanigans with his niece and that he would never allow her to manipulate the young girl of whom he was so fond.

"Maeve, Maeve, stop daydreaming," Dexter said petulantly.

Maeve wheeled away from her blind view out the window, looking down toward San Francisco Bay. "It hurts to remember that it was your cousin who killed my husband . . . and your father."

Dexter glared at her. "She was charged but not convicted. Trish ran because she was afraid of being committed again."

"Are you saying that you don't believe she killed your father?"

Dexter looked discomfited suddenly. "No. I'm not saying that. The police are pretty sure she did it."

84

Maeve stared at him. "Even if that woman you saw on television is Trisha, do you think resurrecting all that old business can bring my husband back to me?"

Dexter shrugged, looked uncomfortable. "No, I don't mean that. It's just that we've moved into Trisha's company, taken over the running of the parent organization without even trying to find her. It's—it's not honest."

"Funny you should get a conscience all at once, after taking a multiple-digit raise last month and signing over the trip to Europe on the Concorde with eleven guests to your cheat sheet," Alan Winston said contemptuously.

Dexter turned white, then he blushed furiously. "At least I'm family. Since when are you to monitor my expenditures? As I recall, your expense account would rival the budget of one of our subsidiaries."

"Why you—" Alan Winston started across the room, hands clenched.

"Stop it." Maeve stepped quickly between them. "We have a business to run and a life to maintain here. We should think seriously about protecting that rather than tearing at each other."

Alan Winston paused, watching Dex for a moment longer. Then he looked back at Maeve and nodded once. "All right, I'll go along with that. How about you, Dex?"

Dex shrugged again, still feeling ill at ease about the situation. "Fine." He looked at the other two, noting the warm looks exchanged between them.

"Damnit, Felice, don't try to cover for the boy. I want to know who the hell this wife of his is and I want to know now."

"Well, you won't get anything out of Sterling by attacking him like a bear," his wife of forty years informed Sterling Galen the elder, called the Commodore by family and friends because of the fact that he had helped win the America's Cup for his country on two separate occasions.

"Felice, I'll be back at dinnertime."

"I'm accompanying you, Sterling." Felice, a small woman with laughing blue eyes she'd bequeathed to her son, studied her spouse in wary amusement. Her hair was a muted golden hue, and with her slender, well-conditioned body on a five-foot-three-inch frame, she looked years younger than she was.

"Why?" Her husband snapped at her, thinking that she looked lovely in the mauve suede suit she was wearing. It had always amazed him that he had loved her for so long. Somehow it had always been in the back of his mind that he would be a philanderer as his father was, who lived in sultanic splendor in Hawaii, but Felice du Lant had captured his fancy when they were both in college, and he found her just as captivating now as he had then.

Felice du Lant Galen watched her tall, stalwart husband, whom she'd loved madly since she was twenty. She fought back a smile as she watched the play of emotions over his face. How he had fought the role of faithful husband and father! But he was her dearest man, and she never chided him about his silliness. How he could ever have thought he was anything like his reprobate of a father, who'd made millions of dollars in his lifetime and bedded every woman who'd acquiesce to his requests, was something she could never fathom.

Felice had liked her mother-in-law and had missed her when she died, but she had never understood how she'd kept from caving her husband's skull in for him.

"Don't you think that I should meet my new daughter-in-law, Sterling?"

86

"I know that you call me Sterling, in just that way, when you're planning something." The Commodore put his arms around his wife and kissed her soundly. "Why do I put up with you?"

"Because you love me, silly."

"That's a stupid reason."

"So you keep telling me, darling."

The Commodore knew there was no sense in attempting further persuasion so he readied himself for the trip into Manhattan with a minimum of grumbling.

Felice du Lant Galen was glad they were being chauffeured into the city from the island. It spared her nerves. Her husband had a habit of looking at whomever he spoke to when driving, taking his eyes from the road.

"Well, what do you think Silver's up to now, Felice?"

"Darling, whatever it is, he will never tell us. He'll just hedge and smile."

"Damned deep man. Makes a good businessman, but an irritating son."

"Yes, he has been that. Nothing irritated me more than his racing."

"That didn't irritate you, it scared you witless."

"You too."

"Damned offspring. I told you not to get pregnant so many times."

"I had help."

"That's no excuse."

Felice put her hand through his arm and felt his fingers thread with hers as he pulled her closer to him. "I think I shall call the others and invite them to the house. Since we do have a new daughter-in-law, we should have a celebration."

"I like it better when it's just the two of us in that big

house. That way I can chase you into any room I choose."

"Devil."

The car cruised into Manhattan, at once getting caught up in the cacophony of sound from traffic and pedestrians.

"I always forget this part of it." The Commodore glared out the window at the traffic.

"I should really have made an appointment at Charine's to have something made if we're going to have a get-together."

"Good. We'll call her right now." The Commodore pressed the automatic dialer and in minutes was talking to the fashionable salon. "Yes, but my wife would prefer early afternoon. Wednesday would be fine. Wait. Better make it for two."

"Who is the other person, Sterling?"

"Our new daughter-in-law might need clothes."

Felice didn't answer him, quite sure it would be of no use to point out to her stubborn mate that perhaps this new relative would wish to choose her own designer.

When the car purred to the curb, the Commodore was out before the driver could come around and do the job.

"Come along, my dear. Don't dawdle."

"I should have worn roller skates."

"Don't be silly, Felice, you'd mark up the lobby floor. That parquet tile was handmade in . . ."

"Madrid. Yes, I did know that, darling."

Her husband kissed her cheek hard. "Faithless creature. I should spank you."

"Oh do, Sterling, but wait until we get home."

When the old-timers of the Galen Building saw the Commodore enter the building, many rushed forward to greet him.

"Hello, Joe. I thought they pensioned you off."

"They did, Commodore, but I went crazy, so I came back." Joe Hardy grinned at the man for whom he'd worked for forty years.

"Didn't put you on half pay, did they?" the Commodore asked loudly enough to turn heads in the lobby.

"Oh no, sir, the young master is doing fair to middlin'."

"Humph. That'll be the day. Take care, Joe. I'll come in one day and we'll have coffee. You can catalogue his mistakes for me."

"I'll look forward to it, sir."

The Commodore put his key in the elevator and turned it. "Don't tell me he hasn't changed the locks yet!"

"I think it would be wiser if we went to Silver's office first," his wife told Sterling Galen softly. "He might wish to introduce his wife to us."

"He should have thought of that before marrying secretly, then announcing to the world that he and his wife have miscarried a child. Damned impertinence!"

"Which? Marrying, or the baby?"

"You're as fresh as you always were, Felice." When the elevator doors closed, the Commodore put his arms around his wife and kissed her long and hard.

When the elevator opened into the foyer of Silver's apartment, they were still embracing.

"I beg your pardon." The nurse stood there staring at them, haughty and offended. "I shall call security."

"Good. Then I'll have you tossed out of here. Where is Mrs. Tillson?"

"I'm here, sir. Good morning, Commodore, Mrs. Galen. It's so good to see you." Mrs. Tillson wrung her hands and rolled her eyes.

89

"If it's so good to see us, why do you look as though you've just been caught with your hand in my wallet?"

The nurse gasped in outrage.

Mrs. Tillson didn't change expression, quite used to the Commodore's plain speaking, as he called it. "Ah, sir, why don't you and Mrs. Galen sit down in the living room and I'll bring a tray with some tea—"

"Don't want any damned tea. Get me a cup of coffee, the real stuff. I'm going to talk to my daughter-in-law. Upstairs or down?"

"Down, sir," Mrs. Tillson answered faintly.

"Make that decaffeinated, Mrs. Tillson, and don't worry," Mrs. Galen told the old retainer before following her husband.

"Wait. My patient is resting." The nurse came to life.

Mrs. Tillson put a restraining hand on her arm. "Don't go in there. You'll set off the Commodore, and believe me, you won't like seeing him in a tirade." Mrs. Tillson looked at the door leading into Silver's office. "I'd better call Mr. Galen . . ." She looked back at the nurse. "And when he comes through, you'd better duck. It's like two bulls hitting forehead to forehead when the Commodore and his son go at it."

Felice Galen came up behind her husband in the darkened room, touching him lightly on the back.

"She's asleep," her husband told her, sotto voce.

"So I see. Perhaps we'd—"

"Who is it?" The bedclothes ruffled, then were pushed down as a sleepy face peered over the hem of the silk sheets, focusing on them. "Hello."

"Damnit, she's young, Felice."

"It would seem so," Mrs. Galen responded, keeping her voice neutral. What had her son done now? He was as unpredictable as his father at times. Felice Galen knew that nothing about her son could ever affect her as much as the terrible accident he'd almost died in, but now she felt a niggling of worry as she looked into the haunted eyes of the young woman with the bedclothes pulled up to her chin. "We're Silver's father and mother, my dear. I'm Felice and this is my husband Sterling, though everyone calls him the Commodore."

"How do you do." Pan, who had been so glad to get rid of the nurse who had fussed over her for an hour after she insisted on taking a shower and not having a bed bath, wished the woman would appear at that moment. The insanity between her and Silver was mushrooming to include his whole family. It had to stop!

"How do you feel, child? Miscarriages are bad. Felice had two. Scared me to death. Told her not to have any more children, but she had three anyway. Never could take an order."

Pan stared at the gruff man in front of her, who was an older version of Silver—tall, spare, very handsome, with graying wavy hair, his stern mien belied by the warm snap in his gray eyes. "Oh."

"Adopt the next ones. Easier on you," the Commodore told her sagely.

"Thank you, sir," Pan responded faintly.

"How are you feeling, dear?" Felice Galen went to the side of the bed and leaned down, smiling.

Pan thought her quite lovely, with her slight, trim figure in the mauve suede suit, her hair beautifully coifed.

"I dye it blond because my children would like me to go gray now that I'm a grandmother." Felice Galen had interpreted Pan's look.

Pan responded to the roguish smile with one of her own. "Would you like—that is, I could ring—"

"Having coffee sent in," the Commodore interrupted, pulling up a side chair close to the bed. "Come sit down, Felice." He pulled up another for himself after he'd seated his wife.

The door banged open, ricocheting off the wall as Silver stormed into the room. "Mother. Commodore, how are you?"

"A lot you care," his father bellowed, then looked at Pan. "Sorry, my dear," he told her in a stage whisper. "Mustn't shout in the sickroom."

"I'm not ill, sir," Pan told him, warming to the gruff older man, who was obviously uncomfortable.

"Is that what he told you?" The Commodore's voice rose again as he looked at his son. "Put 'em right back into the fields, is that it?"

"No," Silver thundered. "She will have every care."

Pan stared at the two of them as they faced each other like pugilists in a ring, noting the resigned amusement of Silver's mother as she watched her husband and son. "Sir, I'm fine, not ill at all."

The Commodore looked back at the bed and smiled. "No, of course you're not. Strong girl."

"Commodore, I think we should go out in the other room—"

"No, Silver. Coffee is being brought in here . . ." Pan faltered at Silver's fulminating look, wondering why he was so angry. "Do come sit down and join us for coffee."

Silver looked from his serene mother to his scowling father and shrugged. "Why not." He walked over to the bed, kicked off his shoes and got under the covers with Pan. "There. Are you comfy, darling?" Silver kissed Pan's agape mouth.

Felice had to steady herself not to fall from the chair as she studied her son's rapt expression. So, it had happened to Silver. Somehow she had always felt that he might be a throwback to his grandfather and go from woman to woman until he died.

"For heaven's sake, is that good for her? She just had a miscarriage."

"I know that, Commodore," Silver said testily, putting his arm around Pan and cuddling her close to him. "We didn't expect guests this morning."

"Testy, are you? Had to leave a meeting to rush in here and rescue the fair damsel there from the dragon?" His father glowered at him.

"Something like that. Pan has to rest for the next few days. Then I'm going to take her to Bermuda for a holiday."

"Why didn't you tell us about this marriage?"

"You don't understand—" Pan began before Silver, realizing that she was going to tell his parents about their charade, bent and placed his mouth over hers again.

"What my wife is saying is that we chose to keep it secret, but now that it's out in the open we intend to live like any other normal married couple. Of course Pan won't be able to conceive a child for at least a year or more."

"Any fool knows that." The Commodore smiled at his daughter-in-law, who looked from her husband to his father and back again. "Might keep the adoption idea open. She's quite tiny—and young, too." The Commodore glared at his son.

"Pan is twenty-four years old."

"What kind of name is Pan?" The Commodore looked at his wife.

"It's a combination of Patricia and Ann, Father. Pan Belmont Galen," Silver instructed, tightening his hold on his "wife."

93

Felice didn't take her eyes off the couple, even after her glance at the third finger of the bride's left hand. "Marvelous idea, Bermuda, but I think we should have a small gathering of family before that just to introduce—Pan to everyone."

"Mother—" Silver began.

"Good idea. Then we can show her that nice house you have on Long Island not too far from us. Good place to raise children."

"Good God." The new bride sounded as though she were choking as she pulled the bedclothes over her head.

"Darling . . ." Silver joined her under the covers, murmuring to her.

"Shy little thing, isn't she, Felice?" The Commodore looked unsure of himself.

"I think she's wonderful. I'm delighted," Felice murmured, beaming at her puzzled husband.

"What are they doing under the covers, Felice?" the Commodore whispered.

"I think our son is whispering love things to her."

"Damned indiscreet, if you ask me."

CHAPTER FOUR

Pan's normal health was quickly restored by the tender, almost overpowering care of Silver Galen. Though she felt a stinging pathos at the loss of her child, Silver's support helped her face that, too, with equanimity.

At times she looked at him askance, thinking he must be getting bored with the whole picture, but he not only showed no signs of boredom, he seemed to delight in planning the trip they would be making to Bermuda and alluding to other things they would be doing together in the future.

One evening as they were sitting out in the great room in front of the fire with colorful travel folders in their laps, Pan turned in the curve of his arm and looked up at him. "I should be looking for a job." The arm on her shoulder convulsed, and she was brought closer to him.

"No. You need more rest. It's only been three weeks and—"

"Our bargain was struck for four weeks, so I should be well past the planning stage and into action by now."

"The bargain was struck on the implied premise that you would be healthy all that time. Losing the child and recovering from it mitigate strict adherence to what we decided." Silver sounded out each word as though he were making a speech to his board.

"You're hedging." It never ceased to amaze Pan how comfortable she felt with him, how absurdly safe.

Silver turned her in his arms, his lips feathering across her cheeks to her lips. "I don't want you to leave me. I want you to marry me."

Pan pulled back from him, trying to mask her breathlessness behind a laugh. "Now that's not being a good businessman. You haven't even tried the product and you want to buy." Mirth bubbled out of her.

"Brat. You know damn well I want to try the product, as you put it, and when you're well enough I'm going to do just that . . . but I want to marry you too."

"What if I'm frigid, or even a nymphomaniac? Then what will you do?"

"Easy. Make love to you until you melt if you're frigid . . . and until you're sated if you're a nymphomaniac. Then I'll give you an aspirin and call you in the morning —so we can do it all over again!"

"That sounds crazy to me."

"So does your implication that you should leave me."

"Finding a job doesn't imply anything else but looking for work."

"Good. Right after we're married I'll help you find a job."

"Silver, we—" She gasped when he took hold of her and turned her so that she was lying on the couch and he was reclining over her, his mouth on hers, tasting her as though she were ambrosia to him.

Even with just their lips touching, heat exploded between them as it had since the first day they'd met and Silver had kissed her once, lightly.

Pan felt as though part of her had floated away from her body and grafted onto him. It both frightened and intrigued her how easily he was able to pull her apart emotionally, demanding and getting her total concentration.

Silver balanced his weight so that there was no pressure on her and lifted his head so he could look down at her. "We're very good together, Pan, even without sex." He grinned at her. "It boggles the mind to think of us that way. We might move the building off its foundations."

Pan was irritated when she felt the blood rush to her face. She knew that it delighted him when he could disconcert her, and she noted how his grin widened. "Conceited!"

"Ummm, about us I am. We're so great."

"I don't think you're looking at us clearly," she told him dryly.

He kissed her gently, his mouth coursing across her cheek. "Yes, I am, darling. *You're* not looking at us fairly."

"Silver, do you know the rate of divorce just in this state alone?"

"Roughly, I do, but I don't intend that we'll ever take that route. We're going to stay married, solve our problems when we have them, but even if there are loose ends in our relationship, we won't part."

"We could go around and around on this." Pan's finger traced his lips. She enjoyed touching him and felt a quiver run through her at the velvet toughness of that mouth.

"Let's take a chance on us." Silver let his body rotate gently against hers.

"Now, you know what happens when you do that." Pan felt heat rise in her body as she melted toward him.

"Yes, so don't make any cute remarks about taking a cold shower."

"Would I do that?" To Pan's chagrin her body betrayed her and undulated back. The startled look on Silver's face was replaced by heated delight.

"Wonderful, but if you keep this up I'm going to embarrass myself," he told her, leaning close and nuzzling her neck.

"I'm sorry, that was unthinking of me."

"Great is the word, but I have a low tolerance for your magnetism, love." Silver groaned and moved away from her. "Let's stop this nonsense and get married. Even if I have to keep away from you then, at least I'll know you're my wife and that will help . . ."

All at once he tensed and looked around at her. "Didn't you see Dr. Seanu today? I should have asked you right away. Damnit, it's been on my mind all day, but the minute I saw you all thought went out the window." He leaned down and kissed her roughly. "Stop trying to put me off with that sexy body of yours."

"I wasn't trying to do that." Pan laughed when his chin came out. "You look like a frustrated mule."

"Tell me what she said."

"She told me that I'm fine, that I can resume all normal activity—except maybe skydiving and things like that." Pan's laugh trailed away at the passionate look on his face. "What are you thinking?"

"I'm thinking that we should get married. Since you can resume all normal activity."

Pan stared up at him, mouth agape. "But you can't—we didn't—we haven't."

"So? We can begin tonight, can't we? You're not going to leave me, are you? Even with seventy-five thousand dollars in your bank account? You can't. I won't let you."

"The money isn't in my account yet." Pan paused when she saw him nod. "Is it?"

"The money's been in there since the second day you've lived here."

"It has?" Pan felt lightheaded. She had to decide now! The bargain wasn't in the future. It was right this minute!

Silver leaned over her again. "Stop fretting. I don't want to intimidate you, I want to love you."

"Maybe that's the same thing." She smiled at him weakly.

"In some cases it might be, but not in ours. We'll fight against anything that might hurt our union."

"You're not Abraham Lincoln." Pan tried to battle out of her corner.

"Won't you take a chance on me?"

The question hung there between them. The silence stretched, vibrated. Their eyes were locked.

"Oh God, yes I will." Pan wanted to laugh at the stunned look on Silver's face but she felt too teary.

"What? What did you say? No, don't repeat it if you're going to change one syllable."

"I said yes, I will."

Silver kneeled next to the couch and put his face on her abdomen. "Pan, darling, you won't be sorry." He could feel her thready uncertainty vibrating into him.

Her hands moved through his hair, holding his head pressed against her. She was sorry already. Damn! She didn't need such an overpowering commitment in her life. Why did she have to fall in love with Sterling Galen III? Silver was a complication in her life, but by the same token she didn't know how to eradicate him. He had insinuated himself into her heart and soul.

He read her feelings, all her misgivings, the sense of doom she had about the future. There wasn't much he could do about that at the moment except keep her with him and try to convince her in slow sweet steps that they would be wonderful together for all time. "Tomorrow night when you meet the horde, I'll tell them that we'll be in Bermuda for three weeks instead of two. That way we can fly somewhere for a quickie ceremony. Everything will be taken care of from now on, love."

"It sounds like a roller coaster to me."

"Stop building barriers to our life. It will be fine, you'll see."

"About meeting your family . . ."

"No need to fret about that. They'll love you."

Pan looked up at him helplessly. "Silver, you don't know that."

"I do. Besides, I don't give a tinker's damn if they hate you, but they won't." He scooped her up into his arms. "How would you like a nice glass of cold milk after you have your shower?"

"Silver, you don't need to wait on me anymore." Her arms curled around his neck.

"I want to do things for you. Would you like to sleep upstairs or downstairs tonight?"

Each night he'd asked her the same question, because he always slept with her. When she tried to argue that it wasn't necessary, he always brought up the scare she'd given him when she'd fainted at the supper club.

"From now on we'll be sleeping together anyway."

"We have been right along."

"I know, but this makes it official." Silver grinned down at her.

Pan saw past the smile to the uncertainty he felt with her. "True."

Silver stopped in his tracks as he traversed the great room, holding her easily, inhaling a sharp breath. "So? Where do we go?"

"Let's try your room this time, shall we?"

"Let's." Silver felt a rush of triumph. She had never suggested that they go up to his room. He felt as though he'd just taken a giant step in their relationship.

"Wait. Put me down. I should get my nightgown and—"

"Don't worry. I'll get everything you need." Silver took the curving stairway two steps at a time. He hurried into his bedroom and placed her in the middle of his huge bed, going down with her so that the two of them sprawled dead center. It was the first time she'd been in his bed, and he was in thrall at the feeling it gave him. Then he rolled off the bed. "I'll be right back."

Pan looked around at the beige and cream room that she'd visited once before, on the first day she'd stayed at the apartment.

When Silver reentered the room he saw her sitting Indian-fashion where he'd left her, and his heart thudded against his chest wall. She was a child-woman, vulnerable, beautiful, exceptionally naive and canny at the same time. What magical forest had she sprung from?

Pan turned and saw Silver staring at her. She smiled at him. "What sleepwear did you bring?"

"The pale pink one. I like it with your hair."

Pan stared at the filmy garment and grimaced. "That cost more than I lived on last year, I'll bet."

Silver watched her get off the bed and take the nightie from him and amble to his bathroom. He was so elated to have her there he could have jumped up and smacked the ceiling. So he did.

Pan reopened the bathroom door. "What was that thump?"

"I hit the ceiling with the flat of my hand."

"Oh. Why?"

"Because it's there, Red." He sprinted out of the room,

laughing when he heard her call out, "Don't call me Red."

Silver showered downstairs in half the time it usually took him, his hair still damp when he went back to Pan, who was waiting with her sexy nightgown on, solemn and wide-eyed.

"We don't have to make love or do anything that would make you uncomfortable, darling," Silver told her softly.

"I know." She lifted her arms.

Like a somnambulist Silver approached the bed, eager but wary, passion-filled but determined to be coolly affectionate. "I've never wanted to get into my bed so much in my life," he whispered. "But I feel as though my knees have turned to water. Am I welcome?"

"It's your bed," she told him huskily.

"So it is." Silver slipped under the covers, noting her barely perceptible flinch even as she schooled her features to a soft smile. He sat up next to her, the coverlet sliding to his hips, barely showing the tops of the pajama bottoms he wore. His index finger lifted her chin a trifle so that he was looking into her eyes. "It's tough on me being near you, but not impossible to handle . . ."

Pan tried to jerk her chin away, but his fingers caught it and turned it toward him again. "We've been through this."

"So we have . . . but since it's very important to our future that you trust me, I think it should be stated over and over, don't you?"

"Don't you think it's equally important that you trust me? Do you?"

Silver inhaled, seeing the challenge in her eyes. "I know there are things you either can't or won't tell me . . ."

"True." Gritty determination was in her voice.

"But . . . I do trust what you tell me, because I think you are a very honest person."

Shaken, Pan looked away from him. "You don't know me well enough to say that."

"I know you very well, darling, and I did the first time I saw you making soup from ketchup and hot water. Spunky, innovative, courageous, outrageous and delightful."

"Is that all?" Pan swallowed, her smile wobbling, her hand coming up in a tentative caress to his cheek, and finding shock waves at the touch.

Silver's arms closed around her, falling back against the pillows, cradling her gently against him. "Comfy?"

Pan nodded, wriggling in a relaxed way, her body reacting in comfort to the warmth of his.

"Ah, could you please not do that, love? We have to have a few ground rules if I'm going to be celibate for a time."

Pan looked up at him, her eyes brimming with mirth at his grimace. "Martyr."

"True." When she undulated slowly once more he groaned, his body betraying him at once. "Pan, baby—please."

Pan shared his excitement, and felt a sense of want that she'd never experienced with anyone, an anticipation that rumbled the blood through her veins. Feathering her hands over his bare chest, gently tugging at the hair there gave her a tingling awareness of how Silver had, like osmosis, entered her being. She wanted him, and that stunned her. With Sydney it had been different. She had wanted to make him happy; her desire for him had been laced with respect and liking. At the moment, with Silver, it mattered not a penny if he was likable or not. Pan wanted him with an earthy desperation that was alien to her.

"Darling?" Silver watched her closely, ticking off in his head the number of things Dr. Seanu had told him about Pan. No matter what frustration he felt, he would do nothing that could make her fearful in any way. It had become his habit to phone the doctor often because he'd had so many questions about Pan's well-being, and their last conversation popped into his mind.

"Mr. Galen, your wife is returning to full strength by leaps and bounds, and though you haven't asked the question, I want to reassure you that normal marital relations are in order as well."

"Ah . . . thank you, Doctor."

Now, as Silver looked down at her, he had to smile just thinking of what Pan would say if he told her of the doctor's words.

"What's so funny?"

"Nothing special, darling; just thinking about you, as usual."

"Oh." Pan felt a tightness in her throat, her breath coming painfully from her windpipe, as she touched the masculine nipples, then impulsively put her mouth there, before lifting her head to gaze at him again.

"God!" Silver's hoarse mutter accompanied his hands convulsing on her, his mouth seeking hers.

The kiss was like no other for Pan. She felt as though she'd exploded from her ankles to her hair. Her body was no longer hers, but fragments seeking to belong to Silver Galen. Pan expected roughness. Instead she got ineffable gentleness that threatened and excited her as nothing had ever done. When his mouth slid down her, caressing and touching every pulse point, passion engulfed her, making her feel at once both helpless and powerful, giddy and alert.

Silver felt her tremble and sensed her uncertainty and trepidation. He tightened his hold, his caresses becoming more urgent, turning her pliant and willing in his embrace.

Then he pulled back from her, at once seeing the panicky question in her eyes. "It's all right, darling. I'll be right back. I want to take precautions with you."

Pan watched him race across the room to the bathroom. He was back in seconds, even as she felt a cooling off, a reticence. When he reached for her again, she stiffened.

Silver felt her reluctance as he began to kiss her again, coaxing her, urging her back to the heated plateau where they'd been. Her body stiffened when his lips traveled down her body and entered her in a most intimate way. "Shh, darling, it's all right. I'm loving you. You are so lovely, my mysterious Pan."

"Not mysterious. Down to earth." She managed the words through gasps of delight as he continued to kiss her.

"Whatever." Silver felt as giddy as a boy. Never had anyone taken such hold of him. It was a whole new experience, making love to Pan, and he felt clumsy, inept, unfledged and more excited than he'd ever been.

"This is wonderful," Pan blurted when he kissed her behind the knee, turned her over and worked his way slowly up her spine and back and forth across her back.

"For me, too, darling." Silver shuddered as his mouth pressed against her nape and the red curling hair caught at him like a loving snare.

"I like it very much."

The surprise in Pan's voice had him chuckling. When

105

he turned her over, she felt silly with building joy. Boneless and made of melting wax, she couldn't seem to make a fist.

He gently entered her, his body careful and hesitant. Reaching up, she clutched him, instigating the rhythm that carried them beyond sexual banter to a pulsating aura that took them away, body glued to body, feverish touching of hands, beings quivering as they sought and found the answer of the ages, the passionate avowal of a man's love for a woman and hers for him, the golden grail of lovers.

Passion burst from them at the same time, eliciting cries of excitement, groans of fulfillment.

For a long moment they held each other, loath to release themselves from the precious bond of love.

After some minutes Silver pushed the damp tendrils of her hair back from her forehead, his eyes searching hers fiercely. "Are you all right?"

"Yes."

"Was it good for you, Pan?"

"Astonishing!" Pan made a face when he laughed, tucking her face under his chin.

"For me too."

"Really?" Pan leaned away from him, searching his face for signs of sarcasm but finding none. "I can't believe that the big-time race driver with all the groupies would find anything astonishing about sex."

"You're fishing for compliments on your expert technique, Patricia Ann Belmont."

Pan rose on one elbow, pummeling his chest. "That's an awful thing to say."

"Ummm, maybe, but when you move like that, your gorgeous breasts quiver on my chest. Love it."

Pan laughed out loud. "You are outrageous."

106

Silver caught her tight against him, kissing her roughly. "And you're the sexiest lady I've ever known. Not even Venus herself could make love as you do. And now you're mine."

"Silver . . ." Pan began before a huge yawn overtook her. "Oh, pardon me."

"Go to sleep, little one. We'll talk tomorrow."

Pan nodded, laying her head on his chest, thinking she'd never felt so comfortable or safe.

The next day when she woke, Silver was gone.

By the time she was out of the shower and dressed in a pair of silky cotton sweats, Mrs. Tillson had brought her breakfast to the bedroom.

The older woman frowned delicately at Pan when she came out of the bathroom. "You should really have had some juice before you rose from bed, Miss Pan."

Pan had grown to like the severely formal woman who was completely devoted to her employer. "I feel just fine, Mrs. Tillson. In fact, I wish you wouldn't bring my breakfast to me . . ." Pan paused, embarrassed, as she realized that she was in Silver's room, but the other woman seemed not to notice her hesitation.

Mrs. Tillson shook her head. "Mr. Silver said that you are to have your breakfast in bed for at least two more weeks, miss."

"Good Lord. Mrs. Tillson, I'm not an invalid."

A smile flitted across the older woman's face and was gone. "I'm afraid you'll have to take that up with Mr. Silver."

"Don't think I won't." Pan grimaced at the other woman before taking the tray from her and putting it on a small table in front of a floor-to-ceiling window.

"Mr. Silver said to remind you that you are going out to Highview for dinner this evening."

Pan closed her eyes. "The family dinner."

"Yes." Mrs. Tillson poured her coffee. "You mustn't mind them, you know. They are a noisy, boisterous group but they have good hearts."

"They eat people," Pan muttered at the woman's back as she went out the door and closed it behind her.

She read a little during the day, took a walk with Ladder along Fifth Avenue, did a small amount of shopping on the way, but she couldn't entirely rid herself of her jumpiness.

"Edgy?"

"I'd like to find a job, Ladder, and—"

"You don't relish meeting the family at Highview."

Pan nodded, enjoying the stroll but glad for her fur. The May morning was blustery, more like March than the lovely month of tulips. Still, flowers were everywhere and the riotous colors gave warmth and delight to the eyes among the austere glass-and-steel buildings that loomed into the blue sky.

"You don't have a thing to worry about, because Silver wouldn't let any of them bother you if any of them were so inclined, but they won't be. The Galens are a stunning group but they're not unfriendly."

"I know. I think I've met his mother and father. It was such a bizarre moment, I'm not quite sure."

"Good people. I would have loved to have been at that meeting." Ladder chuckled.

They returned from their walk with Pan feeling refreshed but ready for a nap.

She was woken by a tickling sensation on her nose. When she went to swipe at it, she heard Silver's light laugh and was smiling before she opened her eyes.

"It's five-thirty, darling. We should move."

"No!" Pan yelped.

"Yes." Silver laughed when she pushed past him off the bed and sprinted toward the bathroom. At once her lithe body ignited a familiar want in him.

When she slammed the door of the bathroom, he rose from the bed and stretched, his eyes still on the door. It both irritated and amused him how much power she exercised over him, yet she seemed unaware of it. Self-control was all that kept him from breaking down the door and making love to her on the spot.

Ambling up the stairs to his own suite, he decided he would have Ladder purchase a car for her, something sporty but safe, so that when she was feeling better she would have a way of getting out to the country if she chose. She wouldn't need a car in Manhattan because Ladder would chauffeur her, but there would be times when she would want to drive herself.

Silver laughed out loud at himself. He was conjuring reasons to give her presents—anything he could do to bind her to him he would do, and it mattered not a whit to him if it bordered on blackmail. Pan was going to be his wife, and if he had to beg, borrow or steal her, he would do that too. Any way it took to get her would be the way to go.

As he stared in the mirror, the puckering skin on the right side of his face gave him pause. He rarely thought of the scarring anymore, and if Pan was bothered by it she gave no indication . . . yet at that moment he wished with every fiber of his being that it wasn't there. Damn! How he wished she could have seen him as he once was, not with the cursed scars.

Damnit to hell, why did they have to go out to his parents' home to dine this evening? He didn't want any questions about his "marriage," and he knew his sister would pounce on that. Once Pan wedded him the whole damned world could go to hell in a basket and ask any bitchy questions they wished, but right now he didn't want her badgered by them. Being alone with her to cosset her, to coax her into being his wife, was all-important. He would strangle any and all of them if they tried hounding her.

He barely glanced at himself after he was dressed. It was so automatic for him to wear well-tailored clothes without being ostentatious that he scarcely was cognizant of it. That the blue silk suit matched his navy blue eyes to a shade, and the white shirt with fine blue tinted hand stitching finished the dashing evening ensemble was not of great interest to him because it was his normal, accepted style.

Before leaving the room he reached into the drawer in his dresser and took out a small wooden box with the name of a well-known jeweler on the lid. He snapped it open and fingered the velvet inner box before pushing back the top of that to expose the violet-tinted marquise-shape diamond that winked back at him. It had taken Ishmael Aram, his Orthodox Jewish friend from university days and a first-rate diamond merchant, quite a time to track down such a unique stone and have it cut and mounted as Silver requested. But Ishmael had done it, and Silver had been delighted with the result.

"It's a perfect stone, Silver, and one of a kind, I'm sure. I don't know why you didn't pass out when I told you the cost. I almost did when it was told to me."

"It's exactly what I want, Ishmael."

"And it costs about the same as the Statue of Liberty." Ishmael had rolled his eyes when Silver grinned and shrugged.

110

No transaction had ever given Silver more satisfaction.

He sauntered downstairs, crossing the room to the corridor leading to Pan's suite. Knocking once, he entered just as she was turning in front of the mirror. "Wow," he whispered, grinning when she turned to face him, chin up a little, expressionless. He approached her, leaning down to kiss her gently. "Double wow, actually. That violet silk sheath is perfect for you. You have a great body and even better legs, Pan." He took her hands and stepped back from her, his eyes going over the deeper-hued violet leather medium-heeled sling pumps with the matching clutch purse, her only jewelry a gold chain at her throat. "Your hair is glorious piled on your head that way—your throat is alabaster and so slender."

"You sound like a PR man selling a product," Pan told him tartly, trying to tamp down the golden warmth spilling through her at his words, but failing.

"I want to sell you on me. Am I succeeding?" Silver brought both her hands to his mouth and kissed each finger.

His words made her dizzy for a moment, and her hands clutched at his before she tried to free them, to no avail. "I think we're late."

"Maybe a bit. There's time for you to put this on. I think it'll go with that dress." Before she could answer him, he lifted her left hand and slipped the violet-hued diamond on her third finger. "There. Perfect fit."

"Silver, I can't . . ."

His hands closed over hers, effectively blocking any removal of the ring. "You can. We should marry soon so that you have another one that will fit just behind it."

"Silver, listen to me—the original bargain was that we live together. Now it's marriage."

"You said yes, lady."

"I know, but maybe we were too impulsive."

"The hospital and my parents think we're man and wife. I think we should make it legal so that hospital doesn't feel it can sue me and my father won't try to take me apart."

"That's fudging and you know it."

"So sue me . . . but after we're married." He steered her toward the door, watching the reluctant admiration in her eyes when she looked at the ring. "Don't take it off, Pan. Please."

"All right." She stared down at the large stone that reached to her knuckle, the slender fire of it beguiling. "It is so beautiful. I don't think I've ever seen a diamond like it."

"It's as unique as you are." Silver put the Portuguese wool lace shawl that matched Charine's creation around her shoulders, and they went down in the elevator to the garage.

"Oh, you're going to drive us."

"Yes, unless you'd rather. I can give you directions."

Silver led her around to the driver's side, opened the door and ushered her under the wheel, dropping the keys into her flaccid grip.

"Oh God, you are going to have me do it. I think once was enough," Pan whispered when he got into the passenger seat and put on his seatbelt. "You'd better drive. You see, though I've kept my driver's license current, I haven't really done that much driving in the last three years."

"Good practice for you. It's still light, darling, and I'll direct you. Start her up."

"Chauffeuring a race car driver is not my idea of getting my confidence back as a driver," Pan muttered, engaging the gears and revving the engine before easing into

112

reverse, the car bucking just slightly at her touch on the unaccustomed gearshift. She steered out of the underground garage, exhaling in relief when she made it to the street without incident. She glared straight ahead of her out the windshield when Silver chuckled at her deep sigh.

Manhattan traffic was hairy, but she didn't pay any attention to the drivers who tooted at her slowness. She had all she could do to concentrate on driving the powerful car.

To her surprise the drive was not only enjoyable but, after leaving the city proper, they made very good time. Pan was able to handle a recalcitrant driver who roared around her to pass on a two-lane stretch on Long Island. "Same to you, fella," she shouted after him when he made a discourteous gesture. She shot a pleased look at Silver and did a double take. His mouth was cemented tight and his face was pasty in anger. "Oh, I'm sorry. Did that make you angry?"

"That bastard! I'll kill him for making that gesture to you. Pull over. I'm driving."

"Oh no, you won't kill him." Pan was glad that he wasn't angry with her. "I won't let you drive, so we won't catch up to him." She glanced at him again, aware that she was getting to know this man who'd insinuated himself into her life very well. "It isn't like you to get up a head of steam about something so infantile."

"I never have before, but I couldn't stand that creep doing that to you." Silver spoke through his teeth, his anger rising again. He would have taken the bastard apart with his bare hands.

Pan didn't look at him again, but her one hand left the wheel and he clutched it, at once bringing it to his mouth, making her blood bubble through her. "Poor baby."

113

"I can't stand anyone not giving you the respect you deserve."

"I'm not the bloomin' Queen, you know."

"To me you are, my Pan."

Pan laughed, but she felt a frisson of uneasiness. Silver had become too attached to her, too fast. If he ever found out about her background, she had the sick feeling he would want to discard her just as rapidly. That fact seemed immutable to her.

The rest of the ride was in silence, both Pan and Silver deep in thought.

"Good Lord," Pan said softly sometime later when Silver indicated the estate with the gates standing open and a curving drive leading up to a classic Tudor mansion that sprawled over a hill. "Buckingham Palace, as I live and breathe. You and your family and your pots of money," she muttered shakily.

"You can give away as many pots as you want, love, if that bothers you, as long as you leave a little to pay the taxes and buy shoes."

"No one could pay the taxes on that pile of stone and stucco . . . but it is beautiful."

"It is, and it was a fun house to grow up in. The hiding places are in the hundreds." Silver grinned at her when she parked the car in front of the fan-shape steps.

"If you have a butler named Jeeves, I am not staying," Pan said faintly when he helped her from the car and she stood staring up at the facade. When the front door opened she moved closer to Silver, who put his arm around her at once.

"His name is Jud and he's a former wrestler—Greco-Roman, I think."

"Heavens." Pan stared at the hulk of a man who came down the steps, his hamlike hands extended to her, his face looking as though his features had been fashioned by a kindergartner with silly putty. "I'm Pan." Her hand was engulfed.

"I'm Jud. Welcome to the homestead." His gravelly voice had a warmth that drew Pan at once. "So you're the one who cracked up the big shot, are you? The Commodore described you but he didn't do you justice."

"How would you like it if I punched your lights out, Jud?"

"You can try, Silver, boyo, you can try." Grinning crookedly, the giant ambled to the car, popping open the trunk from the switch near the dash. "Where's your luggage?"

"We're only staying for dinner," Silver answered shortly, glaring at the large man.

Jud whistled soundlessly. "Oh, oh. I think the Commodore expects you to stay for a few weeks."

"What? That's insane. I have my work and—"

"Not you, Silver, boyo; the little lady is the one staying." Jud's rubbery face creased into a wider grin when Silver's teeth cracked together. "Not so, boyo?"

"Not so. Pan stays with me."

As Jud opened his mouth to reply, the Commodore himself came out of the house. "What's all the talk out here? Oh. I might have known. Silver, are you arguing with Jud again? Ah, there you are, my dear." The Commodore ignored his glowering son and held his arms out to Pan, who walked into them quite naturally. "What did I tell you, Jud? Isn't she a beauty?"

"Even better than you said, Commodore." Jud chuckled when Silver glared at him. "And she's got him by the jugular."

The Commodore was still laughing when Silver swept Pan into the house.

"You should laugh with them. It would be easier on you," Pan told him softly when they were standing in the huge foyer.

"I don't feel like laughing about us," Silver said harshly.

Pan faced him, her hand going up to his tight mouth, loving the feel of those lips when they softened and began to caress her fingertips. What was going to happen if he ever found out about her past? Then he would hate her.

"What are you thinking, Pan? Secret thoughts again?"

"Yes."

"Damn, I hate that."

"I know." She tried to free her hands. Instead she was pulled tighter to him, his mouth coming down hard on hers, worrying her lips, parting them, then his tongue touching and playing with hers as though he would entice her to confide in him, be his.

The temptation to become only his was growing in her, and despite all her adjurations to herself to pull back, her hands slipped around his face and she gave herself up to the wonder that never ceased to amaze her. Silver could draw her out of herself as no one could. It frightened her that he might plumb her secret from the very core of her. Then all thought faded as a curling delight built in her. The house and its surroundings faded away, and they were alone on a pulsating plane of love.

"Wow. No wonder you don't want her to meet the family, brother," a voice said behind them, shattering the aura, making Pan struggle against Silver's hold.

Silver dragged his mouth from Pan's but didn't release his hold on her. "Braden, damn you, I don't suppose you'll go away."

"I won't."

Silver turned, keeping Pan in the crook of his arm.

"All right, then, I'll introduce you to my wife. Pan, this is Braden Travis Galen, the youngest and worst of the Galens."

"I thought you were," Pan murmured, eliciting a guffaw from Braden and a smile from Silver.

"The Commodore said she had you on a string. I didn't believe it, but now I do. No female other than Nancy Barrows ever talked that way to you."

"Pan isn't quite broken in yet," Silver said, his mouth closing over her expected riposte, the kiss roughly gentle. Silver lifted his mouth from hers. "But she's getting better."

"Twit," Pan burst out, her high heel coming down on his instep getting a muffled imprecation from Silver and another burst of laughter from Braden.

"What's going on?" The Commodore came through the door, scowling.

"God, it's wonderful, Commodore. She hits him high, she hits him low, and the Wonder Boy is reeling," Braden told his parent gleefully.

"Didn't I tell you so? Good for you, my dear. Have to keep him in his place. Hope he hasn't put you back to work yet—"

"I had no intention of sending—"

It was Pan's turn to lean up and kiss Silver's surprised mouth. "Shh, darling," she purred.

"See that, Commodore?" Braden was all but crowing.

"See what?" Felice du Lant Galen strolled from the back of the house, looking absolutely elegant, gazing at each of her family in turn with cool amusement on her face. "How long are you men going to keep Pan standing there before you bring her out to the sun room?" Felice walked over and kissed Pan on each cheek, murmuring welcome.

117

"Allow me, sister-in-law." Braden stepped to her side, hooking her away from Silver, who had been momentarily diverted when the Commodore muttered, "Seems to me he's too anxious to get her back into the fields again."

When Silver turned around again, he saw that Pan was already disappearing down the hallway with his younger brother. "Braden, damn you, wait."

"She'll be fine, Sterling, dear. Braden won't eat her."

"He hadn't better do a thing," Silver growled.

"Heh, heh, never thought I'd see the day when you were snagged by a slip of a thing, son." The Commodore laughed out loud.

"Why not? You were," Silver shot back before striding after his "wife" and brother.

The Commodore glowered at his wife when she chuckled. "He's as fresh as you, Felice. Damned if I don't knock him on his backside one day."

His wife saw the smile he was trying to suppress and leaned up to kiss him. "You love it when they're all here."

"Yes. Damned if I know why." He kissed his wife long and lingeringly. "I don't know why I keep you either."

"I do." Felice batted her eyes at him.

"Shameless. Let's go in and see what they're doing to the lamb."

"Don't worry about Pan. She'll handle all of them—easily."

"Then she must be exactly like you." The Commodore kissed his wife again and led her down the wide corridor leading to the back section of the huge home.

The two older persons stopped in the doorway of the three-sided glass-walled sun room and watched the by-play of their children meeting the wife of the favorite and famous brother.

"Actually I'm from all over but I was born in California." Pan didn't like giving out that much information and she noted that Silver was eyeing her alertly. He didn't need very much to ferret out the truth! She had come to realize that despite his devil-may-care attitude with her, he had a mind like a steel trap that could compile, compute and conclude with menacing accuracy. Pan had suspected from the first that his offhand acceptance of her was a little thin. The more she'd come to know him, the more sure she was that he wouldn't be satisfied by the status quo for long, that a showdown would come.

She shook off her dolorous thoughts and tried to concentrate on what was being said to her. "Pardon me. What did you say, Sasha?"

"I asked you where in California you were from."

"Don't pester her, Sash," Silver interrupted.

Felice entered the room and crossed to Pan's side. "Sterling is right. Don't quiz Pan. She'll tell us what she wants us to know."

"Sounds mysterious." Silver's brother-in-law Ben grinned when Silver gave him a warning look. "What do you think, darling?" Ben leaned over his wife's chair and kissed her hair.

"I think she's absolutely stunning. That hair and those eyes! What a combination. I don't blame Silver for marrying her quickly so she wouldn't get away," Sasha said quietly, her eyes going from Pan to Silver, then smiling at her brother when he shot her a grateful look.

"Well, now that that's settled, perhaps we could have a little wine before we have our dinner." Felice pressed a button, and in a moment, Jud had wheeled in a drink cart.

Pan was sipping her sparkling grape juice, letting the coolness of it salve her spirit as she watched each of the Galens in turn. Being introduced to them had been like meeting an avalanche head-on, but a friendly landslide just the same.

"Why don't you wear your wedding ring, my dear? Was the one my son gave you not right for you?" The Commodore barked the questions, then glared at his son, who stared back at him woodenly.

"Some women don't wear their wedding rings because they interfere with the engagement ring, Sterling, dear," Felice answered for Pan.

"I've never heard of such a thing."

"Neither have I, Father," Braden said slowly, peering at his brother closely.

"I think I have," Sasha said haltingly, her face creased in thought.

Pan put down her glass and turned to face Silver's father, her shoulders back, her chin up, purpose in every line of her body.

Silver was quite sure she was going to level with his family, but before she could open her mouth, he put his arm around her. "I'm getting Pan a new wedding ring before we go to Bermuda. It will be one that will suit her."

"I should hope so." The Commodore looked over his half-glasses at his son, then at Pan. "She's a good girl. I like having her in the family."

His family stared at the head of the house for a moment in silence.

"Heavens, that is high praise," Sasha said in amusement. "You only got a handshake, Ben."

"But a very good handshake, sir," Ben added quickly when his father-in-law scowled at his daughter.

"Shall we go in to dinner? It's all ready, isn't it, Jud?"

"It is, Mrs. Galen."

Pan had to smile when she saw the dining room. "No doubt this could seat two hundred comfortably?" she whispered to Silver.

"Something like that." He grinned down at her.

"I wish you would tell your parents we're not married."

"No need to. We'll be married before we go to Bermuda."

"Silver, I'm not sure—"

Silver held her back from the rest of the family, who ambled to their chairs. "Pan, I won't let you off the hook on this one."

"You don't know me . . . and I don't believe in divorce . . . and once—I mean, if you ever find out about me you'll want one . . ."

"No! We'll work out the troubles we have as we go along, but we're not going to build fences ahead of time."

"Silver—"

"Shh, let's have dinner."

Pan would have said more but she noticed that all eyes were on her so she subsided.

Dinner was fun for Pan despite her worries. When they finished, she automatically refolded her napkin, placing her silver carefully on the plate.

"Oh no, she's making points with Jud," Braden said with a groan. "Now she'll be held up to us by him as some vestal virgin or something and he'll harp about her forever."

"A vestal married lady, maybe," Pan interjected, then bit her lip, the color rising in her face when the Galens laughed.

Silver pushed back her chair and scooped her out of it

121

and onto his lap. "She has Ladder in her back pocket, too, Brade. A very charming lady is my bride."

"What are they doing now, Felice?" The Commodore rumbled, rolling his eyes at Silver and Pan.

"Just cuddling, Sterling."

"Well, I suppose it's not as bad as when they scoot under the sheets, but they should have some control, Felice. We wouldn't do that at the table."

"Under the sheets? Commodore, when did you see Pan and Silver under the sheets?" Braden laughed.

"Young fool, stop that braying, you'll upset your new sister-in-law. Besides, it was perfectly legitimate. Your mother was there with me, weren't you, Felice?"

"Yes, dear, I was."

"What were they doing under the sheets, Commodore?"

"Sasha, don't be indiscreet. Ask your mother."

"Well, Mother?"

Everyone was chuckling except Pan, who was trying to wriggle off Silver's knee.

"Your family is outrageous, Silver, and you're worse," Pan whispered, panting slightly from her exertions.

"Yes, but even they would tell you that I never give up anything I want to keep. And I want to keep you, my darling Pan."

CHAPTER FIVE

The houses in Bermuda looked like pastel-color bonbons, and the ocean looked like turquoise silk.

Pan waited for Silver at the top of the bluff path leading to the ocean where they would be going swimming and snorkeling. There were no Portuguese men-of-war in the water today as there had been yesterday, and the weather was perfect. She stopped scanning the expanse of ocean and looked at the circle of gold on her left hand. Her wedding ring! She wouldn't wear her diamond when they went swimming even though Silver had asked her to wear it all the time. She couldn't take the chance of losing the beautiful ring that she loved. It irritated her that Silver could be so cavalier about such a wondrous gem, though it wasn't the value of it that concerned her but the fact that Silver had chosen it for her. Not that she wasn't aware it was an expensive ring; she was. Chance remarks that the Commodore had made about the diamond had telegraphed to her how unique it was. Yet she loved her wedding ring no less.

Pan shook her head, staring at the wedding band that had come to mean so much to her in the last two weeks. What had made her marry the man called Silver? She had acquiesced to his proposal as though it had been something she had expected since the beginning of time.

How ironic that she could feel that way about a man she'd known such a short time! Pan couldn't quite face the answers to this enigma, admit to the emotion that swamped her when they were together. Love was ridiculous! It couldn't be that.

The wedding was still dreamlike to her. She hadn't put up even the merest struggle against his insistence that they marry.

A week before they came to Bermuda, almost two weeks ago, they had driven to upstate New York, where they were married by a justice of the peace. No family, no friends, just the two of them and witnesses supplied by the justice. Plain and no frills, as Silver called it, but Pan had been as nervous as though she were being married at the St. John the Divine Cathedral in New York City.

"Ready, darling?"

"What?" Pan jumped, startled out of her reverie. Turning to look at her husband of almost three weeks, she admired the strong torso even though it was still scarred from the many grafting operations he'd had, including one long inch-wide scar down his chest and abdomen that would be dealt with cosmetically at some later date. None of these in any way detracted from his male beauty —his long strong legs, the well-muscled arms and chest, the wonderful shoulders, the litheness of his body.

"You know, I'm the one who wants the job modeling, but I think you could go after a career in it. What a body!" Pan laughed when she saw the color rising in his face.

"I'm glad you like what you see, bride, because it's what belongs to you, what you get to keep."

Now it was Pan's turn to be disconcerted. "Lecher," she muttered before he pulled her into his arms, kissing her thoroughly, drawing the passionate response from her that seemed to grow every day.

"Yes. I admit I lust for you, darling. I did think that might abate after we were married. Instead it increases each time we make love. I think by the time you're ninety, you'll be tired." He felt a flash of irritation at his admission.

"Not as tired as you," she shot back, trying to bite back the smile. It had been such a happy time with Silver. Oh, she had been happy with Sydney, too, but not this way. There was excitement and passion with Silver that she had never thought possible. When she woke in the morning there was an instant rosy aura when she accepted that she was now Pan Belmont Galen.

"Either you stop looking at me that way right now, or we go back into the house, up the stairs and into bed," Silver said, tightening his hold on her. "Your eyes are almost purple."

"Are they?" She scored her fingernail down his cheek on the left side of his face, loving the velvet harshness of that skin. Silver had even let her shave him one day when they hadn't gotten out of bed until two in the afternoon.

Now she put her hand on the puckered flesh on the right side of his face, not pulling back when he flinched. "This is part of you, too—and you said that all of you belongs to me."

"So I did," Silver answered stiffly, the tingling sensation of someone's touch that was not a doctor's or his own sending an alien vibration through him. Never had he wished so strongly that the scar would disappear.

"Since it is mine, I would like you to have a good attitude about it. I do," Pan told him softly.

"I know that."

"And did you know that the scar might as well not be there for any notice I take of it?"

Silver kissed her forehead. "I know that, too, wife. I love you, Pan Belmont Galen."

"Does that mean that you won't throw a wrench in the works when I decide to pursue modeling as a career?"

Silver grimaced. "Pan, I don't like the idea of you doing anything so strenuous. You need rest and a life of ease for the next year, and modeling is a tough, tension-filled occupation."

"You are a stubborn man."

"C'mon, wife, let's explore the deep."

They swam and snorkeled for almost two hours, Silver staying at her side and checking constantly to see that she didn't become fatigued.

That evening they dined on the luscious Maryland crab that Silver had flown in. Since they were alone in the house, except for a houseman and gardener who came every day, they were able to have all the privacy they craved.

"I wonder what Captain Frith would think about us staying at Blandfield?" Pan mused, referring to the wonderful house where the celebrated Bermuda pirate was supposed to have lodged a time or two. She was feeling replete and lazy from the good food and a day in the sun and water.

"Well, since the kitchen section was built in 1620 and he was supposed to have stayed here and eaten here more than once, I would say he probably is grumbling into his beard about now."

Pan laughed, feeling carefree. "I love this house, and what you told me about how they quarry the white coral stone they use for the roofs fascinates me—and the pink

126

color of the stucco with the green shutters. Ummm. It's like something from fantasy land. Wonderful."

Silver looked at her over the rim of his brandy snifter. She was so unaffected, so natural, so pleased with the world around her. If at times her eyes were shadowed and distant, that was something he intended to tackle a little bit at a time. He would finally know what it was that caused the sadness in her eyes, that made her draw back from him at times. "That's why I've taken steps to purchase this house from Reggie for you, because you like it so much."

Pan had been staring out over the water at the sparkle of stars that silvered the ocean. Her head slewed back to him, making her curling red hair fly across her face, catching on her lips and eyelashes. Her trembling fingers lifted the strands free as she stared at him. "What did you say?"

"I said that the house is to be one of your wedding presents from me," Silver told her blandly, leaning forward in the dim after-twilight to brush the hair from her face. "Did I ever tell you that I love your hair?"

"Many times," Pan answered absently. "I can't take a house from you. It's too much."

Irritation filtered through him. "You're my wife—and you're going to be my wife through this and ten other lifetimes. Nothing is too much for you."

"You think too big," Pan said faintly. "I have trouble planning tomorrow."

"Then leave the planning to me. This house will be yours, Pan, and I don't know how many others you might have, but I want to please you and make you happy. That's what makes me happy."

"Not having soup made of ketchup and hot water makes me happy." Pan reeled with what Silver had done

127

since their marriage. If she had thought him generous before, now she thought him downright foolhardy. "Giving me material things is very nice, and I love what you give me, but you mustn't bury me in—"

"Am I making you uncomfortable?" Silver rasped, feeling a pain in his heart.

"Yes . . . no. I don't know." Pan spread her hands and looked away from him for a moment.

"Look at me, darling." When Silver saw the uncertainty in her eyes, he reached for her, lifting her out of her chair and settling her on his lap. "I love giving you things, and if there is a lacing of blackmail in the giving —well, I told you I'd do anything to keep you."

"But you don't need to give me anything to keep me." Automatically her hands wove through his hair as they most often did when they were making love, her fingers tingling from the crisp ebony strands touched here and there with gray. "I don't want to leave you."

"God, angel, I wanted you to say that so badly." Silver bent over her, his lips coursing her cheek before they settled on her mouth, then remaining there to drag in sensual slowness across her face.

In a burst of love Pan pressed her lips against the puckered pinkish scar tissue of his face.

Silver hauled in a painful breath. "Darling. Don't."

"Must I remind you that you said you belong to me? This is part of you. How could it disgust me?"

"Pan, my baby. I love you. I want you." He surged to his feet with his wife clasped close to him.

"We certainly retire early in Bermuda, don't we?" Pan chuckled in his ear.

"Yes, damnit, we do." A harsh laugh escaped him when he carried her up the carved wooden staircase to

128

the large octagonal room with the wood-burning fireplace and the canopied bed.

All at once Pan's hands tightened on his neck. "Don't expect too much of the future, Silver. Just take what we have and enjoy it."

"I intend to—but I intend to have our future as well, wife," Silver pronounced through clenched teeth, irritated with her veiled references to their possible parting in the future. He dumped her unceremoniously in the middle of the bed. "And whatever it takes to prove to you that we won't be parting will be done too." He dove after her onto the huge bed.

"Stop, you monster. You'll break this lovely old bed." Pan couldn't stop laughing, glad to put away the dark thoughts that pursued her like a specter.

"Then I'll get it fixed." Silver unbuttoned her silky cotton strapless dress that opened down the front. "I love your breasts."

"Did you know you have a habit of repeating yourself?"

"Yes. I tell you that every time we make love. Get used to it; I intend to continue."

"Good." Pan closed her eyes when she felt him begin to slip the dress and underthings from her body. She was wearing very little clothing. She had begun to know that it was a waste of time with her husband, who only removed them.

It had been a shock and a delight to discover what a voluptuary Pan was. Each time they made love, Silver was more fascinated by her. There were times when he couldn't remember a life without Pan, and the thought of a future without her was enough to make a cold sweat break out on his body. He had withstood the pain of fire when he'd had his accident, but he wasn't sure he could tolerate the loss of Pan from his life. He'd bleed to death from a thousand cuts.

"You are a very sexy man, Silver Galen." Pan had learned what pleased him, and it excited her very much to make him passionate, and now as she kissed the firm male nipples she could feel her own libido heat in response.

It had been both a sadness and a joy to her when she'd accepted that she loved Silver Galen, that all her admonishments to herself that such love didn't exist on this or any planet had not stemmed the feeling. In fact, it grew stronger every day. It would be an everlasting punishment to be parted from him. Wiping the thought from her mind, she began to caress and kiss the man who'd brought such sunshine into her life.

Each tried to give the other more joy, and as a result, the passion built between them with lightning speed.

Silver heard his own groans muffled against her skin even as Pan moaned his name.

"Silver!"

"Yes, darling, I know." Silver slid up her body again, feeling the series of shudders that racked her, the surprised glazed look to her eyes as she clutched him to her. In gentle thrusts he took her, feeling the answering motion as she joined with him in the rhythm of life. They crested together in the liquid explosion that welded them in the thundering passion of the ages.

Silver soothed her shaking body as he always did, feeling the same sort of shuddering aftermath. "Wife of mine, not only are you a voluptuary, I think you invented lovemaking. Never, but never in my life has anyone taken me apart as you do, time after time. And I love every minute of it."

"Me too," Pan told him, still slightly out of breath. "It is special, isn't it?"

"Very."

"I could stay in Bermuda forever. I've never felt so good."

"And you look wonderful, too, darling. You've gained color and weight and lost a great deal of tension, too . . . but not all of it."

Pan smiled at him ruefully. "I am better, but—"

"Never mind the buts. We'll take them one at a time."

Pan touched his nose. "You are an arrogant man, thinking you have the answers to all the questions in the universe."

"Yes. When you hold me and love me as you've just done, I'm sure I have all the answers."

"Cocksure, I call it."

"Being a Cockney again, are you?"

"Maybe." Pan yawned and laughed at the same time, loving it when he cuddled her close to him. She couldn't ever have imagined how much she would love sleeping in Silver's arms. She snuggled close to him now. "I suppose you're going to waken me at dawn to make love again."

"Unless you waken me first, as you did yesterday."

"Rat! You're not supposed to remember that."

"Darling, I'll never forget it."

"Roué." Pan's eyes fluttered shut. She felt safe and loved. Perhaps, by some outlandish miracle, Silver could chase all the monsters away.

They slept until the sun came up, making love as they always did before breakfast. It was their last day. They would fly back to New York late in the afternoon.

In the middle of the morning they walked out of the ocean, their arms around each other, drying themselves, then lying under an umbrella as the sun rose to its zenith.

131

Silver lathered her body with lotion to protect her skin from the elements, insisting that Pan not remain long in the direct rays of the sun.

The private beach was quiet. The only sounds were the cries of the gulls and the constant *whush* of the surf on the sand.

"Now let me put lotion on your back, Silver."

"My tough skin doesn't need it, but I love to have you touch me, wife. Ummm, that feels cool."

Pan gazed at the rippling muscles on his back, the fading scars of his accident showing white against his tan. He had a beautiful body. "Silver, I do want to look for a job when we return to the mainland."

Silver turned his head so that he was looking over his shoulder at her. "I'll hate it when you go to work, but I won't stop you."

"Thank you."

"Kindly take that grin off your face. I don't like to think that you'll be happy away from me all day."

"I'd be away from you anyway, silly. You work long hours, mister."

"I've cut my work in half since you came into my life, lovely."

"What? You couldn't have! You work ten hours a day as it is." Pan stared at him. He had hidden his own pain in work just as she'd hidden hers behind a wall of coldness. Neither of the walls had held up. She leaned down and kissed his ear. "Now that I'm your wife I'm going to set some ground rules. I don't want you working that hard. Clear?"

"And I don't want you working too hard either. Bargain?"

"Bargain. We'll always have time for each other." Even as she said it a sense of pathos touched her. It was being borne sharply in on her more and more how important the time with Silver was to her. Damn! She wouldn't even consider modeling if she weren't sure that at some juncture along the road there would be a comeuppance and she would need to have a way of making a living. There would be no way that she would take anything from Silver once they parted.

They played like children until afternoon, when it was time to pack their things. If there was a measure of desperation in their play, neither commented on it.

The sun was descending rapidly as their private plane rose over the golden isle. Pan looked down in nostalgic longing, hoping that every moment would be etched clearly in her memory for the time when she would have to dredge up each precious pearl to savor in her loneliness.

"Don't look blue, darling. We'll be back often. As soon as the papers come through and you're the proud owner of a Bermuda home, we'll have a second, third and ad infinitum honeymoons."

"Yes." Pan smiled at him weakly, trying to mask the voice inside her that chanted, "Never again."

New York was its usual busy, chaotic self, and the first few days back Pan spent orienting herself into the routine of their life in the Big Apple. Silver helped arrange some interviews for her, but at the same time he urged her to consider a position with Galen's instead of modeling.

But Pan wouldn't consider that, and so, a week after their return from Bermuda she prepared for the first of her modeling interviews. Once she and Silver were separated, he would understand fully why she had ignored his overtures for a job with his company.

Dressed and ready, she left the house shortly before nine in the morning. With Ladder to chauffeur her, she made her nine o'clock appointment with the Rendoll Joyce Agency with a minute to spare.

"Hello, I'm Letta Joyce, Miss Belmont. I have your résumé and your recommendations here in front of me," the thin, hawk-faced woman told Pan. She smiled slightly, her heavy makeup, though expertly applied, giving her thin face a masklike appearance. "I'm pleasantly surprised, I assure you. You have wonderful cheekbones, and your long neck and legs are an advantage. I can't help but wonder why we have not seen you before now." The chic woman rose to her feet. "Let's go through to the studio and see what Hodge thinks."

Pan had heard of Hodge Dickenson and read about him in trade publications. He was tough and he was noted for being able to tell in a matter of moments if someone was right for modeling. It gave her a nervous flutter to think of such an expert, clinical stare running over her. Then she lifted her chin and followed Letta Joyce through the door into a cavernous room with cameras, arc lamps, lights and cables all in disorder. In the center of the room a man crouched over a camera, aiming it at a piece of scenery.

"Hodge? Surface, will you?"

The man uncoiled his sinuous, skinny length and turned, squinting at the two women through thick-lensed glasses. "Yuh?"

"This is the applicant I wanted you to screen. All right?"

"Yuh."

Pan looked after Letta, then back at the slouching man, who approached her. "Hello."

"Hi. I'm Hodge."

"I'm Pan."

"Catchy name."

134

"It's my real name."

"Interesting."

Pan was about to tell him to take a flying leap out the window. The man acted as though he were on a cloud sailing over the rest of humanity, with no need to contact mortals.

"Get on the podium, will you." Hodge turned his back on her and began fumbling with his camera.

For forty-five minutes she turned, twisted, smiled coyly and brightly and sweetly, until she thought her jaw would have a permanent ache.

"Fine. All done. Be back here tomorrow. Eight sharp with no bags under the eyes. We're rolling at nine." Hodge went back to his camera, ignoring her and not saying good-bye.

When she returned to the outer office, Letta Joyce was sitting on the edge of a desk talking to another woman who Pan assumed was an assistant. "I'm to come back tomorrow."

Letta and the other woman looked impressed.

"Hodge must have loved you. He usually gives five-minute auditions," Letta told her, inhaling deeply on a cigarette in an exotic holder.

"Or less," the assistant added, rolling her eyes.

"Hodge is very fussy," Letta explained, then tamped out her cigarette and stood, holding out her hand to Pan. "Congratulations. You're on the team."

"Thank you." Pan was torn between elation and a desire to tell Letta that she would not work for a wooden-faced man like Hodge Dickenson who barely acknowledged her presence. "I'll be back here at eight tomorrow," Pan told Letta.

When she arrived home there was barely enough time for a quick shower before dinner. Elated with her news,

135

she dressed in a pair of Charine's silky "harem leisure pajamas."

Silver came through from the office as she was coming down the stairs, and Pan ran to meet him, her arms outstretched.

"Ummm, I love it," Silver muttered, his arms closing around her and holding her tightly. "Your breasts are pushing against me, love. I think we'll have to put dinner off for an hour."

"How can you think of that after the long day you've had?" Pan moved back so that she could look up at him, laughter bubbling from her.

"Easy. I've thought about it all day. You're having a disastrous effect on the Galen holdings, my love."

Pan pushed her fingers through the thickness of his hair as she loved to do. "I have the most wonderful news."

"Oh?" An instinctive wariness had Silver watching her closely. "Tell me."

"I went to the Rendoll Joyce agency today and they've asked me to come back for a shoot tomorrow morning. The photographer was awful. He thinks he's God but it's a start."

Silver sucked in an angry breath, trying to mask his feelings. "Didn't I tell you that you could have a job with Galen's?"

Pan inched back from him, her smile fading. "Yes, you did, but I told you that I wanted modeling."

"There are other ways of expressing yourself, Pan. You don't have to lock yourself into one field."

Pan shoved against his chest. "I am not locked into a field, I just want to model."

"You're being stubborn."

"And you're being arbitrary."

"Damn you, Pan." Silver reached for her as she tried to flounce away and scooped her up into his arms. "Stop wriggling. I'm not putting you down."

"I just dressed," Pan told him, her arms circling his neck as he took the steps to the bedroom two at a time. "And I don't like you."

"Once we're in bed it will all be forgotten."

"Problems aren't solved in bed."

"Oh yes they are," Silver answered. "That's the only way I can keep you from arguing with me." He placed her on the bed and undressed rapidly, throwing his clothes at a chair.

"Don't be so careless with your clothes," Pan told him absently, already affected by his naked body. Damn Sterling Galen for taking her over the way he did!

"Get them later," he responded, throwing himself down beside her and reaching for her at once. "This silky thing is driving me crazy. It's like a second skin on you."

"Silver," Pan whispered, accepting that she wanted him as much as he wanted her, that she needed him.

"Yes, love," he murmured, gently removing her silky garments, then pressing his face between her breasts, moving his mouth back and forth across the satiny globes.

"Love games again?"

"Yes. Do you mind?"

"Not at all."

The loveplay between them increased in intensity. They held each other with the desperation of new lovers, but also with the sweet touch of all lovers down through the ages.

It never ceased to amaze Pan that she could feel that burgeoning heat that was like hot lava, and no one could give her release except Silver.

Passion exploded between them as it always did, and Silver felt the helpless yet powerful feeling of taking his woman and being taken by her. Nothing in his high-powered world had ever prepared him for the excitement and satisfaction of making love to his wife. As he held her, his chest heaving, he vowed that he would never let her leave him. He couldn't.

Silver noticed how quiet she was and turned her in his arms. "Still irritated with me?"

She pushed some strands of hair from his forehead. "No, but I do want to try this so much . . . and I want you to be understanding about it."

"I'm too possessive with you at times, I know that."

"You're good to me and I love being with you . . . but I want to try this."

"All right, darling."

When they rose from the bed, Silver gave her a twisted smile. "I'd better change in the bathroom. Watching you dress would put us right back in that bed again."

"Where do you get the strength?" Laughing, she watched him shrug and grin at her.

Pan reveled in the heat of his smile, but she didn't miss the cynical twist of his mouth. It still rankled him that she hadn't chosen Galen's as a place to work. Pan inhaled, her hands trembling slightly. "All right. I'll meet you downstairs. Shall we have a drink before dinner?"

"Please. I could use one." He left the room at a jog.

Dressing slowly, she checked her makeup and ran a comb through her hair, leaving it hanging loose, and left the bedroom to go downstairs.

Silver stood under the needle spray, cursing his own heavy-handedness with her. Damnit! He handled a sprawling international corporation with ease, yet he had himself in a constant sweat over a slip of a woman who

138

had him cupped in her hand. He didn't know what made him angrier—the fact that she did hold him, or that he accepted it as truth.

When he went downstairs he saw her in the dining alcove, putting the last touches on the dining table. He paused, watching her, the fine-boned sculpting of her features silhouetted in the window by the dying sunlight, which also outlined her too-slender figure. Nothing in the world was going to keep him from seeing to it that she was in the best health possible, so that she would always be the glowing, happy woman she was meant to be.

"Darling?" Silver murmured, seeing her raise her head, the quick smile on her face. "You're lovely." He leaned on the railing. "Will you forgive me for trying to bind you to me too tightly?"

Pan felt tears well up in her. "Oh, Silver, Silver . . . you dope." She flung herself across the room as he jumped down the last few steps to the landing.

He caught her and swung her around in the air before pressing her close to him and kissing her fiercely.

"You're a nut," she told him, out of breath.

"And your eyes are purple at this moment, my wife. Does that mean we should go back upstairs?"

"Not until we've eaten, you roué."

Silver nibbled at her neck, chuckling. "*You* can take the blame for that, lovely one. Every time I see you I start pawing the ground. Any control I ever had went out the window when I met you."

"To be honest, I'm not much better with you."

"And it tears you up to admit it, right?"

Pan sighed, tucking her head under his chin. "I didn't think there was anyone like you on the planet, Silver. You confuse me."

139

"Good, because you've damned near knocked me off my pins—permanently."

Pan looked up at him, feeling warm, safe, more comfortable than she'd ever been in her life. "Let's eat."

"God, you and your appetite."

"My dear sir, I have gained a great deal of respect for regular meals and I don't intend to waste this one."

"That must be the reason for the check you sent out of your personal account to African Famine Relief."

They had been approaching the table with their arms around one another. Pan stopped. "I should have known you would find out right away, but I really didn't need all the clothes you'd ordered for me from Charine's. So I returned some of them and figured out the cost."

"And remitted the total to the African relief fund." Silver kissed her nose as he was holding out her chair. "That's fine, darling. I applaud the thought, and I added something to your check, but I also had Ladder retrieve your clothing from Charine's. The things were designed for you and no one else. They're back in your closet." He seated himself across from her and smiled at her shocked expression.

"But—"

"No buts, darling. You can send as many checks as you want where and when you want, but please don't take away my one indulgence. I enjoy buying you clothes, and Charine tells me that you're a dream to design for."

"You're a generous man, Silver Galen."

"I'm a man in love, Pan Belmont Galen."

After dinner they sat and listened to music.

"I have tickets for the ballet on Friday, love. Would you like to see the Corps de Ballet Russe?"

"Oh, yes. In fact, once when I was in Germany I had

140

the tickets to go to Moscow and see it there, but . . ." Pan's voice trailed.

Silver hated that faraway look in her eyes. It seemed the only time he had her intense concentration was in bed. Despite his impatience to know everything about her, he didn't quiz her about the tickets to Moscow.

That night they made love as always. The heat and passion were intense, but Silver felt the tension in her, as though when she'd mentioned living in Europe she had crawled back into her cocoon and was hiding from him.

The next morning when Pan woke, Silver had already risen and showered. When she went down to breakfast, there was a perfect white rose at her plate and a note.

Knock them dead, my beautiful redhead.
Love, Silver

She held the rose to her lips, fighting tears when Mrs. Tillson came through from the kitchen with a plate of grapefruit slices, a bowl of oatmeal and a glass of milk. Silver didn't accept that she didn't eat breakfast, so they'd struck a bargain that she would eat something every morning as long as the portion was small.

After eating and putting the rose in water in their bedroom, she readied herself for the day. She left the apartment at twenty minutes to eight, glad to have Ladder do the driving.

In the studio with the taciturn Mr. Dickenson, she was handed over to the makeup artist and then dressed in a slinky gold paper satin strapless dress that clung to her figure and was slit to the knee. With it she wore four-inch-heeled gold slings, and her red hair was swept upward by the hairdresser so that the curls rioted downward from her crown.

When she was ready, Pan walked out of the dressing room and waited just at the door. Dickenson must have heard the movement, though he hadn't turned to look at her. "All right. This is a perfume ad and a fairly new account, so it will mean a good bit if it goes well. Step up on the podium . . ."

Pan stepped into the light and up on the dais. She heard a whispered blasphemy and thought it must have come from one of Dickenson's helpers.

"Looking good," Dickenson mentioned flatly.

Then the shoot began and so did the fantasy. Pan had the sensation that she had fallen down the hole with Alice in Wonderland.

They broke for lunch, and then the frenzied pace began again.

After what seemed like eons, the ads broke on the billboards and in magazines.

One morning, several weeks after Pan had begun with the Rendoll Joyce Agency, she came into the studio and found it in an uproar. Pepe Rendoll introduced himself to Pan, and then he and Letta Joyce began a sort of jig, holding each other and laughing. Dickenson toasted her with a glass of champagne—at eight o'clock in the morning!

"Champagne for Pan!"

Pan shook her head, amazed and amused at the usually taciturn Hodge. "Did someone win the lottery?"

"Better." Hodge grinned at her. "We have secured one of the plum accounts of the world, and it's all due to you!" Hodge put down his drink and put his arms around Pan, dancing her around the outer office. "You are now the Torrid Girl for Benet Lasal Inc. That means their clothes, cosmetics and perfume, kiddo."

"Benet Lasal? Really?" Pan remembered when she had been in Paris and seen the main building of the world-wide couturier firm. Now it had branched out into many fields, growing and expanding until it was second to none in fashion products. "I didn't know you were photographing me for them." Pan smiled faintly and sank into a nearby chair.

"I feel a little shaky myself, Pan. Who would have thought when you walked into our offices so many weeks ago that we would land the big fish?"

"Not me."

The others laughed at Pan's remark, and Hodge took hold of her arms and lifted her to her feet. "C'mon, star, no time off for you. We have to shoot the Torrid Girl." Hodge threw open his arms, making the others laugh and lift their glasses in another toast.

Once they were back in the studio, Hodge turned to face her, pushing his glasses back up on his nose. "In case I haven't said it before, you've been a dream to shoot, Pan."

"No, you haven't said it before, and I appreciate the words." She smiled at him.

Hodge shook his head. "You are very beautiful, Pan, top to bottom, but your facial bones are outstanding, maybe the best I've ever seen."

"That's the most you've said to me since I started here."

"So? I'm excited."

The days that followed were hectic, but the new shoot went forward in leaps and bounds.

The first time Pan saw herself in the ad on the street-vending kiosk inside the Galen Building, she felt self-conscious looking at the sexy-looking lady with the fly-away red hair and the strapless gold gown, her pouting mouth looking kissable as she lifted her chin and sprayed Benet Lasal perfume on her neck.

"Heavens," she muttered out loud, noticing that most of the magazines were gone.

"That's not what Silver said." Ladder spoke behind her, amusement in his voice. "He bought every copy, but the distributor showed up with another shipment."

Pan bit her lip, trying not to laugh. "Was he irked?"

"Irked? Oh no, he was just trying to bite through the concrete column over there when he first spotted your picture." Ladder grinned. "I couldn't stop laughing even when he threatened to toss me out my office window—on the thirtieth floor!"

"Oh Lord." Pan laughed then and was still chuckling when she reached their penthouse apartment. As the doors opened, her mirth died as she looked into her husband's eyes that had gone from navy to steely blue. "Hi."

"Do you know that there's a billboard of you atop one of the buildings here in town? That the whole world is looking at my wife, the Torrid Girl?"

"I heard about the billboard from Letta but I haven't seen it." She watched him warily. "I won't quit, Silver."

He put out an arm and hooked her to him, his mouth coming down on hers. "Damn you for being so beautiful. You're mine and I hate sharing you with the world." He kissed her again. "I bought a hundred copies of the damned magazine. Stop laughing."

"I can't help it. Stop. What are you doing?" Pan threw her arms around his neck when he scooped her up and carried her across the foyer to the stairs leading to their bedroom. She pushed her face into his neck. "I wanted you to be proud of me."

"I am proud of you, damnit. I just don't want anyone else looking at you."

When he strode into their bedroom and placed her on the bed, Pan was still laughing. "I'm glad we're not going to fight over this."

"Who says we're not going to fight? I feel like wrestling a bear, lady." Silver tossed off his clothes, then threw himself down next to her, bringing her close to his body and beginning to undress her. When the phone rang next to the bed, he cursed roundly. "Don't answer it," he told Pan.

"Don't be silly. Keep me warm while I talk," she told him coaxingly, admitting to herself that she was irritated by the interruption. "Hello. Oh yes, Felice, I saw the spread." Caution entered her voice. "What? You liked it! My goodness. I'm pleased. The Commodore likes it too. Oh, good. I didn't think that—"

Silver took the phone from her hand. "Mother, please don't encourage Pan. She doesn't need any. Yes, I'm a little irked. She's laughing . . . but she won't be for long after I hang up this phone. Never mind, Mother." Silver covered the mouthpiece with his hand. "They want us to come out to dinner Sunday. Do you want to go? We don't have to if you'd rather not—"

"Tell her yes."

"Yes, we'll come. Mother, I'm hanging up on you. Yes, a very special appointment. I don't care if you do understand or not, and stop laughing." Silver hung up the phone and reached for his wife again after switching the phone to the answering machine. "The women in my life seem to be enjoying a joke at my expense."

"Poor baby," Pan murmured, her eyes closing in delight as her husband began the slow sweet rhythm of lovemaking that was a very important part of their life together. Imagining life without Silver and his love was not something that she could face anymore, and she had buried the unwelcome idea of leaving him at some future date. Leave Silver? The thought sent chills up her spine! He had become paramount in her scheme of things. Day by day was the only way to handle it. Let tomorrow take care of itself.

The subsequent days were increasingly busy for Pan and Silver. It became a matter of prime importance to schedule their moments together, and they did it carefully so that they could have optimum time together.

"I don't want to make social engagements. I see too little of you now. I don't want to surround us with other people and make inane cocktail conversation."

"Fine with me," Pan told her husband when they were cuddled together on their couch after dinner one evening, the calendar on their laps. "But we have to see your family now and then, and I don't want to shut Ladder from our lives."

"Agreed." Silver kissed her hair, loving the curling softness that touched his skin. "Your hair always arouses me."

"Everything arouses you."

He nodded. "Everything about you does." He kissed her nose when she looked up at him. "You get sexier and lovelier every day."

"So do you."

"I don't think anyone's ever called me lovely until now."

"That's because they don't know you."

"Let's go to bed."

It stunned Silver that not only did he want Pan every moment she was with him, but that she was always in a side pocket of his mind, so that in any free moment in the

146

day she was there in front of his mind's eye. Each day they were together he needed her more, and he had stopped trying to discover the reason. Many times the secretive side of her angered him, but he masked his emotion, biding his time.

One day when Silver was late in the office and she and Hodge had quit early, she encountered Mrs. Tillson as the housekeeper was leaving for the day.

"There was a message for you, Mrs. Galen, from California. Good night."

Long after the housekeeper had gone, Pan stayed where she was, rooted to the spot, absorbing the shock that she had been discovered by the forces she'd run from in California. California! It had to be one of the Drexels calling. She had had a funny, shivery sense of acceptance that she would hear from them, especially since the Torrid Girl ads had taken off and were now spread all over the world. Relief and dismay warred within her. Had she been aiming herself toward this moment? Was her insistence on taking up modeling entwined with a need for confrontation? Her knees felt weak with the revelations.

"I'm glad they called." Pan spoke out loud as she moved step by step toward the library. "It's about time I faced this thing." Silver. Silver. Silver. Would he hate her when all the mess was laid before him? Her marriage was so important to her.

Standing at Silver's huge mahogany desk that had belonged to his grandfather, she picked up the message. Wilson Carpenter had called. Pan inhaled a deep breath. She remembered him. He had been the lawyer for her uncle and had represented the Drexel holdings. Call anytime, the message concluded. How had he gotten the number? From the Rendoll Joyce Agency? Pan knew that Wilson Carpenter had many connections on both coasts.

Pan dialed the number, realizing that because of the three-hour difference Wilson would be in his office. "Yes. Could I speak to Wilson Carpenter, please. It's Trisha Drexel calling." Pan hadn't spoken the name that she'd been known by most of her life in such a long time that it sounded alien to her. She knew in that moment that no matter what was ahead for her, she would keep the name of Pan.

"Trisha? Trisha, is it really you?"

"How are you, Wilson?"

"My dear, I'm just fine. Are you well?"

They talked of many things the first few minutes, and Pan was grateful for the warmth in the lawyer's voice, but she was also impatient to come to the point. "Wilson, what's going on?"

There was silence at the other end of the line. "Not good things for you, my dear. That's why I decided to make contact with you before your stepaunt and Alan Winston could do so through the lawyer they've retained."

"Go on."

"They are making noises about charging you with the murder of your uncle, that they're not just going to have you confined but that they are going to have you jailed." Wilson paused when she gasped. "Listen to me, child. I think you can beat this. I've gone over and over the evidence and I don't think you can be fingered on what there is against you. I think a verdict of person or persons unknown is more than likely—but you must come back to fight this."

"I didn't do it, Wilson, and I'm mentally capable of standing trial and defending myself against such a charge. Will you help me?"

"Of course I will do all I can. There could be complications because of my association with the Drexels, but we will work something out. I tell you this: I will stand by you and I will make sure you have excellent representation in court—if you decide to come back, which I urge you to do."

"Do you really think so?"

"Yes. You are welcome to stay at my home with my wife and me, Trisha."

"Thank you. I have a few things to settle here; then I'll get back to you. But I think you can count on my coming." Pan had a momentary desire to flee, but she thought of Silver and it was like putting steel into her spine.

After she broke the connection she went upstairs, undressed and climbed into the hot tub in their bathroom, the swirling hot water allowing her to relax somewhat.

"Hey, what's this? I'll join you, darling."

Pan watched her husband through half-closed lids as he disrobed quickly, throwing his Savile Row clothes every which way in his hurry to join her. Her body swayed in the small tidal wave he made as he sank into the water and pulled her close to his side.

For many minutes they were silent, holding each other, their hands massaging each other in sensuous exploration.

"What's the problem?" Silver felt Pan jerk in his grasp. "Something's gotten to you, darling."

"Yes." Pan toyed with the idea of keeping Silver in the dark. She hated to tell him even one sordid detail of the California incident. As she was dwelling on that time, the phone on the tile deck of the hot tub rang.

"Damn. I should have put the system on the answering machine." Silver watched as Pan lifted the phone and spoke, then he saw her color fade and her eyes dilate. He tightened his hold on her.

"Darling?" She seemed not to hear Silver's query, her hand tightening on the receiver.

"Yes. I know that my stepaunt and Alan Winston know where I am, Mr. Slate. I have already talked to the Drexel firm's lawyer. No, I don't know you or your law firm, Mr. Slate, but I accept that you are Mr. Winston's solicitor . . . But that doesn't mean . . . Mr. Slate, I have done nothing wrong. I intend to return to California soon and prove that."

Silver could feel his temper heat as he saw her fight the agitation she was feeling, her chin lifting as it always did when she was upset. It took all his forebearance not to yank the phone from her and demand to know who dared disturb her in such a fashion.

Pan could feel her indignation building as the man on the other end piled innuendo on implication. It seemed to her that Slate was trying to intimidate her, that despite his words to the contrary, he was trying to keep her from going to California. No! Now was the time to face things. She was a Drexel heir and the legal owner of the Drexel Holding Company. She had a right to it because she'd done nothing wrong. Pan blinked when the man raised his voice, realizing that he had said some things she'd missed.

"Yes, Mr. Slate, I hear you," Pan told the lawyer. "But you may tell your clients that I will contact them in the next few days about our meeting and that they will have no say whatever in my future." Pan slammed down the phone, her whole body shaking.

"Darling, darling, what is it? Who dared do this to you?" White lightning was in Silver's voice.

As upset as she was, Pan had to smile when she looked

at him. Silver was thunderous. Maybe now was not the best time to tell, but she was going to do just that. "I don't like having to tell you what I'm about to tell you, Silver, but it's time, I suppose."

Silver nodded, cuddling her close to him.

"My name is Drexel. Belmont is my mother's maiden name. I ran from my family because I was found near my uncle's body after he'd been shot. There was no hard evidence to convict me—it was all circumstantial—but a case was building just the same. I didn't do anything to harm my uncle. I loved him very much, but I felt threatened, so I ran." Pan inhaled a trembling breath. She prayed that Silver would not be able to tell that even now she was not telling him the complete story. "That's when I started wandering, first in Europe, then here."

"And now you're going back?"

Pan looked at him for the first time, seeing the determination in his gaze. "I have to go."

"You're not leaving me." Fury erupted in him and he pulled her across his lap, loving her, taking her fiercely right there in the hot tub, feeling grim delight in her ready response and active participation.

"Silver," Pan said softly, her voice sultry, replete, her eyes heavy. "You are the most sensual man on earth."

"With you, I am."

Pan touched his face, her finger tracing his features, lingering on his mouth. "Silver, I have to face my past. I never wanted this confrontation before I met you, but you've made me stronger than I ever was. Now I know I have to go back. I have to try to clear myself. No more running."

Silver surged to his feet, their dripping bodies pink from the heat. At once he oiled her with a fragrant emollient, then dried her with a fluffy terry cloth bath sheet. "Would there be another man out in California?"

Pan pushed back from him, wanting to slap his face for asking such a thing. "I don't think that requires an answer."

"Why the hell not? You've kept a library of things from me since our first meeting, wife."

"And you knew that there was a reason for that. I didn't pretend I didn't have things to hide."

"And now I think you should level with your husband."

"Don't get tough with me, Silver Galen. I don't like it."

They glared at each other like adversaries.

CHAPTER SIX

There were long periods of silence between Silver and Pan during the next week, and there were a few eruptions of temper that left them feeling irritable.

Though they made love with the same passion, with the added intensity of desperation, the rift between them subtly widened until their conversations were sometimes stilted and forced.

Pan was glad to go to work and she worked harder than ever, trying to forget her problems with Silver and what she would have to face in California.

One day when Letta was in the studio watching the shoot, Pan asked her to wait for a moment until she was done.

"You want to take time off to go to California?"

"Hodge told me that we are way ahead of schedule because we'd doubled up on so many of the shoots."

"True, but I was hoping to try you with Keeley Femina."

"I thought I had an exclusive with Benet Lasal."

"You do." Letta shrugged. "But we could have figured out something."

"Can't we leave it until autumn?"

Letta shrugged again. "Pepe won't like this, but what the hell, go ahead—as long as you come back to us."

"I will. Thanks, Letta."

"Hodge will have a basket of kittens about this. He finds you so easy to shoot."

"Why doesn't he tell me that?" Pan quizzed dryly.

"He's a rat." Letta smiled at Pan.

"That was some meeting," Ladder observed laconically, his feet propped on Silver's desk, the jar of candy open in his lap. "You managed to insult the entire board in one fell swoop."

"Take your damned feet off my damned desk." Silver glared at his best friend.

"Touchy, aren't you?" Ladder popped a pink candy into his mouth but didn't remove his feet. "Had an argument with Pan?"

"Yes, and it's none of your damned business."

"True, but I do know you'd better learn to separate your private life from your business life or we'll end up without a board." Ladder smiled blandly when Silver glared at him. "I never thought I'd see the day when anyone could throw you the way that little lady has."

"Shut up."

"The Commodore and Lady Felice think it's terrific."

"You stop feeding them information from this office."

"I don't tell them anything. The board members call the Commodore, he tells Lady Felice and she calls me."

"Nice little network of spies," Silver said with a sneer.

Ladder stared at his friend, his smile fading a little. "You know better."

Silver stared back, then nodded slowly. "I know better, but I'm damn well buffaloed by my bride. There's more than what she's told me about her life in California."

"Tell her how you feel . . . and don't let her go alone."

Silver ground his teeth together. "I have no intention of letting her get away from me for even a short time."

"I can handle the Lendel merger, and if I get in a jam, I'll call the Commodore or ask Braden to work with Lindley."

Silver nodded. "Damnit, Ladder, I'm not worried about how things will be handled here, I'm worried about Pan. Something's eating at her . . . and whatever else happened in California that she's not telling me frightened her enough so that she ran from her home, changed her name and wandered alone and penniless across two continents." Silver snapped the pencil in his hand in half. "I will know whatever it was that did that to her."

Ladder smiled knowingly. "I have no doubt in my mind that you will, old chum."

Lawrence Slate faced the man and woman across the desk from him after he hung up the phone. "Things are getting a little sticky."

"Meaning?" Maeve snapped.

"It seems that Wilson Carpenter had already contacted the heiress before I called her."

"What?" Alan Winston leaned forward in his chair, his glance sliding toward Maeve and away again. "How did that happen?"

"I imagine he has seen the ad for the Torrid Girl and recognized Trisha Drexel just as you did, Alan. Carpenter has vast sources of information, and I imagine it didn't take him long to discover how to contact her," Mr. Slate said dryly, noting how tight-lipped Mrs. Maeve Drexel looked. She wasn't a woman he ever wanted to be on the wrong side of, and he was pretty sure she ran her stepson with the same iron hand she used to run the Drexel company.

"So she knows. And she is coming back here, you say?" Maeve asked silkily.

Slate nodded.

"Good. Alan, you might contact Judge Needham and remind him of the court order still outstanding against Trisha. I do think that since she was to be confined for a complete mental workup at the time of her disappearance, the judgment of the court should be carried out now."

"She's older now and will know she has the right to contest such a judgment," Slate offered cautiously.

"True, but if she is once confined as ordered by the court, it will take a series of court decisions and psychiatric judgments to free her. I think her previous instability will manifest itself, and we can carry on at Drexel's as we have been," Maeve answered coldly.

Slate noticed that Alan Winston relaxed and nodded at her words. "I wouldn't be too sure of running her, Maeve. She sounded pretty sure of herself on the phone when she told me that she would inform me when she was coming."

Maeve smiled, though her eyes remained agate hard. "Really? Well, we'll just see how my stepniece does when she sees the barriers that face her, not to mention the board of directors who are pleased with the way the business is going."

Slate coughed into his hand. "I must remind you that there isn't any hard evidence against her—"

"But a substantial amount of circumstantial evidence. That will be taken into account, I'm sure."

"And there is our word against hers about what we heard and saw," Alan Winston interjected.

Slate nodded slowly. "I still think we're not dealing with the same girl who ran from California."

"And I tell you, Lawrence, that justice will be served. My stepniece will be confined as ordered, and then, since she will be in my custodial care . . ." Maeve shrugged. "She still has the cloud of murder over her head, and I intend to see to it that if she wants to walk free after killing my husband, she will have no hand in running his business."

Alan smiled at her and patted her hand.

Mr. Slate coughed delicately. "I always thought that the Drexel Holdings belonged to Patricia Ann Drexel—that she is the legal heir to them."

"Perhaps she was at one time, but it was my husband's company at his death and I have no intention of letting the person who killed him take over his business. If you don't think you can support me on this, Mr. Slate, I shall find another attorney who can."

"Oh I support you wholeheartedly, Mrs. Drexel. It's just that I don't think we can bring Wilson Carpenter around to our way of thinking. The few times I've spoken to the man, he has been adamant about finding the real heir and having her properties and estate put into her hands."

Maeve smiled coldly. "That's because he's under the mistaken notion that my stepniece is innocent. I know better."

Mr. Slate smiled. "All right, Mrs. Drexel, we'll go ahead with this and hopefully we'll have it settled in a short time."

Pan didn't look forward to speaking to Silver after dinner. She knew that what she had to tell him would set off another argument, and it seemed to her that they had done little else since she'd told him that she was going to California.

157

She went upstairs to their room after telling Mrs. Tillson that she would take care of the final steps of the hot spinach salad.

Pan was stripping off the clothes she'd worn all day when she heard a sound behind her. Her mouth dropped at the sight of her naked husband leaning on the bathroom doorjamb. "Silver!"

"Hello, darling. I've been waiting for you."

"Mrs. Tillson didn't tell me that you had finished in the office."

"She didn't hear me come in, and I didn't feel like talking to anyone so I came right upstairs. Care to get in the hot tub with me?"

"Ah, sure, yes, I'd like that." For some reason she couldn't define, Pan felt shy with him and she turned her back while disrobing. They had been at odds for several days; now he was talking to her much the same as he always did. She felt out of balance. When she heard his low whistle she stiffened, turning her head to look at him over one shoulder.

"That is the loveliest backside on the planet, love, and your wonderful white skin is perfection. Venus, you have turned me on mightily. Hurry over here before I come over there and grab you."

Laughter melted away her inhibitions and she turned, arms slightly upraised and outstretched. "Here I come, ready or not," she told him throatily, chuckling when he groaned, his aroused body telegraphing his desire.

Silver waited until she was about a foot away from him, feeling a film of perspiration coat his body, his heart hammering against his ribs. Then he leaned forward and scooped her up. "Well, lady of my dreams, do you feel triumphant knowing you have me in your spell?"

"No one controls you, Silver Galen," Pan murmured,

threading her fingers through his hair, the tactile sensation running through her like a caress.

Not releasing her, Silver took her through to the bathroom and lowered her gently into the tub, following her at once. He was aware of an air of tension about her, aware that she had something on her mind. But the fact that he had made a new commitment to her, and what he had decided that very afternoon after talking to Ladder, made him more amenable to whatever it was she was going to tell him that evening.

They washed each other in slow enjoyment, their gazes locked, their hands telegraphing all the sensuous meaning in the world.

Finally Pan pulled back from him a fraction. Silver knew that whatever it was she had to tell him, it would be now.

"I've told Rendoll Joyce that I'm taking some time off next week to take care of the business in California." She bit her lip, staring up at him.

"Fine, but I wish you'd given me a little more notice. But it doesn't matter; the company will be in Ladder's hands, and in a pinch the Commodore will step in to help."

"But . . . but, you're not coming."

"Yes, I am, darling. Did you forget I told you we wouldn't be separated?"

Pan's mind spun out of control. She hadn't counted on Silver accompanying her. "You have no idea what you're getting into, husband. We're talking tough turkey here."

"Lady," he told her in measured tones, "you haven't seen tough—but you're going to, very soon."

Pan clutched his shoulders, trying to read the opaque hardness of his eyes. "You—I—don't you see there are

159

things about this situation that I'm not sure of, that I could be guilty of—"

"You said you didn't believe you were guilty, that you couldn't have done what was said. Isn't that true?" Silver smiled slightly when her chin came up a trifle.

"I loved my uncle. He was kind to me, he talked to me all the time about how he wanted me to work in the business so that I would be ready to take over the reins when he retired."

"Didn't he have children?"

"Yes, my cousin Dexter. My uncle brought him into the company but he was always reprimanding him because he thought him too extravagant." Pan smiled slightly. "Uncle could be very austere, but he loved both of us."

"Did he?"

Pan seemed not to notice the inflection in his voice. She had a faraway look in her eyes. "Dex liked fancy cars and clothes but he didn't seem any different from anyone else to me. We were close when we were young, but later we had our own sets of friends. Dex was always on the go, but I liked to stay home and read."

Silver nodded, reading volumes into the two short sentences. Pan had been lonely. She had gravitated to her uncle, but there had been few other persons in her formative years.

"Tonight we have a lobster casserole in the oven, with caesar salad." Silver changed the subject, noting that he threw her off balance and that she was watching him warily. "Scoot. Let's get dressed. I'm hungry."

He watched her go toward the closet, turning to glance back at him. Then Silver left the room and went down to the kitchen, banging pots and pans though there was no need to do so, since Mrs. Tillson had done all the preliminary work on the meal. He made tea because Pan preferred it to coffee and it had become a welcome change to him after a long day of coffee drinking. There was no way she was going to keep anything from him, and tonight when they were drinking tea in front of the fire, he was going to extract the information from her any way that he could.

Though the table was already set with flowers and cutlery, it pleased him to check it over and make sure there was everything necessary for the intimate dinners they enjoyed so much. They rarely dined out except for an occasional dinner with his parents or siblings. Silver had never pictured himself as the type to be satisfied with one woman, let alone being content to eat alone with her each night, then spend a quiet evening chatting or reading. Not only hadn't he thought he fit in such a picture, he would have laughed had anyone suggested it. Now it was what gave him the greatest joy.

"Hi."

Silver wheeled to face his wife, who was wearing silky leisure pajamas in a violet color that captured the tone of her eyes. "Love the harem slippers." His eyes traveled up her form, noting her slight blush and aware that she had fought to stem it. "Not to mention the pajamas. If you're trying to take my mind off work, you've succeeded. But you aren't going to keep me from asking you more questions about yourself."

She glared at him.

"I think we should dine before you execute me, darling," Silver said with a slight smile.

"You're a know-it-all, Silver Galen," Pan blurted, then sank into the chair when he held it for her. "There are certain situations that maybe even you can't handle."

"Sarcastic, darling? How unlike you." Silver leaned

161

down and kissed her neck, feeling the skin quiver there. "Don't worry. Everything will be taken care of and after dinner you can tell me all the worries you've been having about this."

Pan tipped her head back, her gaze holding him in place as he leaned over her. "What if what I tell you sends you away?"

"Then I'll take you with me—we'll do a little dancing, have some champagne."

"Silver, it isn't funny."

"No, but you are, thinking that I would let anything come between us, that I would let anything part us." He kissed her hard, relishing it when she flinched. Nothing made him angrier than when she showed little faith in him.

Pan picked up her spoon and picked at the fresh fruit cup in front of her. Silver had insisted that she eat fresh fruit every day, drink milk and have green vegetables. She looked up, startled, when she felt the movement of the table and the noise of a chair being scraped back. Pan stared at him when he settled himself next to her.

"There. I want to be closer to you."

Pan sighed and nodded. "I want that too."

"Good. Then just stay close to me all the time. I mean to stick to you like glue."

"That should make for interesting board meetings." She smiled faintly when Silver laughed.

Pan relaxed after that, and they chatted about many things as they worked their way through the caesar salad and lobster casserole. "Umm, that was good. Mrs. Tillson is a wonderful cook."

"So are you, wife. I love the meals we make together on the weekends." Silver pulled back her chair when they finished, making no demurral about clearing the table.

Pan was adamant that they not make extra work for the housekeeper.

When they carried the tea into the living room, Silver turned on the disc player while Pan set out the things on the low table in front of the mammoth white couch that sat at a ninety-degree angle to the fire.

They settled themselves close to each other, Pan sitting in the crook of Silver's arm as she always did, sipping the fragrant tea and listening to the low, sweet strains of Rudolph Serkin playing the piano.

"Tell me what happened in California, and don't leave out one detail or I'll get the detective agency that works for the corporation to get the information I want."

Pan sipped her tea, barely aware when the scalding liquid touched her lips. She looked up at him, seeing the etched-metal look on his face, knowing that there would be no putting him off with half-truths. Trying to pull away from him proved futile, so she stayed where she was and looked into the fire, welcoming its warmth and the heat of the man who held her. It was a comfortable spring evening, but she had the feeling she was in the Arctic.

"I told you about my uncle and his kindnesses to me, but I suppose I realized that his son, my cousin Dexter, resented the attention his father showered on me." Pan inhaled. "As I said, Dex and I weren't close once we were older, but we were on fairly friendly terms up until my uncle married again when I was about eighteen. Subtly there were changes in Dex. He seemed angry with me most of the time, so I began to ignore him. Shortly before I left California for good, we were veritable strangers."

"Go on," Silver urged her when she paused and stared into the fire.

"When I started college I had a whole new social life,

163

and my relationship to Dex mattered less and less. My relations with my uncle were still good, but I could tell when I went home for weekends or visits that I was a bone of contention between my stepaunt Maeve and my uncle." Pan leaned forward and poured herself more tea. "I could tell that my uncle was pulling closer to me and further from his wife. Often he would even call me at school and tell me not to come home, that it would be better if I stayed at the university."

Silver felt her body tremble for a moment. "And when did your uncle die?"

"I had completed my last year. Commencement was the following weekend, and I had brought some things home from the dorm so I wouldn't have to bring everything in one trip after the graduation exercises." Pan paused, as though the memories had taken over her mind.

"Go on, darling. You're doing just fine."

"Uncle Henry was happy to see me as always, but he was a little reticent. We talked about a job for me, and it surprised me when he suggested I try New York first and get a feeling for working away from California before coming with Drexel. I was stunned." Pan looked up at him. "You see, from the time he'd become my guardian he'd always talked of when I would come into the business with him, and now he was doing a complete about-face. I was hurt, to say the least, and he could see that because he kept trying to comfort me, telling me that there were a few things he had to iron out in the company before he wanted me aboard, that it wouldn't take long and then I would be with him at Drexel and we would be making all sorts of changes."

"And?"

"One evening, just two days before I was returning to

164

campus, I went out with some friends of mine, for a pregraduation celebration. I wasn't out late. It wasn't even midnight . . ."

"Easy, darling," Silver said soothingly when he felt her body quake.

"I'm all right. I've run this around in my head so many times that it sometimes seems unreal." She raised her mouth blindly, taking his lips greedily when he bent over her. When he pulled back she stared up at him, her breath wheezing from her body. "I was glad my uncle was awake. You see, there were so many things to talk about—graduation, a job, going away from home as opposed to staying. So . . . I . . . pushed open the door of the study and rushed into the room. Uncle was bent over his desk. At first I thought he was sleeping. Then I saw the blood trickling down his face. I wanted to scream, but instead I tried to awaken him. I had the sensation that he wasn't dead. Then I reached for the phone—"

"And?"

"Someone hit me, and I went out like a light."

"What?"

"Yes." Pan raised her voice, sitting erect. "I was knocked unconscious." She licked her desert-dry lips. "At first I think the police believed me, but after talking to my stepaunt and her friend, they seemed suspicious," Pan said bitterly. "Even though I had a bump on my head that was plain to see." Pan's voice wavered into silence.

"What happened after the police came and questioned everyone?"

"My stepaunt insisted that when she and Alan came into the room I was bent over my uncle with a heavy

165

paperweight near my hand." Pan was breathing as though she'd run up the side of a mountain.

Silver felt her go rigid, and he suspected something worse was coming. "Tell me."

"At first they believed me—the police, I mean. Then—then little by little I could tell they were starting to doubt my story. There was no forced entry, so there could be no one who had come into the house and burgled it, then hit Uncle and me. They said—they said that we fought over my money. My stepaunt told them that my uncle didn't want me in Drexel's, that he wanted me to leave the state and work."

"Which was a version of the truth."

Pan's head whipped around, and she nodded vigorously. "Yes, yes, it was, but it sounded all wrong, you see . . ."

"It sounded as though your uncle was sending you away, not that he wanted to clear something up before you came into the company."

"Yes, yes, yes." Pan couldn't stem the tears that flooded her eyes and flowed down her cheeks.

"Then what?"

Pan didn't want to tell him any more, but she'd come too far to turn back. "Then there was to be a hearing that would determine if—if I could be brought to trial for my uncle's—but—you see—there—was no tangible—evidence so the judge handed me over for a court-appointed mental workup and prehearing examination."

Silver's arms tightened. "Were you confined in a mental institution?"

"Yes," Pan said softly. "My stepaunt insisted that I wasn't capable of standing trial and that I was a danger to myself and the community. As her husband's heir, she was my custodian until I reached the age of twenty-one, which I would have been in three months. Until then I was to be confined." Her words fell over one another as she tried to make it clear to him.

"So you were kept locked up?" Silver's voice held a menace that Pan had never heard. Startled, she looked at him and nodded.

"But one day when they were cleaning my room, I just walked out of the building. I slipped on a coat that belonged to one of the staff, I suppose. With the change I found in the pocket, I called Wilson Carpenter. He tried to make me come to his office, but I told him I wouldn't, that I wanted to leave the country. I asked him to send my passport and some money." Pan inhaled a shaky breath. "He did and told me to call him when I needed more, but I was afraid to do that, for fear I would be put back in the institution."

"They couldn't have kept you there. You had every right to sign yourself out of there."

"It was a private hospital. Wilson Carpenter told me that he'd had no idea what had happened to me or where I had been taken."

"Now you're going back to clear yourself."

"Yes. You've given me the courage to try, Silver. I feel stronger because of you."

Silver stared down at her. "And it will take courage, my sweet. Sometimes you will feel alone, bereft, unsure. Will you give me your word that you will trust me?"

The old wariness came over her like a musty security blanket. "What do you mean?"

"Can you bring yourself to trust me completely?"

Her cautious core screamed a negative. "Yes. I will trust you." Pan burned her bridges.

"Will you give me carte blanche? Power of attorney?"

"Power of attorney over what? I don't think I have much more than what you've given me, Silver."

"Trust me, Pan."

"All right. I'll give you power of attorney, Silver." She inhaled when he smiled at her and nodded.

"Good. Now tell me about your relatives in San Francisco."

Pan shrugged, putting aside the uneasy feeling that Silver was toying with her, hiding something from her. "There was just my stepaunt and Dexter . . . and a close friend of my aunt who was at the house much of the time—Alan Winston."

"That was it?"

"Yes, unless you count Mr. Slate, who seems to be my stepaunt's lawyer. I think that Wilson Carpenter is still the attorney for Drexel Holdings."

"Tell me about the company."

Pan relaxed, feeling warmer than she had a few minutes ago. "Well, let's see. My father took a small local paper that had been in the family for many years and hammered a publishing empire out of it. We have a news service in Europe that's similar to Reuter's and we own several newspaper chains on this continent, in Europe and in the Far East. Drexel's is by no means the largest— maybe it isn't even in the top twenty worldwide—but it has grown and under my uncle's tutelage it became a very classy, honorable news network."

"So it did," Silver mused, his lips pressed to her hair. "Tomorrow morning before you go to Rendoll Joyce I want you to come through to my office. You can sign the power of attorney then."

"My, you are in a hurry." Pan's skin prickled, but she smothered the warning that sounded in her brain. She didn't pay lip service to trusting her husband; she did trust him, fully!

"Yes." Silver turned her in his arms. "Right now I'm in a very big hurry to make love to my wife." Silver slid to the floor and onto the oriental rug in front of the dying fire.

"Aren't we going up to bed?" Pan's nebulous fears melted away at the look in his eyes when he slowly shook his head. "Decadent."

"Wonderful. We'll have a decadent sexual encounter right here." In slow, sensuous exploration Silver removed her clothes, murmuring love words against her skin as he revealed her slowly. "I don't know how you feel right now, darling, but I think you just blew me apart."

"Good. I didn't want to be the only one."

They began to make love with a terrible urgency. Pan's head whipped back and forth as she lay naked under him, his mouth making her body quake with sexual excitement.

"Shh, easy darling." Silver gave a breathy laugh when she dug her nails into him. "Slow down or it will be too fast."

"Not fast enough." It awed and stunned her at how rapid her responses were to her husband, and as time went on, she seemed to become even more explosive with him. He was her life!

Silver struggled to contain the passion building in him, wanting to please and excite her, but as always, she had taken possession of him and his being shuddered with want. It amazed him how she closed around him body and spirit, keeping him for her own.

Each giving to the other, they climbed to the pinnacle of delight that only giving could achieve. They crested and climaxed, both groaning satisfaction and satiation.

Silver cuddled her close to him. "Nothing on earth is as good as that, my love."

"It amazes me what we can do."

Silver laughed, his joy in her growing with every moment.

The plane ride was uneventful. The food was good in first class and the flight attendants were attentive and thoughtful, but Pan couldn't relax.

It had been two days since she'd told him about her confinement in a mental hospital, and although their lovemaking was as fulfilling and awesome as always, Silver seemed distracted. Pan had an easy time convincing herself it was because of what she had told him and how disturbed he was by it. There were moments when she could not reach him, he was so deep in thought and distant.

On the surface of his mind Silver was aware that Pan shot more and more closed looks his way, but he was so taken up with the project he'd begun that he didn't take the time to soothe away her concerns.

The day after he'd talked to Pan, he'd called Ladder into his office.

"I want the good old boys on this one." Silver referred to the six men left alive out of his company in Vietnam. They'd all been in the hospital together, and Silver had visited them and Ladder at the same time. They referred to themselves as the good old boys, though only one of them had come from the hill country of Tennessee.

Ladder straightened from his slouched position. "Must be very hush-hush."

"It is. I want Lem to get his agency on this, and I want Tel and Will to do some legal work. Marv can handle the advance work. I'm going to lay it out, and you'll coordi-

170

nate it from here. Will this be too much for you, along with handling the corporation?"

"No, but I think I will bring in Braden and the Commodore as you suggested, just in case things get a little hairy with the Lendel merger."

Silver nodded. "Let Braden handle it. He knows those people and he's good in a pinch."

Ladder saw how Silver's eyes slid away from him, seeming to fasten on a fascinating cloud in the sky outside the window. "You're worried about her, aren't you?"

Silver threw his pen down on the desk. "She's been hurt, damnit. I won't let that happen again." Silver turned toward his friend. "She was confined, almost as we were confined in Nam. They scarred her."

"More than you've been scarred, I reckon, or me, but she was able to give me comfort one day when we were walking down Fifth Avenue." Ladder looked at his steepled hands as he faced Silver across the desk. "No one ever got as much out of me as she has. She's a loving, wonderful person and no one's going to hurt her."

"Damn right."

Ladder and Silver had stared into each other's eyes, sealing the silent covenant.

Silver came out of his reverie, looking startled when the flight attendant leaned over him and proffered the canapes. He shook his head, sinking into thought again.

Pan took the food but she felt as though she were eating sawdust.

Why was Silver ignoring her? Had he already regretted his action in coming with her? She felt a stab at the irrational thought that divorce could be the next step. Pan's stomach clenched in revulsion at the idea. It wasn't fair. She hadn't wanted to marry him in the first place, but she had, and now she was quite used to having him, to being

171

his wife, to have him be everything to her. Damn Silver for making her love him! If he walked away, her life would be a huge empty hole. Wrestling her horrible fantasies sapped her energy.

"Why did you sigh?" Silver turned his head, focusing on her.

"Oh, just thinking. It will seem strange to be in California again."

Pan felt more isolated the closer they came to the beautiful Pacific Coast state.

When they deplaned, Silver felt the slight trembling of her body and he tightened his arm around her. Though he meant to comfort her, he sensed that she was in many ways beyond his touch now that she was back in California.

It stiffened Silver's resolve to wipe the slate clean when he saw how chalky faced she'd become and how high she'd lifted her chin. The days ahead were going to be an ordeal for Pan, and Silver felt like killing the persons who were responsible for it. There was no doubt in his mind that Pan was innocent, that somehow there'd been a mistake—or a frame.

"Where are we staying?" Pan stared around her, then turned her head toward her husband. "I'm sorry. I didn't hear what you said, Silver. Daydreaming, I guess."

"I said that we're staying at your home, that I've sent an advance party to make sure that we reside in the master suite. I have also obtained a court order for my accounting firm to go into your company and do an audit of the books."

Pan stared at him, aware that her mouth was opening and closing, but no sound came from her throat. "How can you—they won't let you—you should have said something." Out of breath and stunned at his quick action, she sank back in her seat, forgetting the passing scenery. "You don't know my aunt . . . and Alan Winston."

"And they don't know me, my sweet wife. My lawyers have already ascertained that the business belongs to you in toto. That means, my love, under the laws of California and New York, that I am your heir, unless you specify otherwise. As such, I have legal powers." Silver patted his breast pocket. "And of course the power of attorney reinforces this. I am legally the head of Drexel Holdings, darling."

"But—but—Silver, you don't need Drexel's. It isn't nearly as big as Galen's."

"You're right about that, Pan, but I don't think you realize how valuable Drexel's is. I intend to show you."

Pan stared at the man next to her, noting how the scarred side of his face quivered and seemed to whiten. When he looked at her it was a blind, icy stare that she didn't know. "I don't think we should go to the house," she whispered. "We're not expected. They could call the police. I'll be arrested—"

"You won't be arrested, and they know we are coming because I've informed them. Nothing will be disturbing to you, I assure you. If your relatives refuse to move from the rooms that we wish to occupy, then they will be tossed off the premises."

Pan gasped. "You can't do that. Isn't possession nine-tenths of the law?"

Silver shrugged. "I couldn't say, love; I'm not a lawyer. I do know that my people have had no trouble or I would have heard of it."

Pan's heart began a painful thudding that shortened her breath and made respiration difficult.

When the hired car that Silver was driving left the

freeway to climb into the hills, Pan looked at him. "You seem to know the way."

"My people gave me explicit directions," Silver said as he gunned the high-powered Cadillac up the winding canyon road.

"My people? What is this 'my people' routine? You sound as though you're a dictator or something."

"Tummy upset by the flight, love?"

"No! My tummy is not upset. I just want to know what's going on around here."

"Everything will be explained in due time."

"Silver, listen to me—oh, wait, you missed the turn. The house is up there."

Pan forgot what she wanted to say as the familiar landmarks hit her eyes like a blow. All the reasons for running from this home mushroomed in on her like a black cloud, sealing off sensible reaction. "Let's go. I don't want to stay here."

Silver's teeth came together with a crack. "I told you it would be rough, but you must be tough and you can be. I'll help you." His fear of her cracking when meeting the family had kept him from telling the household the exact time of their arrival. Pan needed every advantage.

Pan nodded, gritting her teeth as they pulled up in front of the large house.

Before Silver helped her from the car, the front door opened and a butler emerged, though he looked more like a bouncer for a pub.

"Are you Gravers?" Silver indicated the trunk of the car and threw the man the keys.

"I am, sir. There was a bit of a wrangle when we first arrived, but the court order that Mr. Lemuel had seemed to settle things." The man stared at Silver woodenly.

174

"One of the staff made a call, sir, so we are expecting higher-level opposition to our plan."

Silver nodded, ushering Pan up the steps and into the foyer, where she stood looking around her, her hands clenched in front of her.

"Miss Trisha. Welcome home. We did not know when to expect you." A plump woman came through from the back of the house, her Latina features alight in welcome, her ample bosom quivering as she rushed forward to enfold Pan in her arms. "I have missed you, *pequeña,* very much."

"Thank you, Maria. It's good to see you."

"I don't think that fancy houseman that Mrs. Drexel hired will stay after the rough handling he had this morning." Maria twinkled at Pan, thinking that the young girl who'd run from California years ago had come back a lovely woman.

Silver reached around Pan and took Maria's hand. "I'm Silver Galen, Pan's husband."

"Pan? *Qué?*" Maria had a puzzled smile on her face.

"That was what my father used to call me, Maria. I don't think you remember him."

Maria shook her head. "No, it was your dear uncle who hired me, *pequeña.*" Her smile widened. "No matter. You are home now and all will be well." A shadow crossed Maria's face.

"Is something wrong, Maria?"

"*Sí.* Your aunt has given me notice. She say that I am too old, but I am not."

"Not to worry, Maria," Silver told the heavy woman. "My wife will want you to stay on here, and this is her home."

Maria's eyes lightened. "*Sí,* that is true. I will run your shower for you. Yes?"

175

"I can do it, Maria. I would rather you were down here making me shrimp tournedos."

Maria threw back her head and laughed. *"Sí.* I have some lovely shrimp, Miss Trisha. I will do it." She turned and hurried to the kitchen, humming to herself.

"So she is the one who helped that appetite of yours along, is she?" Silver teased her, but her smile was twisted when she nodded.

Once they were in the huge room where their things had been taken, Pan looked around slowly. "I have only visited this room before now. First it was my parents' room, then it was Uncle's."

"It doesn't make you uncomfortable, does it, darling?"

Pan shook her head, removing her suit jacket and sitting on the bed.

"Because I intend to show your relatives that you are coming out of your corner with a vengeance, that you are not only getting your life back on keel but that you are going to take over your home and business."

Pan's head whipped up and she stared at him when he laughed harshly. "You make it sound like a vendetta."

"Do I? Well, maybe it is. I'm taking a shower." Silver went through into the bathroom.

Pan stared at the closed door. Three days ago he would have insisted that she join him in the shower. She trembled at the confusion in her life, realizing that her greatest fear was losing her husband, not facing the Drexels and the court hearing.

Like an automaton she rose and began unpacking her clothes, all at once aware that there were more suitcases for her than she'd packed.

When she opened one of the bags she saw several of the silk dresses that had been purchased at Charine's with the shoes and all accessories. She stared open-mouthed at

176

the contents of the bag. There had to be ten or twelve ensembles. She discovered her jewelry roll in one of the bags that Silver had carried.

"Why are you staring into the luggage, love?" Silver came up behind her, rubbed his hand over her backside and kissed her neck.

Pan straightened and gave him a tight look. "Where did all this jewelry come from?"

Silver looked where she was pointing, studying the array of gems, chains and necklaces in the leather-covered box. Then he smiled at her and nodded. "You're my wife. I'll buy you anything I damn well please."

Pan's temper evaporated into giggles. "You should see your face. You look like a pit bull ready for the ring."

Silver's reluctant smile broke through as he reached for her and swung her off her feet, throwing her past the baggage to the middle of the bed.

As he landed on the bed next to her and took her in his arms, the door slammed open behind them, hitting the wall with a resounding bang.

"What the devil do you mean by coming into my bedroom, Trisha? Take your lover or whatever he is and get out of here."

The acid words stiffened Pan, but Silver continued to kiss her thoroughly. Then he touched his lips to her eyes and nose before looking over his shoulder.

"I don't know who the hell you are, but you'd better get the hell out of our bedroom now, because when I get up from here I'm going to toss you out—you and anyone else who speaks to my wife in such a fashion." Silver's menacing gaze touched Maeve from head to foot, then back again. Then he came to a sitting position, his hands folded loosely in his lap. "Get out of here. Now." Silver watched as Maeve's color went from white to red to

177

white once more. Then she slammed out of the room, the reverberation knocking a precious porcelain figure from its niche to smash on the floor. Silver turned to a wide-eyed Pan, grinning. "I take it that's your stepaunt."

Pan nodded, then shook her head. "You deliberately baited her."

"Did I?" Silver shrugged. "I was telling her nothing more than the truth. I don't want anyone in our bedroom. We make love a great deal, and I don't like being interrupted when we're together."

"You were glad she came in," Pan said accusingly.

Silver sprang out of bed and pulled her after him. "Don't be silly, darling. I was just asserting our right of privacy. Now put it out of your mind. It isn't important. Let's make love in the shower."

"You've already had a shower."

"You haven't, so I'll join you."

"Silver," Pan responded faintly when he scooped her up in his arms, carried her into the bathroom and set her in the cubicle, coming in after her. "Dinner will be in less than an hour," she told him as she put her arms around his neck and closed her eyes. "We can't do this," she whispered as she kissed his neck.

"All right, I'll stop."

"Thank you," Pan mumbled as she felt him lift her and let her body slide down his, feeling his moist entry as the most exciting expression of love on the planet. "Damn, I think I love you." She groaned fatalistically.

"Shh, sweetheart, you won't die from it."

"Oh yes I will. When you leave me, I'll die even though I'll be standing up . . . and talking . . . and eating . . ."

"Crazy lady." Silver chuckled. "I'm not leaving you."

They clung to each other as the familiar but brand-new

178

explosion of feeling rocked their bodies, joining them, locking them together in love as the water streamed over them.

Dressing was an exercise in laughter and restraint for Pan. She had never seen such a comic side of Silver. As she was turning to see if her slip was hanging beneath the hem of the pleated silk sleeveless dress in an off hue of aubergine, he came up behind her and slipped his arms around her waist, dropped to his knees and bit her gently on the backside. "Silver." She laughed, appalled and delighted when she looked down into his rakish eyes.

"You are sweet to eat, luscious wife. I think we'll go back to Bermuda and I'll dine on you a few times."

Uncaring of her dress and makeup, she too slipped to her knees. "Oh, I wish we could. Bermuda was so wonderful."

"I agree. We'll take care of this little California annoyance and then we'll get at it." Silver rose to his feet, his strong arms lifting her with him until she was above him, his arm cupped under her buttocks holding her in place. "Just remember that this is only a momentary irritation that we'll soon put behind us." Silver saw the slight whitening of her coloring, though she smiled and nodded at him. Damn all the Drexels to the deepest, hottest inferno.

Pan looked down at her husband, fighting the sting behind her eyes. She couldn't lose him now. He was her world.

CHAPTER SEVEN

Dexter Drexel watched his cousin walk into the huge sitting room and thought her to be the most beautiful woman he'd ever seen. Dex felt a twinge of regret for the lost wonderful relationship they'd had as children.

All at once the memory of when they'd been at school and Trish, two years older than he, had come to his aid when some of the school toughs had decided to harass him, filled his mind. He could taste the terror as clearly as if it were yesterday. Even now it took his breath away when he recalled how she had jumped onto the back of the biggest one and pummeled him. The ferocity of her attack had so stunned the others that they had backed off and stared at the red-haired wild girl who told them she'd bury them if they ever touched her cousin again.

Guilt stung him as he watched her hesitant entrance into the sitting room of her own home. She should hate him. Not only hadn't he supported her, he had allowed his stepmother and her boyfriend to take over this house and the Drexel Holding Company. "Trisha," Dexter said hesitantly, swallowing when she faced him expressionlessly.

"Dexter." Pan didn't know what to say to her childhood playmate, but she felt awkward and cautious. Her glance slid toward her husband, who stood at her side, relaxed, urbane, a slight smile on his face. "Ah, Dex, this is my—my husband, Silver Galen."

Dexter almost didn't shake hands with Trisha's spouse, he was so shocked at the scarred face of her companion. "I was at the Indy when you crashed that day. That was some driving. You would have killed a hundred people if you hadn't maneuvered into the center field." Then Dexter shook his hand hard, feeling the blood rise to his face. He'd been babbling. His glance slid to his tight-faced stepmother and Alan. They looked as though they had just sucked on very fresh lemons. "Ah, Mr. Galen, have you met my stepmother and her—her friend, Alan Winston?"

"Call me Silver. And yes, I've met your stepmother. She came to our room earlier." Silver's hard smile touched Maeve; then it moved to Winston. He inclined his head but didn't offer his hand. "Winston."

"Galen." Alan Winston ground his teeth at the insulting acknowledgment, as though Silver Galen were somehow his superior. "Welcome back, Trish. I'm sure you're eager to get into your old room. It's been kept just the same for you."

"You're wrong there," Silver answered easily for his wife. "We prefer the master suite. That's why my wife's stepaunt has been moved to guest quarters." Silver ushered his wife to a chair in front of the fire. "In fact," he said to Maeve, "I'm sure after my accountants are through at the firm and my people have begun to take over, you and Mr. Winston will want to find other lodgings."

Even Pan gasped at Silver's words.

"We have kept this house in perfect order—" Maeve began.

"And we thank you for that, but Pan and I also value

181

our privacy, as I'm sure you do." Silver smiled, gesturing for Maeve to be seated in a guest chair, seeming not to notice the high color in the woman's face.

"Do not think that you can walk into the Drexel Holding Company and just take over. The board of directors will have something to say about that. Dexter, Alan and I are on that board," Maeve told him, fighting to keep the furious tremor from her voice.

"So I understand." Silver smiled. "White wine or sparkling water, darling?"

"Sparkling water with lime, please." Pan began to relax. Silver's bland amusement was infectious. After all, this was her home! She owned, personally, fifty-one percent of Drexel's, a block of voting stock that assured her a place on the board. "I've been thinking—" Pan paused to clear the huskiness from her throat "—that I would like to put my affairs in order here—"

"Then you will have to talk with the district attorney and the court-appointed psychiatrist," Maeve interrupted. "The court has remanded you to Schilling Institute for a complete workup. Or had you forgotten, Trisha?"

Pan felt her world tilt, and her hands clasped in front of her, beginning to perspire. "I realize that I have—obligations that must be faced and I intend to do that, but I also feel that my father and my uncle would expect me to assume responsibility for the company that belongs to me."

"You have been declared incompetent by the courts, Trisha," Alan Winston said smoothly. "Maeve and I have been running the company and doing a good job. I don't think the board or the shareholders would appreciate someone who has a history of mental illness taking over the helm."

Silver saw Pan's chin lift a fraction, a familiar veil coming down over her eyes. How the hell did she ever last as long as she did against this unholy three? He turned his gaze on Winston, staring at the man.

Alan Winston considered himself unflappable, good in a crisis and an excellent administrator, but when he gazed into the eyes of Silver Galen, that scarred face giving him a malevolent look, he felt a shiver of dread travel up his spine.

"How kind of you to think of the board. But the staff that has evaluated the company and its subsidiaries would disagree with you. In fact, isn't it true that the requests to find Trisha Drexel and bring her back to the company were many? And that they were ignored by you?"

"We didn't ignore them, and most of the requests were made only immediately after she disappeared," Maeve said stiffly. "Besides, we had all we could do to keep the company going."

Silver leaned back in his chair, stretching his feet out in front of him, the silence stretching like a rubber band. "Dexter, what is your position in the firm?"

Maeve and Alan opened their mouths, then shut them again.

"I'm a vice president," Dexter mumbled. "Personnel."

Silver nodded. "Then you are not involved in the fiscal end of the business. Fine." Silver steepled his hands in front of him. "Tomorrow, at the latest, I will have a full report in my hands about the business—its past, present and future. The preliminary study submitted to me showed many fiscal holes." Silver looked at each one of them in turn. "I don't like that."

"Now wait a minute—" Alan began.

"See here—" Maeve said at the same time.

183

"No, you wait a minute." Silver jabbed the air with his finger. "The psychiatric workup you alluded to, Mrs. Drexel, was urged by you. I have brought in psychiatrists from other parts of the country who have talked to my wife and who placed their findings before the judge who chaired my wife's hearing into the death of her uncle. Judge Needham freely admits there was nothing to indicate that she was guilty or that she needed testing, but at your and Mr. Winston's urging, he had ordered it. He has agreed to open the hearing once more. This time my people will be on it. Hopefully the mystery of my wife's uncle's death will be solved, but if not solved, then at least there will be enough evidence to clear her. Certainly the authorities have found nothing that would incriminate my wife in any crime."

Pan stared at her husband. When had he done all this? Why hadn't he told her what he was planning to do?

"I never really believed that Trisha killed my father. She loved him," Dexter blurted, his face reddening when everyone looked at him. "And he loved her better than anybody."

"That's not true, Dex. He loved you, but you were always with your friends and never home. You didn't like to talk to him and be with him. I did," Pan told him quietly. "I would have fallen apart after my folks were killed if it hadn't been for him."

"But you do admit that you were on the edge, mentally speaking, that is?" Maeve said as she stared at her stepniece.

"I was grief-stricken. If that's what you call being crazy, then I suppose I was."

"That's what the courts decided, too, so I don't think there's any need to reopen the hearing. We are custodians of the company and it's doing well, and I'm sure it should stay that way," Maeve pronounced.

"We'll see about that," Silver said silkily, rising to his feet. "Please join us for dinner. Then of course you are welcome to stay overnight, since your things are here. But tomorrow you and Mr. Winston will look for another place." Ignoring their gasps, he went to his wife's side to escort her to the dining room.

"Dex should stay here," Pan told her husband. "This has always been his home."

"Fine, darling, if that's what you want, but if I find anything that smacks of conspiracy here, no one will be protected."

"I can move, Trisha," Dex told her.

"No—not now." Pan didn't look at her stepaunt and Alan Winston. There was no way she would ask them to stay. Being around them made her very uncomfortable.

"We will not stay for dinner," Maeve said angrily. "Tonight we will leave this house, but I will get a court order ousting you, Trisha. My husband wanted me to have this home. It is legally mine."

"No, it is not," Pan told her hotly, her voice strong. "You lived here because you were married to my uncle, but this house is mine."

"We will see about that." Maeve's eyes flashed menace.

Alan and Maeve stormed from the room.

Silver went to the console on the table and pressed a button. A burly man Pan didn't know entered the room and looked right at Silver.

"Go upstairs, where you and Simmons will assist and oversee Mrs. Drexel and Mr. Winston in their packing. Understood?"

The man nodded and left.

"I don't think they'd take anything, but they will fight

for this place. They consider it theirs," Dexter told Silver, grim-faced. "I don't suppose there can be much trust between us now."

Pan made a move toward him and stopped, her smile twisted. "It will take time, Dex. I lost the trust I had in my family."

Dex nodded, his throat working.

Pan preceded Silver out to the hall leading to the formal dining room.

Silver looked at Pan's cousin. "She's had it rough."

"Yes, I know."

"Do you also know that if I find that you contributed to her pain in any way, I shall throw you off the Golden Gate Bridge?"

Dex gave him a shaky smile. "Yeah, I guess I know that too."

The two men followed Pan down the hallway to the dining room.

Pan sat very still in the chair that Silver had held for her, looking around the oak-wainscotted room at the silver tea service that sat on top of a huge oak buffet, blinking at the crystal chandelier that hung dead center over the table. "Hodgkins," she said softly, "would you take the leaves out of the table for our next meal? I never liked the table this way unless we had company."

"Of course, Miss Trisha. I would be glad to do that for you."

"I'm very glad my stepaunt kept you and Maria on until my return, Hodgkins . . . but there are a few faces missing." Pan smiled faintly when Silver nodded encouragingly. "If there is any way that the old retainers can be found and rehired, I would like you to do it."

Hodgkins's expressionless face lightened somewhat,

though his features didn't change. He inclined his head slightly, then retreated to the kitchen.

The shrimp tournedos preceded by clear consommé madrilene with caesar salad and homemade bread touched a palate memory for Pan.

"My compliments to the chef, Hodgkins. That was good," Silver told the older man when he was supervising the clearing of the table before bringing on the cheese and fruit board with coffee. Silver acknowledged the inclination of the retainer's head before the servant disappeared with the kitchen helper. Then he turned to his wife and grimaced. "You have quite a staff here. I feel as though I'm in Buckingham Palace."

Pan smiled when Dexter laughed and answered for her. "My father didn't have the heart to dismiss any of the people employed by Trisha's parents, but Maeve had no qualms about letting people go." Dexter's amusement faded. "I should have stopped her when she fired old Filler. He'd driven for your father and mine for so many years. I don't even think she pensioned him off."

Silver saw the flash of pained alarm on Pan's face. "Not to worry, darling. I'll find him for you and you can amend the situation."

Dexter saw how his cousin's face lit up when she looked at her husband, and her loveliness took him aback. Regret at his own stupidity, his conscious blindness at what had been done to her, assailed him like a flood. "I can find Filler for you, Trish. I'll check it out tomorrow, first thing."

Silver noted how Dexter sat straighter when Pan smiled at him and thanked him. It seemed as though her cousin was sincerely sorry, but he had no intention of taking anything for granted. No one and nothing was going to get at Pan again, and he would see to that, no matter who he had to step on to protect her.

Pan and Silver had been at the big house on the hill in San Francisco for almost a week when the court summons was hand delivered to their door. Pan was called to appear before the same judge she'd faced years ago, to explain why she had refused to obey the court order remanding her to an institution for a full psychiatric evaluation.

When they were up in their bedroom dressing for dinner that evening, Pan kept shooting glances at Silver, feeling the fury coming off him in waves, though his face was bland and he smiled readily at her.

"I knew you shouldn't have baited her," Pan told him, her chin rising slightly, though she was making a great effort to keep her hands from trembling and was trying to smile at her husband.

"No need to worry, darling. I haven't come out of my corner yet." His smile showed every tooth, but Pan shivered at the menace in those eyes. "But I do believe the bell just sounded for the main event—and I'm ready."

Pan nodded and forced a smile, but she had a feeling she'd never met the man who was facing her now. He was, rather, a terrifying stranger.

Silver was seething that Maeve Drexel and Alan Winston had gained the jump on him. He had been assured by his lawyers that everything was moving steadily forward and that whatever was between the two parties could be handled in a law office or, at best, in the judge's chambers. Now there would be a public hearing, and that meant publicity, not only because Trisha Drexel had returned but because she was now married to Silver Galen, the former race car driver. Silver ground his teeth at the thought of reporters hounding his wife.

"You're trying to hide from me that you're very angry at the moment." Pan gave a breathless laugh when he scowled. "You're very amusing when you do that."

"Am I?" Silver reached out and hooked her closer to him. "You're getting to know me too well, wife. How am I going to hide all my little indiscretions from you?"

"Easy. You'll be good. Because if you try anything, I'll bash you. That will keep you from what you call your little indiscretions." Pan let her fingers rove his face, loving the feel of him.

"I'm totally intimidated," Silver said, leaning forward to kiss her lips, his skin goose bumping with delight when she ran her fingers through his hair. It never ceased to amaze him how she could touch his scarred face with such love and tenderness. Though most of the time he never noticed his scar, when he did concentrate on it, his marred face irritated him—more so now that Pan was in his life. Yet he had never seen such feelings on Pan's face. "Do you still trust me?"

"Yes."

Silver tightened his hold, bringing her up against his body. "I want to make love to you, wife. Shall we put dinner back an hour?"

"Since we've been doing that since we arrived in San Francisco, I don't think the staff will be too surprised." Pan hugged him eagerly, wishing for the delightful oblivion she found in his arms, the forgetfulness that only Silver could give her. Not only did she never want to deny him, she was well aware that it was often she who initiated the lovemaking.

Again, as always, their coming together was a burning

away of all that was extraneous, lifting them up and away from earth as they shared their perfect union.

Later, as they dressed, Silver laughed with her and tried to keep the atmosphere light, but before they left the room he touched her arm, turning her to face him. "They're playing hardball, darling, but so can we. I called my office in New York and alerted the Commodore and Ladder. My father was so incensed that I had to hold the phone away from my ear."

Pan gave a watery laugh. "I do love your family, especially your mother and father."

Silver kissed her nose. "They love you. Let's hope that Ladder can keep the family on the East Coast, though. My father seems to think that you need him."

They went down the wide curving stairway, their arms around each other.

Dexter, waiting in the sitting room, turned when they entered, his face flushing when he looked at Silver.

"What's wrong, Dex?" Pan stared at her cousin, puzzled.

"Thank you, Silver." Dex spoke to Silver, then faced Pan. "Your husband arranged for me to supervise a staff change at Drexel's that's been sorely needed, and I appreciated the opportunity." His hoarse voice telegraphed his emotion. "I won't let you down, Silver—or you, ever again, Trish."

"I know you won't."

"I'm counting on it," Silver said almost at the same time.

"I will tell you one thing . . ." Dexter's voice trailed as he was distracted by a noise at the front door. "What the devil is that?"

"Lord." Silver closed his eyes, putting his arm around his wife's waist and pulling her tight to him.

"What is it, Silver? Are you ill?"

"Yes. I think a giant headache has just entered our house."

Mystified, Pan glanced at the closed sitting room door just before it burst open. "Commodore!" Pan looked at her father-in-law glowering in the doorway, his lovely, calm wife at his heels.

"Who the hell is making charges against my daughter-in-law?" he roared, charging into the room, a goggle-eyed Dexter not noticing when his drink tipped and began dribbling on the rug. "Was it you?" The Commodore jabbed his finger at Dexter, who didn't respond.

Silver groaned to himself.

"How wonderful to see you." Pan glided forward to be clasped in a bear hug by her father-in-law. "I hope you've come to stay awhile."

"Don't encourage him," Silver muttered, throwing questioning looks at his mother, who only shrugged.

"Don't worry, my dear," the Commodore rumbled. "No one is going to railroad you, and I'm here to see to that."

"Oh, Commodore." Emotions raised by the events of the past weeks seemed to surge up in Pan all at once, and tears spilled down her cheeks as she hugged the older man.

Horrified, Pan's father-in-law stared at her, then shot a thunderous look toward his son. "You don't take care of her!"

"I do!"

Dexter stared open-mouthed at father and son as they yelled at each other; then his gaze fell on the elegantly serene woman who approached him, holding out her hand and smiling, her well-coifed head and silk suit practically screaming haute couture. Though he felt confused

191

and off balance, he returned her smile, having the bizarre sensation that he should go down on one knee. "I'm Dexter Drexel, Trisha's cousin."

"Is that what you call her? Trisha? How sweet. We call her Pan . . . and though I'd never heard the name, I do very much think it suits my daughter-in-law. I'm Felice du Lant Galen, mother of Sterling Galen the third, whom you call Silver. We have come to rescue our Pan from all the evil Californios who would frighten her . . . those are my husband's words."

Dexter laughed, entranced by the sparkling older woman.

"Excuse me, Dexter. I should extricate my daughter-in-law. She seems to be sandwiched in between those two."

"Damnit, I won't have it, Silver."

"Just listen to me for a moment, Commodore."

"Gentlemen, please," Pan interjected, feeling the first real mirth bubbling up in her since she'd arrived in San Francisco.

"Please, indeed. What are the two of you thinking of? Come along, Sterling. We must change. Will we inconvenience you for dinner, dear? It's no problem to go to a club."

"Will be a problem. I hate clubs," the Commodore muttered darkly.

"And you needn't go to one," Pan said soothingly, putting her arm through her father-in-law's. "We are having one of your favorites tonight—bouillabaisse—and Maria, our chef, has a magic touch in the kitchen. Hodgkins will have taken your things to the wing overlooking the garden. It's very private there."

"You're a good girl." The Commodore patted her

hand, kissing her on the cheek. Then he glowered at his son again. "But he doesn't take good care of you."

"Yes, I do," Silver shot back.

"You'll have to hurry and change, Commodore, so that we can have our dinner." Pan urged the older man toward the door, where the butler was waiting. "And there will be a pot of hot tea in the room for you."

"Make it a tot of Irish whiskey," the Commodore grumbled, leaving the room with his wife and the butler.

"You should have told me they were coming, Silver."

"I didn't know, damnit, but I should have suspected something like this." Silver glared at Pan when she smirked. "You're not funny. Just because he dotes on you, don't think this will be an easy time for any of us."

Pan's smiled faded. "What will they think when they discover that I could be charged with something after the hearing?"

"The Commodore will probably tear the courthouse down if they try anything." Silver was relieved to hear her laugh, and he encouraged her telling Dexter anecdotes about the father-in-law she so obviously liked a great deal.

Later, during dinner, Dexter was barely able to swallow his food, he was so bemused and entranced by the oddly matched couple who parented the great race driver Silver Galen.

"And I have put a battery of detectives on this, Silver," the Commodore informed his son. "No trail is so cold that it won't be picked up by my people."

"I already have detectives on it, sir."

The Commodore waved his hand disdainfully. "I don't mean any of those Milquetoast professionals you employ. I've put my boyos on it."

Silver closed his eyes for a moment, setting his fork on

his plate with a muttered expletive. He saw the questioning looks that Dexter and Pan were giving him and explained heavily. "My father has an underground group that was formed from some of the people who frequent the soup kitchens the family began in New York, then expanded to different cities in the United States. These so-called derelicts have been good friends to us on many an occasion. The Commodore became pretty active with them, and when something goes awry and he needs information he puts out the word in the underground network."

"And does it work?" The older man grumbled a challenge to his son, who shrugged.

"I have to say that it has had a measure of success."

"A measure of success? Bah! The boyos are always right."

Pan grinned at her father-in-law. "I think it's marvelous."

The Commodore smiled back. "How did such a smart girl end up with that son of mine? Too bad he isn't more like me—and don't go scowling at me either."

"Well, sir, I keep trying to bring out those traits in him that are most like you," Pan told the Commodore, her glance sliding toward her glowering husband. She could barely contain her amusement.

"Hear that, Felice?" the Commodore boomed, bringing Hodgkins in from the kitchen, who retreated at once when he saw Pan's signal.

"I think they heard you on Alcatraz, Sterling," Felice responded blandly.

"Told you she was smart." The Commodore nodded fiercely. He fixed his gimlet stare on Dexter. "You weren't part of this nonsense, were you, young fellow?"

"Not at all, Commodore," Pan interjected hastily.

"Dex is working at Drexel's. I haven't told you about the company, have I?" At the Commodore's shake of the head, Pan launched into an explanation of Drexel's, effectively blocking any further questioning of Dexter.

"Sooo, that's the skunk in the woodpile, is it? A growth company!" The Commodore rubbed both his hands together gleefully. "I'll get our people on it right away."

Silver saw Pan stiffen and he tried to catch her eye, but she was staring fixedly at his father. "Darling—"

"No, Silver. I want to tell your mother and father." She sipped her ice water, pressing her lips together for a moment. "The real skunk in the woodpile, as you call it, is that my uncle died under suspicious circumstances and there is to be a hearing to see if I should be remanded over for trial."

The Commodore surged to his feet, his face reddening, his voice booming. "They dared to accuse you?"

Pan realized all at once that this was what Silver had been trying to prevent—that he hadn't been worried that the Commodore wouldn't believe in her but that he was afraid of a blowout.

"Now, Sterling, dear, do sit down. You're making me dizzy pacing around the table that way," Felice du Lant Galen told her spouse gently.

"Father, sit down, please." Silver rose to his feet and took his father's elbow.

The Commodore jerked back. "We're going after those people, whoever they are. They're trying to set her up."

Dexter cleared his throat. "I should have done more, but I never did believe that Trisha had anything to do with my father's death. I always thought it must have been an intruder."

"Who the blazes is Trisha?" the Commodore bellowed.

195

Pan rose to her feet and took hold of her father-in-law and guided him back to his chair. "I was called that by my uncle, sir, but my parents always called me Pan."

"Wise parents." He glared at Dexter. "Call her Pan or Patricia Ann, if you please."

Dexter's face lightened. "Yes sir, I will. I'm glad you're here, sir. I think it will help things."

"Bound to," the Commodore answered, taking his seat, somewhat mollified.

To Pan's relief, her father-in-law praised Maria's cooking and pronounced the dinner wine "tolerable, but not as good as New York wine."

Silver rolled his eyes at his mother, who smiled sweetly.

Felice wasn't too worried about the problems facing Pan. She had a feeling that Dexter must be right and that the uncle could have been attacked by an intruder. In any event, she was convinced that her husband and son would not allow any harm to come to their sweet Pan. Her well-made-up face softened when she looked at her son. The change in him was astounding, but she was quite sure only a few persons close to him would notice. Ladder had seen it, and when she had called the office the other day, he'd mentioned it.

"I never thought to see him so truly well, Lady Felice. He's like a new man. I caught him whistling at a board meeting the other day."

Felice had laughed. "I see it too, Ladder. She's very good for him, isn't she?"

"She's good for everybody. She makes me feel good."

Now as she watched him covertly, she noticed how often her son looked at his wife, how his features softened so that even the ugly scarring on the right side of his face seemed to all but disappear. Yes, no matter what they had to go through, Pan had to be protected. She was good for Silver. She'd made him human again.

"Felice? You'll pour the coffee in the other room. Right? Can't stand sitting around a table all night." Again the Commodore rose, aiming himself for the door.

Felice looked at her daughter-in-law, who chuckled.

"Please pour for all of us." Pan rose and came around the table and kissed her mother-in-law on the forehead. "It's so good to have you here. It makes me feel so much better."

Felice laughed. "The Commodore has that effect. He either destroys or elevates."

For the first time in many days Pan was relaxed. Conversation was good, stimulating. Pan looked around the sitting room of the house she'd always loved and felt truly home.

Felice poured the coffee, and Silver dispensed hundred-year-old cognac that Hodgkins had brought into the room. Silver held Pan close to him on the settee. If only they didn't have that damned hearing to face. He would have to call his people and have them nose around the courthouse. It wouldn't hurt to see if there was any scuttlebutt about it.

Somewhere in the house a phone rang, and in a few moments Hodgkins glided into the room.

"Phone for you, sir. Will you take it in here?" Hodgkins looked at Silver.

"Ah, no, I'll take it in the study."

Pan watched her husband sprint from the room, puzzled that he wouldn't take the call in the sitting room.

Silver lifted the receiver on the oversize oak desk in the paneled study and identified himself. "What? Are you sure about that? Oh, yeah, right. Sure, we'll think of something." He hung up, leaning back in the overstuffed leather chair, his brain building and knocking down solutions to the problems that faced them.

"Silver."

Silver spun in the chair so that he was staring at the door. "Commodore. Come in."

"Something isn't going right."

Silver nodded. "That was one of the men from the detective agency. The judge who instituted this hearing is the same one who was on the bench for the first one, and though there is no concrete evidence against her, the picture isn't rosy. The detectives seem to think it could go either way for Pan, since the judge has some doubt about her because she ran away the last time. So despite many murky areas as far as evidence goes, she could end up defending herself in a court of law." Silver's breath rasped from his throat. "She could be going into that hearing with the deck stacked against her." The chair shot forward with him in it and he looked at his father with tortured eyes. "I—won't—let—them railroad her."

The Commodore squinted at his son for a moment, then went to the phone, dialing a number. "The boyos will help us on this. They're at the mission downtown. With the network of underground information they have, they'll find out something for us."

Silver stared at his father. "What did you do? Fly them in?"

"Don't be foolish. The men from St. George's mission called the San Jacinto mission out here and—yes, yes, this is the Commodore. Right. Put him on, please. Yes, Miguel. Right you are. Well, it's a Mexican standoff, but my son feels that she could be railroaded. Something about the judge being angry because she ran from a judgment . . . right, that's it. No, there was supposed to be no hard evidence that would hold her over for trial.

198

Good. I appreciate it." The Commodore replaced the receiver and looked at his son. "It will take a little time for them to nose around, but we should have something by late tomorrow. When is the hearing?"

"Next Wednesday," Silver told him in a colorless tone.

The Commodore sank down on a chair on the opposite side of the desk from his son, his chin sunk on his chest.

"I'll kill anyone who tries to take her from me, Commodore."

"Of course." Silver's father eyed his son, a slight smile on his face. "It's a blow to find something so precious in your life, isn't it?"

"Yes," Silver responded hoarsely.

That weekend Silver received calls from his sister and brother-in-law.

"No, there's no need for you to come. Well, yes, I know you feel you should be here, but we're handling it. The Commodore is out every day with his boyos and each day he comes back with something new, no matter how small, but we're putting together a strong rebuttal. Every night the lawyers are here and—yes, Ward Battle will be coming from New York with some colleagues who are expert in this sort of thing, and they will be coordinating with a man called Wilson Carpenter, the Drexel lawyer. Don't worry. Give my best to Ben and Braden. Bye."

Each night when they went to bed Pan and Silver made sweet love until both were limp and sleepy.

"You never want me to sleep," Pan said and yawned.

"I do, darling. It's just that I prefer you to sleep in the day and play with me at night."

"Lecher." Pan laughed into his neck.

"Yes, but admit you enjoy it."

"Oh, I do. And it's such a surprise that it keeps getting better."

"I think I've been insulted."

Pan giggled. "That's not true and you know it. You're acting like a little boy." Pan went still in his arms. "Speaking of little boys, I wonder if we shouldn't—"

"No!" Silver tightened his hold on her. "We are not getting pregnant."

"*We* wouldn't be, silly. *I* would."

"Not until the year is up. Then we'll think about babies, but you can't conceive until your body has fully recovered from the miscarriage," he told her grimly.

Wriggling free of his hold, she reared up and leaned over him, her weight on his chest. "We don't have to be sticklers about this." She touched his face gently with her fingertips.

"Wrong. We are going to be very fussy about this—or I am, and you're going to listen. We'll have children, Pan, but only when your health is perfect."

"Perfect? Good Lord, are you running me through a wonder machine that can tell you that?" She chuckled at his scowl.

"It isn't funny. I take this very seriously."

"So I noticed," she told him, laughter bubbling through her words.

Silver heaved up and turned her on her back, pinning her beneath him. "Listen, lady love, you're the most important thing in my life and don't forget it. Hey, did I hurt you? Why the tears?"

"You're not supposed to make a woman feel as important as the moon, foolish man." Pan sighed when Silver kissed the tears that were running down the side of her face to the pillow. "I don't know why I'm being watery."

"I love you, Pan, and I'm going to take care of you." Silver pressed his face to her breast. "I need you."

The simple declaration rocked her, and she clung to him. "I want us to be together."

"No need to wish for that, Pan." Silver's voice was muffled against her skin. "There's nothing on earth that can part us." He lifted his head when he felt her body quiver with laughter. "I'm dead serious."

"You still sound like a little boy."

He grinned at her. "And you are looking very young and beautiful at this moment." For a second a shadow passed over her face and he tightened his hold. "We'll get through this quickly and easily, and we'll be back home in no time." He probed her face, his mind searching for ways to distract her. "What if we let Dexter continue to live here in the wing he's been using; then we'll use the house whenever we visit this coast? Would you like that?"

Pan stared at him as though he'd offered her moonbeams. "Do you think it will be settled that this house does belong to me?"

"I do." When a smile trembled over her face, he felt as though his heart had moved over three inches in his chest.

"Then I would like to do that."

Long after she was sleeping, cradled in his arms, Silver rubbed his cheek over her hair, staring at the pattern of moonlight that danced on the ceiling. Something wasn't ringing true. The detectives he'd put on the case were somewhat baffled as well. Though the evidence against Pan was murky and circumstantial, so was the evidence against there having been an unknown intruder. There had been no forced entry, no signs that Pan's uncle had been surprised by an outsider or put up a struggle. Yet there was no other way for it to be, because the other possible suspects had been away from the house—Maeve at a banquet, Dex at a party, Alan out of the city on business when the incident occurred.

Too many things were fragmented. Nothing came together, jelled or fit.

Silver turned his head a bit so that he could look down at Pan, her lips slightly apart as she sank deeper and deeper into sleep. If only she could remember what happened before she came to on the floor of the library with her uncle resting on his desk, dead.

In less than a week there would be another hearing. Silver's skin crawled with the feeling that she was being set up, that this hearing was being called not to clarify things but to nail down Pan's coffin.

When Pan moaned in her sleep, he loosened his grip on her that had tightened convulsively with the turmoil that plagued Silver's mind.

Before the hearing they had to have enough ammunition to mount an offensive against those who would let Pan Drexel Galen be swept away by circumstantial evidence. It was clear to him that neither Pan's stepaunt nor her boyfriend would be too unhappy if Pan was found culpable in the death of her uncle. It would certainly make it easier for them to assume the reins of power of Drexel's permanently. Pan's inheritance would go down the drain, and her reputation with it. No! He was the head of Drexel's now. Though now, as a Galen, she didn't need the money or the company, he would see to it that she didn't lose either. Silver was determined that no one was going to use her good name as a stepping-stone to wealth and financial security.

Silver fell asleep, his mind set on protecting his wife, freeing her from the burden that had been hers for too long.

202

* * *

The following day Felice prevailed on Pan to accompany her shopping in San Francisco. "My dear, the Commodore and I visited here some years ago, but I hadn't realized the city had grown so much," Felice told her when Pan drove through the shopping area and parked.

"It's a beautiful city," Pan said quietly. "My parents thought it was the only place on earth to live; so did my uncle."

Felice took her arm after they'd parked the car and were strolling past the shops. "You were very close to your parents and your uncle."

"Yes . . . but now Silver and all the Galens are my family."

The two women smiled at each other, discussed the merits of a knitted silk dress in the window and then turned away to cross the street.

"Ghirardelli Square is not far from here. Shall we go there?"

The person in the black car with the darkened windows watched Trisha Drexel Galen walk with the elegant older woman. Damn her for coming back to San Francisco! It had all been so simple before she'd returned and upset everything.

Reaching toward the ignition, turning on the engine was a fluid move. It would all be timing.

When the two women were in the middle of the crosswalk, others passed them by in both directions, but then for a moment they were alone in the center of the thoroughfare.

The driver gunned the car, fixing on Trisha Drexel Galen. The tires squealed as the vehicle bore down in deadly purpose.

Whatever made Pan look up, grab the older woman and throw her toward the sidewalk would never be known by the driver, who felt a grinding frustration when the auto just grazed the intended target.

Cursing fluently, the driver saw the arrested shock on the passersby; then the powerful car veered around a corner and was gone.

"God, oh God, get help someone." Felice put her clutch purse under Pan's head, watching her eyes flutter open with a rush of relief.

"What—what happened? No, no, it's all right, the car just touched me. The fool must have been drunk." Pan tried to sit up but people kept telling her to lie still until the ambulance and police came.

In short order an ambulance arrived and emergency attendants were efficiently examining Pan.

"Yes, of course, you're fine, Mrs. Galen, but I don't think you should stand just yet. We'll take you in and let a doctor decide your condition, shall we?" The attendant soothed Pan when she tried to rise.

"The man is absolutely correct, dear. I've never been so frightened in my life as when I saw you bounce off that car." Felice looked up at the policeman who was listening to her attentively. "My daughter-in-law pushed me out of the way, otherwise she could have jumped clear of the car." Felice's lip trembled, and the policeman patted her shoulder with a hamlike hand. "Sir, would you contact my husband and son and tell them where we're going?" Felice scribbled on the back of a personal card, then handed it to the officer.

Pan sat up in the ambulance, assuring Felice over and over that she was fine. "Have you checked my mother-in-law's blood pressure?" Pan whispered in an aside to the attendant while Felice conversed with the other one. He nodded and mouthed that though it was slightly up and her pulse had been a bit thready, she was fine.

At the hospital the doctor concurred that although Pan had a badly skinned arm and knee and a minor concussion, nothing was broken and she and Felice could be released.

Both women were still conversing with the doctor, Felice in a chair, Pan sitting on a gurney, when the double doors leading to the anteroom were flung open with such force that they banged backward against the wall.

The doctor, nurses, Felice and Pan stared openmouthed at the grim-faced pair who stormed into the examining room, the older man going at once to Felice's chair, dropping to his knees and scooping his wife into his arms, his breath sounding loud in the sudden silence.

Silver went to Pan, catching her up and cuddling her close to his body before turning to glare at the doctor. "Has she had every care? Is anything wrong? I want her to have the best."

The doctor's mouth opened and closed, irritation flashing across his face for a moment. "I assume that this is your wife and you are Mr. Galen."

"Yes." Silver's face was tight and angry.

"Both women are fine. They were shaken up by the incident and your wife was bruised and abraded because the car hit her . . ." The doctor watched the man in front of him turn ashen, the scars on his face standing out in livid rejection. "There is no lasting injury, Mr. Galen, I assure you of that."

"My wife is very delicate," Silver said through his teeth.

"Really? She doesn't seem the least infirm, sir, you can be reassured of that."

205

Pan put her hand to Silver's face, turning his gaze on her. "I'm fine, truly. He missed both of us."

"Not really," Felice interjected, rising from the chair with her husband still holding her. "The fool must have been drunk. He bore down on us as though he didn't see us. Pan saw him at the last minute and pushed me out of the way. If she hadn't taken the time to do that, the car would never have touched her. She saved me, Sterling." Felice raised her face and patted her husband's cheek when he kissed her gently.

"My child, you have been dear to me since that first day when we came to visit you and you were sliding under the bed covers with my son." Silver's father had tears in his eyes.

"Commodore," Pan said laughingly when she saw the doctor's eyes widen and the nurse stop straightening the instrument table to stare at them.

"Now," the Commodore continued gruffly, "you are more special than ever. I'm forever in your debt, child, for saving my Felice."

Pan would have gotten down from the table and gone to the Commodore, but her husband wouldn't release her. "Silver, we should go. I'm sure the doctor has other patients . . ."

"Are you sure you're all right?"

"Positive. Just a little headache that the doctor says is normal with concussion."

"You're going to bed when we get home."

It took all Felice's and Pan's persuasions to keep the two men from ordering wheelchairs to get them to the car. Once they were in the high-powered Rolls-Royce brougham, the Commodore picked up the phone in the back and dialed a number.

"Commodore, are you calling the mission?" Silver

handled the car and listened to his father's terse conversation.

"What is he doing?" Pan whispered to Silver, wanting to press her hand to his scarred face and wipe away the tension she saw there.

"Just checking something." Silver thought he would burst with anxiety as he listened to his father. It wouldn't matter what the "boyos" told the Commodore. Silver didn't have good feelings about the "accident," though he had no intention of telling either his mother or his wife about his suspicions until he could have the incident investigated.

"Ignoring me?" Pan said lightly, though her insides churned knowing something was bothering Silver. She had not lived with him long before she came to recognize that navy blue metal look to his eyes; the tight-lipped, iron-jawed attitude; the infinitesimal quivering of the scarred side of his face.

Silver's head whipped her way, his eyes roving over her and riveting on her bandaged arm and leg. "Never have I been so scared." He reached out an arm and brought her in to the curve of his shoulder. "Not even when I couldn't get my canopy off the car when it was on fire did I experience the raw fear I had when the police called and told us you were on your way to the hospital after being in an accident. I couldn't breathe until he reassured the Commodore and me that you were conscious and seemed unhurt."

"Silver, I'm sorry you had to go through that when there was nothing wrong."

"You call being struck by a car nothing." His teeth clicked together on the words. "If I ever get my hands on the bastard who struck you, I'll tear him apart."

"You know you wouldn't do that to a drunk."

207

"You saw him?"

"Ah, no, the windows were black glass and I couldn't see anyone in the car."

"Or even if there was more than one person?"

"Or even that."

When they reached the house the doors were flung open and Silver's sister flew down the steps to the car.

"Damn," Silver muttered, getting out from behind the wheel and going around to help his wife from the auto, noting that the Commodore was gripping his wife with unusual fervor. "What are you doing here?"

"Mother, you're all right. Hodgkins said that you both were fine." Sasha hugged her mother and Pan, not ceasing talking all the while. "Don't be crabby, Silver. It will give you ulcers. We're all here except Ladder and he might be flying here on the weekend. We thought you'd need us and you do, letting Mother and Pan be hit by a car. It wouldn't have happened if I'd been with them."

"Good Lord," Silver moaned into his wife's hair. "It will be a nuthouse. Damnit, they're going to a hotel."

"Don't be silly, we have loads of room," Pan told him, nipping at his chin.

"I want to be alone with you," Silver told her, a moist sheen to his eyes. "I could have lost you, Pan, and I'm having a damned hard time dealing with that."

CHAPTER EIGHT

For the rest of the days before the hearing, Silver didn't let Pan out of his sight for long. Even the Commodore commented on it, and he was never far from Felice's side.

"Can't be her shroud, boy, oughtta know that. I'll bet she feels smothered," the Commodore roared at the dinner table, where he sat at the head at Pan's insistence. "Don't you, Pan?"

"No, sir. Silver doesn't smother me." Pan smiled at her father-in-law.

"Loyal little thing, isn't she?" the Commodore said sotto voce to his son-in-law three places away from him.

Ben lifted his glass, smirking at his glowering brother-in-law before turning to smile at Pan. "To a loyal lady who is very special."

The family echoed the sentiment, raising their glasses. Silver rose and went around to her chair and leaned down to kiss her. "Very special indeed."

Pan felt a glow as the Galens' caring fell about her like a golden net. Feeling safe with Silver had become part of her life, but now she felt truly part of his loving family.

"And we won't give in to any type of coercion from your family either—"

"Sasha," Ben said warningly.

"What do you mean?" Pan asked Sasha but her gaze

slid to Silver's hard mien, noting, too, that Dex looked very uncomfortable.

"I'll talk to you later, darling."

"Talk to me now. Everyone else seems to know what you're referring to, Silver." Pan didn't mean to sound so tight-lipped, but fear crawled through her as she saw how the family looked at one another, then back at her.

"Never should have told any of them," the Commodore muttered.

"You're right about that, Father." Silver nodded grimly. Then he looked at his wife, seeing how chalky she'd become. "Darling, it's nothing big, truly. Your stepaunt and her boyfriend have filed for committal of you into Schilling Institute as ordered by the previous hearing. We have no intention of doing that. Wilson Carpenter along with Ward Battle and the battery of Galen lawyers tell us that they won't have a problem in getting such an order rescinded, and they are in the process of taking care of it even as we sit here."

"No one will touch you, child," the Commodore rumbled, his face creased with concern.

The world spun around Pan. Before she could formulate a response, Silver was at her side, kneeling next to her chair, his arm around her. "I'm all right," she told him breathily.

"Do you trust me?"

Pan nodded. "Even if you weren't here I wouldn't allow them to get away with that," she told him raggedly. "There is nothing wrong with my mental capacities and I won't let anyone stampede me again."

"Good for you, Trisha," Dex muttered.

"Except for marrying my brother, I would say you're as sane as anyone I know," Braden said.

"Considering whom you run with, baby brother, that would hardly be a compliment," Sasha retorted.

Pan laughed with the others, feeling the momentary tension drain away, but not the wariness. So, they were at it again. That was what had happened to her when her uncle had remarried. Right after the death of her parents, her uncle and Dexter had moved into her home. Slowly she had come out of her cocoon of pain, until his marriage to Maeve. After that the changes were subtle, but she had felt them. Even though everyone was kind to her, she began to feel awkward, unattractive and stupid. She hadn't liked her stepaunt, even though the other woman had never been mean to her, but she was made to feel increasingly uncomfortable in her own home.

When she had been accused of perhaps being involved in her uncle's death, her stepaunt had turned on her. It was then that Pan had run. But not this time! She wasn't the impressionable young creature who thought her family wouldn't harm her. She could understand her stepaunt's antipathy if she really did think she had hurt her husband, but Pan was innocent. Even if they never found the intruder, she would make them believe she could never have hurt the man who had been a surrogate father to her. Forewarned was forearmed! If they wanted a battle for Drexel they would get it.

"Don't worry, Pan. We'll fight them together. We have quite a bit of ammunition and we'll get more." Silver pulled her up from her chair and brought her next to him.

The conversation went on around Silver, whose mind was on other things. One of the detectives he'd hired had called to speak to him before dinner, but Silver had put him off until later. Now the urgency in the man's voice seemed to seep into his bloodstream, and nervousness itched him. When the family adjourned to the living room for coffee and liqueur, Silver excused himself and went into the library to make a call. He was about to dial a number when Hodgkins came into the room and told him that there was someone to see him.

"His name is Walzer, sir, and he says he's with the Stanwyck people."

Silver replaced the receiver and nodded that he would see the visitor. His body was as tense as a bow when the man was shown into the room. He didn't speak until Hodgkins left the room. "Walzer. What is it, man?" Silver's voice was rougher than he had intended, but foreboding had taken him over and he felt snared by it.

Walzer, a round man with a rather pudgy face and shining, alert brown eyes, lowered his girth into a chair on the other side of the large desk from Silver. "I think it could be important, sir. I was questioning people at the intersection where your wife and mother were hit by the car. Most of them didn't see anything unusual." Walzer took a deep breath. "But I questioned the man in the paper kiosk at the corner. He's been there for years and people know him and he's pretty observant. He said that the car had been coming up the street slowly, that it stopped when your mother and wife were crossing. He couldn't see the driver because of the black glass on the windows, and he noticed that because most cars don't have it.

"Pavia, that's the man who owns the kiosk, says that it looked like the car waited until the women were dead center and alone in the street before gunning it and going right for them. When I asked if the car weaved at all, as a drunk would do, he said it was like the car was aimed at the women."

Silver wasn't really surprised because he'd had a gut

212

feeling, but still, the affirmation made the fine dinner he'd just eaten rise in his throat. "So it was deliberate."

"I would say that we have to look at it that way, even if it isn't, sir."

Silver nodded. "I want people on the house and garage at all times. When I'm not with my wife, I want two people covering her and a person on every member of this household."

"It will be expensive, sir."

"Do it."

Walzer rumbled to his feet, staring at Silver, who was now standing as well. "I know the background, sir, and your wife's involvement. We will take every precaution."

"Right."

After the man left, Silver sat down in the leather swivel chair behind the desk, his eyes going around the room that he had come to enjoy. The oak paneling and floor-to-ceiling books defined a place meant for cogitation. Damnit, nothing was going to happen to Pan. Tomorrow was the hearing. From what Wilson Carpenter and the other lawyers had told him, it looked good for the court case. If only there weren't the bad feeling about the accident, things would be in order.

When the door opened and Pan stood in the doorway, he lifted his arms and she walked toward him and sat down in his lap. "Umm, lovely, let's go to bed."

Pan could feel his hardening body, but she also knew that her husband was trying to put her off. "Was that a detective who just left?"

"Uh-huh," Silver whispered into her hair, fully committed to lying to her in order to keep her calm for the next day.

Pan leaned back so that she could look into his face. "I

213

think you don't want me to worry, but that you are upset by the accident still."

"I'm going to get you some tea leaves so you can start working part-time telling fortunes." The smile left his face. "I am still concerned and I will be while we're in California, but the way things look, everything should be as smooth as silk."

"But you're still concerned."

"Yes. You might have bounced back from that accident, but my imagination keeps telegraphing me about what could have happened and it eats me up." Silver closed his eyes as her hands feathered over his face.

"Let's go to bed and I'll make you forget all that car nonsense."

Silver felt a dart of joy. He scooped her up in his arms, thrusting his body out of the chair. "Wonderful idea."

"You are a very strong man to be able to come out of a chair that way," Pan told him musingly, her arms tight around his neck.

"You make me strong, love. The thought of you taking me to bed makes me feel like Atlas."

Pan laughed, for a moment able to push aside the specters that beset her life. "Let's shower together. I feel a little sticky."

"God, woman, are you putting me off?" Silver groaned.

"Not at all. Who knows what could happen in the shower?"

Silver laughed out loud, allowing her to slide down his body. Then the two of them strolled out of the room, across the hall and up the stairs. He didn't stop in the bedroom but headed her straight through to the bathroom, where he began undressing her himself. "It's a good thing this is one of those giant old-fashioned bath-

214

rooms. By the way, did I tell you that I love your house. And we can come here as often as you want?"

"Yes you did, and I wish you would stop saying and doing such sweet things." Pan glared at him. "I don't want to love you so much."

"I know," Silver said soothingly. "But you didn't want to marry me, either, and see how easy it's been."

"It hasn't been easy," Pan said, getting into the large shower with him, her hands pushing her hair from her eyes. "I've fought you every step of the way, but you keep on coming."

"Inexorable me," Silver crooned. "God, you've got me excited as hell just by being here with me."

"I should hope so." Pan stretched her body against his, feeling the familiar sensuous wonder that Silver always engendered in her.

Silver smiled at her as she lifted her face to the spray. He wanted her so much. Each time they made love he wanted her more, and it awed and shook him to the core that she could do this to him time after time. There was nothing he wouldn't do to keep her.

"Hey, are you forgetting about me? I'm all ready." Pan laughed out loud when Silver looked astonished, but when he lifted her up along his body, the laughter faded in the magic of sensual power between them. When Pan felt him lower her so that he could enter her gently, she gasped with the wonder of it.

In slow, insistent rhythm they began to love each other until they were breathing in ragged bursts, their love murmurs trembling over each other.

When the explosion of love abated, Pan was gripping Silver, her nails digging into his shoulders. "Oh, I'm sorry, I did it again. I'm so primitive with you."

"Don't be sorry. I loved it. When I'm alone I like to

215

reach inside my shirt and feel those marks. It's very exciting, like having you always naked and in my arms."

Pan stood in front of him, limp in the aftermath of love, gazing up at him as he soaped her gently and then let the warm water sluice her body. "You're a terrible lecher." She started to giggle.

"My being a lecher causes such mirth?"

"No, it isn't that. I was just thinking that anyone else trying to shower might be getting cold water because we've been here so long."

Silver lazily lifted her clear of the cubicle and began to oil her wet body. He kissed her neck as she dried him, then, arms around each other, they ambled back into the bedroom.

It was late. Dex was tired; he felt trapped and afraid. He dialed the number and noticed that his hands were shaking, so much, in fact, that he had to dial twice to get it right.

On the third ring it was answered. "Hello."

"Maeve, it's Dexter. Are you going to be at the hearing tomorrow?"

"Of course."

"I think you should tell Alan to back off, Maeve, and please don't tell me that you don't know what I'm talking about, because I won't buy it. You and I both know that Pan is sound in mind and body and that any examination will prove that, so call off the witch hunt."

"Since when have you become such a supporter of your cousin? Don't you know that if she comes through this hearing without being indicted she will be back as head of Drexel's? I'll be out as CEO, but so will you, Dexter. And I doubt if Trisha will allow any of us to be officers of the firm once she takes over."

"Let the future take care of itself. I just know after spending time in my cousin's company that she is more than capable of handling—"

"You miserable wimp! So you want to cave in, do you? Well, you listen to me, Dexter—no one is taking the Drexel Holding Company away from me and I will fight to keep it. So will Alan."

Dexter frowned. "The law might have something to say about ownership, Maeve."

"The company belongs to the people who have worked for it, expanded it and brought it to the level of excellence it now enjoys."

"Are you implying that it wasn't an excellent company when you took it over? Because if you are, the figures will refute you. Despite my differences with my father—"

"And there were many."

"I still admired the way he handled the company. He was respected countrywide—no, worldwide—for his business acumen."

"You don't have to describe your father to me, Dexter. He was my husband. Remember? Do you also recall that he was nothing until he took over Drexel's from Trisha's father?" Maeve paused. "I was the one who gave him the push, the impetus to run Drexel's the way he did, and—"

"That's baloney and you know it. My father promised himself that he would make Drexel's the best company of its kind in the world so that Trisha would have something to be proud of when she inherited."

"And how you hated that, stepson," Maeve whispered.

"I thought that I deserved some recognition, yes," Dexter shot back, stung.

"Recognition? For what? For being the playboy of the month by running up debts in all the nightclubs in town?"

"I changed my ways." Dexter's voice had risen. "Don't take shots at me, Maeve."

"No? Well, then, I'm sure you wouldn't mind revealing the problems you had with your father. I'd also like you to dwell on the fact that if Trisha is exonerated and there are still some unanswered questions, we will become the cynosure of all eyes, judicially speaking . . . if you get my meaning, Dexter." For a long moment Maeve wasn't sure if they had been cut off. "Dexter?"

"I understand you."

"Good. Now, no one is asking you to go against your cousin if that's your choice, but just remember that when the dust settles I will be running Drexel's, and I like people around me who are loyal."

"Fine, but I'd like you to remember that I'm a stockholder with more shares than you, so don't try to ice me out, Maeve. I won't allow it."

"And you just remember that when Trisha is convicted, I will be in control of her shares, Dexter."

"Look, Maeve, I won't be—"

"Let's just table this, shall we? Things will stand as they are as long as neither party upsets the other."

"What if they decide to question us more closely?"

"Dexter, just relax. And I think we've talked long enough on the phone. Who knows who could be listening in on an extension?"

"Don't be melodramatic, Maeve."

"Good-bye, Dexter. I'll see you at the hearing."

"Good-bye."

Dexter held the phone in his hands, staring at the instrument, listening to the buzz of the broken connection. His mind felt like cotton wadding. Thoughts bounced off his head, but nothing penetrated the thickness there.

There had to be some way he could get out of this mess. He felt caught in a particularly tight and painful web.

Maeve's words had brought back vivid memories of his father and those long, wrangling months they'd had before he died. Pain and regret cut at him.

Dex finally replaced the receiver in the cradle, his hands clasped and hanging loosely between his knees as he sat there. The bitter wish that he should have talked to his father more ballooned in his head again, as it often did. It might have changed things. If only he hadn't borrowed from Drexel's treasury to pay some gambling debts he had; if only he hadn't fought with his father about it; if only he could remember the events of that evening more clearly . . .

He undressed and readied himself for bed, knowing that the bad dreams that had dogged him since his father's death would come again to haunt him.

"You look tired." Alan came up behind Maeve and slipped his arms around her waist.

"Not that tired." Maeve didn't like to be reminded that she was tired, and older than Alan.

"Tomorrow will be over soon and we'll have won."

"I hope you're right." She turned in his arms, letting her fingers trace the strong planes of his face. Alan had a beautifully masculine look and he knew it and he did everything he could to promulgate it. "It would be wonderful to think that we can get back to work and back to our house."

"I can't wait." Alan hid his face in her hair, his hands going over her in sensuous exploration.

"Don't. We should get to the office. I want to keep an eye on that watchdog crew that Galen sent into Drexel's." Maeve's face tightened, and she seemed to forget that Alan was caressing her. "Who would ever have thought our little Trisha would snag a catch like Silver Galen? I still can't believe it. What does he see in her?"

"You sound jealous."

"Ridiculous." Maeve tried to pull back from him, attempting to mask the sourness of spirit she was experiencing. "Let's get out of here. This hotel room depresses me."

"What? This is a very spacious five-room apartment, for God's sake."

Maeve shrugged and tried to wriggle free. "I don't like living like this."

"No. We have time, Maeve."

Maeve saw the look in his eyes. "Well, maybe a quickie."

The day dawned bright and clear in San Francisco, but when Pan looked out the window down toward the bay, she didn't see the sunshine or the puffs of clouds scudding across the blue. Images of her first court hearing mushroomed in her mind, and she saw the bewildered, almost beaten figure she had been then, and she cringed at the mental picture. It had been months after that, when she'd been on the run for some time, that she'd begun to be herself again, to assert her personal strength, to fight back, to be a person. The very destructive force that had made her lose her personal courage to a great degree and had caused her self-esteem to be badly dented were the basic reasons she hadn't returned to San Francisco. It had taken Silver and his grit to give her the courage to face the people who had destroyed her self-confidence and made her so confused.

But now, at this moment, a snake of terror wound its way through her and she wanted to run. Pressing her teeth so hard into her lip that she tasted blood brought her back to the present. She had to clear her name. When all the unpleasantness was over, she would establish a scholarship in her uncle's name and she and Dexter would oversee it.

"Hey, what's going on, wife? How can you be dressed before me? Trying to ruin my image?" Silver saw the slight relaxing of the tension in her face, but he noted that her hands were still tightly clenched. His first impulse was to sweep her up into his arms and carry her out of the house, away from San Francisco, out of the country, off the earth to the moon, where he could keep her safe and to himself. Nothing was going to hurt her again. The love he felt for her was so overpowering. He both loved and hated it, feeling strong and enervated at the same time. That was the only barrier between them. Neither of them could quite give way completely to their feelings. Damn! It was like readying to jump into a deep, dark well with no bottom. Love was the damnedest thing!

"Why are you scowling, Silver?" As her glance went over his scarred face, she marveled at how few times she really saw the mar on his strong features. "That's your little-boy look."

"Oh, it is, is it?" Silver reached out, noticing how she laughed and tried to avoid him as he caught her close to him.

Pan braced herself against what she thought would be his punishing mouth. To her surprise, his lips feathered over her face, touching her eyebrows, her eyes, nose, ears, then finally her lips, the gentle pressure increasing until Pan heard the groan in her own throat turn to a moan of desire. Her arms coiled around his waist, tightening. She pressed herself against him, slanting her body so it fit to

221

his in a familiar, sensuous way that had her blood pounding through her veins. "Silver."

"My sweet one," he said breathily without lifting his mouth. "We have to leave here—now. Goddamnit, I'm taking you to bed the minute this charade is over and keeping you there, and I don't care who is in the house with us."

"Silver," she sobbed into his neck, her arms tightening around him. Not once had he doubted that there would be a happy solution to the problem. He didn't see any scenario in which Alan Winston and Maeve Drexel would be coming back to the house. Pan wished that she could be as positive, but she couldn't stop recalling the shock she'd felt years ago when she'd first realized that the judge was going to have her confined for psychiatric testing. The second body blow had been discovering that her stepaunt Maeve had become her guardian and would have the say on whether she would remain confined or be free.

"Be strong, darling. Nothing is going to happen to you. At the very worst I'll kidnap you and take you to Tahiti."

Pan laughed shakily as she pushed away from him. "If that's the worst, I'll take it."

Silver kissed her nose, smiling at her, but the moment she passed him his face hardened, his eyes glinting with purpose.

Dexter was waiting in the downstairs hall when the two of them descended from their wing of the house. Maeve might believe that all would go her way today, but the look in Silver Galen's eyes told Dexter that he could and would hold back a flood with his bare hands to protect his woman.

"Drexel, are you ready? You haven't seen my parents and the rest of my family, have you?"

"Yes, they left a few minutes ago. They said Pan might be more comfortable if there was just the three of us in your car."

Silver nodded and opened the front door for his wife, ushering her out in front of him.

The flash of cameras and a portable television unit with its lights blazing hit Pan full force, making her stumble back against Silver, who caught her and swept her behind him.

"What the hell is going on?" His clipped, angry tones made the cameras aim his way.

"Mr. Galen, isn't it true that your wife was involved in a mysterious death some time ago and—"

"Unless you want to eat that camera, get it out of our faces. We have no comment. None."

Pan could feel Silver's anger percolating into the atmosphere as he shepherded her to the car.

Silver gunned the engine and sped out of there so fast that no one would be able to follow them. "I have pretty good instincts about where we're going, Dexter, but if you see me going wrong, shout, because we're moving on this one." Silver spoke through his teeth.

"Turn right at the next corner, then go straight for four lights," Dexter said excitedly, shooting glances over his shoulder as he sat forward in the small back section of the sports car. "My God, I've never gone this fast in the city."

"Well, I don't usually do it, either, on city streets and it has been quite a while since I've opened up on a road, but I think we'll be able to put some space between us and them."

Pan gripped the side bar just above her head, her eyes glued on the landscape that flew past their windows. She felt full confidence in Silver. "I've never driven this fast either. It's crazy, but exhilarating."

Silver chuckled low in his throat. "When we're in Tahiti, my love, we'll get a dune buggy and race along the beach."

"Only if I'm driving."

Silver laughed out loud, her dart of humor doing more for him than anything could. She was fighting back!

In front of the courthouse were several groups of people. In the center of one of them the Commodore was arguing with a cameraman, shaking his finger in the man's face. When Silver roared up the plaza, his father turned goggled-eyed to watch his son skid into a turn, do a three-sixty and come to rest next to the curb.

"Silver, damn you, are you trying to kill her? Get back, all of you." The Commodore leaned down and opened Pan's door. "He was driving like the Hounds of Hades were after him. Were you frightened, child?"

"Not at all. It was wonderful. I'm going to talk him into taking me around a track sometime."

The Commodore laughed with her before turning to scowl at the cameramen who were in a half moon around them. "Get out of here. Boyos, get over here and scatter this vermin."

Pan was startled when a group of rather casually dressed persons of all ages charged across the area in a flying wedge, scattering cameramen in every direction. Soon there was a great deal of yelling and pushing. Pan felt herself lifted with Silver's strong arm around her waist and the Commodore on the other side of her. Then they were charging up the steps, into the cavernous building, their footsteps echoing on the parquet tile floor.

Once in the courtroom, the silence was immediate and intimidating. Pan almost preferred the push and noise that they'd faced outside to the sudden facing of reality when the bailiff asked all to rise, saying that the court was now in session, the Honorable Harry A. Needham presiding.

Judge Needham banged his gavel, pushed up the voluminous sleeves of his black robe and squinted at the courtroom through his half-glasses. "Ladies and gentlemen, as you know, this is a preliminary hearing to see if there is culpability of a person or persons in the death of one Henry Drexel." He looked down at the papers in front of him, shuffling them. Then he looked up again. "There is also the matter of Patricia Ann Drexel defying a court order to—"

"Your Honor, I beg the court's indulgence. I am Wilson Carpenter, counsel for the Drexel Holding Company, and in this capacity the lawyer for Mrs. Sterling Galen, formerly Miss Patricia Ann Drexel, and these are my consulting colleagues on this, Your Honor—"

"Yes, yes, I have the names on my list, Mr. Carpenter. Very impressive, but there's no need to go through the ten names."

"Thank you, Your Honor. I just wanted to stipulate that my client would never have considered running had she not been in a state of shock over her uncle's death and the implication that she might have been in some way involved. My client is not now nor never was mentally ill, Your Honor. She has had great stress, of course, but she is perfectly able to make decisions that could affect her life and the company that belongs to her."

"I object." Lawrence Slate, the lawyer who was representing Maeve and Alan, leapt to his feet.

Silver sat back in misleading indolence, taking in all that was said, sometimes scrawling a note and sending it over to one of the battery of lawyers that sat alongside his

225

wife. He rarely took his eyes from her, though he paid close attention to every nuance and dialogue. In dark amusement he watched his father scratch something on his note pad and pass it to another of the lawyers who were sitting in on the case. More than once Ben DeWitt, his brother-in-law, did the same thing.

Silver was going to clear her name and there was no doubt in his mind that he could do it, but he also was fully committed to breaking the law, if need be, by snatching up Pan and running from the courtroom if it looked like the judgment could go against her. No way would she be stampeded. He knew she was innocent. His glance drifted across the aisle to where Pan's stepaunt and her boyfriend sat. Silver caught the glances that they shot toward Dexter, and he pondered the meaning of that. Were they holding something over Dexter Drexel's head?

According to the teams of accountants Silver had sent into the company, Drexel's looked in pretty good shape, but there had been one or two gray areas that warranted closer scrutiny. Appleton, the chief accountant, had told him that it looked like there could have been some modest skimming, but since the company was in such good shape, further digging was probably unnecessary. Silver had told him to keep digging.

Startled out of his reverie when Pan rose to her feet and walked toward the witness box, Silver had a moment of panic. Who the hell had called her up there? His restless anger communicated itself to the lawyers in front of him and one turned around and smiled, nodding his head in reassurance. It didn't lessen Silver's anger one iota, but he sat back, his eyes glued to his wife. His wife! The thought of Pan and what she meant to him made his chest expand painfully. He was going to kill the first per-

226

son who upset her. Then he focused on her fully, realizing that she had begun to speak.

". . . and I had been out with a friend. It wasn't late and I saw the light under Uncle Henry's study door, so I knocked and walked in, as I usually did." Pan paused and licked her lips, feeling the pain that she'd experienced at that time. "Then—I—at first I was sure he was napping at his desk, though he'd never done that, to my knowledge. But he was a hard worker and put many long hours into the business, so it didn't seem too unlikely to see him with his head down on his arms on the desk. It was only as I got close to him that I noticed the blood on his face . . ."

"Go on, Pan," Wilson Carpenter urged.

"That's all. Something hit me from behind, and when I came to, I was on the couch and there were a great many people in the room."

"Thank you."

The other lawyer jumped to his feet. "Isn't it true, Miss Drexel—pardon me, I mean Mrs. Galen—that a doctor testified at the first hearing that the blow to your head could have come from falling rather than being hit?"

"Yes, but—"

"And isn't it true that there was no other person in the room but yourself and that when you realized what you'd done, you fainted in horror because you'd killed your uncle?"

"No!" Pan shouted.

"Your Honor, I object." Wilson Carpenter was on his feet, glaring at the other lawyer, then at the judge. "My client consented to this hearing and she is being cooperative, but she is not on trial and I resent my colleague's attempts to turn this into a witch-hunt."

"Objection sustained. Counselor, you will confine your questioning to the issues at hand and you will refrain from drawing any more conclusions. This is a courtroom, not a three-ring circus, and if I see that anyone is trying to grandstand I will find him in contempt."

"I have no more questions, Your Honor." Mr. Slate smiled at the judge.

When Pan returned to her seat and looked over her shoulder at her husband, he was sitting forward, his eyes on Slate. Clearly Silver was in the grip of a terrible fury!

At day's end the judge reminded the lawyers that he expected all the pertinent information to be in front of him by tomorrow. At the end of the week he would make a judgment whether there would be an indictment.

Dinner that evening was a subdued affair. Conversation was desultory. Persons glanced at one another, then away again without speaking. After dinner they all adjourned to the spacious living room.

When Dexter approached her, Pan smiled at him. "Sit down."

Dexter sat next to her, looking at the others as they chatted about many things. Ben, Silver and the Commodore sat in a corner with their heads together. Sasha talked to her mother. Braden was sitting at the piano, picking out tunes. "It was awful for you today, wasn't it, Pan?"

"It brought it all back, that's for sure."

Dexter continued to look down at his hands hanging loosely between his knees. "I never thought you killed my father."

"I know that, Dex."

"But you didn't know I was drunk that night, did you?"

228

Startled, Pan stared at him, shaking her head. "I didn't even know you were around until the next day."

"I wasn't, not really. I slept off my drunk in Alan's apartment over the garage. Do you remember he used to stay there sometimes when he worked for my father?"

Pan pressed her hand against her forehead for a minute before nodding her head slowly. "Yes. Now I do recall. I forgot that he used to stay there if there was something crucial at Drexel's so that he would be close at hand if Uncle needed him."

"Not that my father thought he was that clever. He didn't," Dex blurted.

Pan smiled. "Uncle Henry was such a perfectionist, and he didn't suffer fools gladly."

"God, no. He once almost fired the entire fifth floor when he discovered they were having twenty-minute coffee breaks."

Pan smiled, shaking her head. "I never heard that one. I'll bet it's one of those legends all heads of companies have about themselves."

"No, this was true. He really did almost can everyone." Dexter squinted at her. "You never did see the hard side of him, Trisha. He loved you so much he never wanted you to think anything but good of him."

"He loved you, too, Dex."

Dex shrugged. "We should have talked more." Dex's face tightened. "It's too late for that now."

"I think he knew. He used to talk about you all the time to me—about how you had the right stuff to work alongside me on the paper."

Dex eyed Pan wryly. "Did he? That's good to hear. I like the work at Drexel's and wouldn't like to think I was there just because I'm family."

Pan's smile twisted. "No way. Uncle Henry was a

hard-headed businessman who believed in getting the best for Drexel's, and he mentioned more than once that you were capable of handling an executive position." Pan's smile faded when she saw the sheen of angry tears in her cousin's eyes. "Dex? What is it?" Pan put out her hand, but he pulled back.

"No! Don't touch me. I'm fine," Dex told her, gazing right and then left. He saw that Braden had left the piano and joined his father, brother and brother-in-law. "Hey, why don't you play and we'll sing, Trisha. We used to be pretty good. C'mon."

Pan knew he was fobbing her off but she didn't push him. She sensed he was on the razor edge of his emotions.

When Pan sat down at the piano, memories were awash in her mind and she felt as though time had shot her backward. Her hands trembled over the keys for a moment; then she began to play an ancient Scottish ballad much loved by her uncle. "Ye banks and braes of Bonnie Doon," Pan sang, Dex's strong tenor joining her mezzo-soprano tones in close harmony.

The others in the room turned one by one to listen, one after the other moving closer to the piano.

Silver watched his wife, going to her side to stare from her nimble fingers to her face, his heart thudding against his ribs when he saw how the music seemed to relax her and take her away. But when he looked at Dexter he was taken aback. There were tears in the other man's eyes.

Song followed song as the Galens joined in the singing, the pleasant amalgam of voices filling the room.

That night when Pan and Silver went to their room, Silver went into the shower at once, locking the door behind him. Pan stared at the closed door, feeling irritated. It was awful being shut away from Silver! After all,

230

he was her husband! Weren't husbands supposed to invite wives into the shower? She grimaced at her own foolishness, trying to banish the lost feeling that invaded her. In minutes he was out of the bathroom, and she swept past him without a word.

"Hey, Pan . . . what—?" Silver jerked back when the door slammed in his face. Frowning at the door, he began rubbing his damp head, then he tossed the wet towel in the corner before donning his maroon silk pajama bottoms. He never wore anything to bed, but part of him was still modest with Pan. He didn't want her to have any fears of him.

"Silver." Pan opened the door and just stared at him for a moment, taking note of the determined gleam in his eye as he stood waiting, arms akimbo.

"Yes, Silver, your husband. Now, tell me why you're angry with me."

Pan took a deep breath, fully committed to dissembling with him. "I don't like it when you march into the shower and don't even ask if I'd like to be in there with you," she blurted. She watched in fascination as his dark eyebrows arched. The harsh line of his mouth softened in sensuous satisfaction, and the hard line of his jaw quivered in sexy amusement.

"Darling, pardon me. The next time I'll know better. It was stupid." He grimaced. "To tell the truth, I was a little scorched that you played and sang with your cousin this evening and you'd never done that with me. Damned stupid."

"No, not stupid, but we are silly with each other sometimes," Pan said in amused irritation. "Everyone needs some privacy. I know that."

"Of course." He stepped closer until millimeters separated them but they were not quite touching. "But I do

231

love it when your naked, wet body rubs against mine."
He touched her cheek with one finger. "Blushing? Because of husbandly devotion?"

"You are the most explicit person I know," Pan told him tartly.

Silver chuckled softly. "I was afraid the events of the day might have tired you too much. That was the major reason I didn't carry you right to the bed the minute we entered the room."

"I'm not tired."

"Neither am I." Silver closed the tiny space between them, his hands still at his sides as he began to undulate against her. "As you may have guessed."

"Could be." Pan sighed, letting her body lean toward him, loving the feel of that hard form taking the weight of hers easily.

Silver bent down until his lips were feathering her ear. "I want to love you, Pan. What do you want?"

"The same, I think."

"You think?"

"Well, your ego is large enough. I don't want your head to swell so much that we can't get it through the door." Pan placed her head on his chest, smiling when she felt the vibration of his heavy heartbeat.

"No chance of that while you're around to keep me on keel, love." He bent down suddenly, one arm holding her under her buttocks, and lifted her straight up his body. When they were nose to nose, he grinned at her. "Have I ever told you that I think you're very sexy?"

"A time or two."

"You are." His lips touched hers and clung. When he felt her tongue intrude into his mouth, his blood boiled through his veins. "Witch," he breathed.

Pan's arms crept around his neck. "Yes."

232

"Bed?"

"Yes."

Silver laughed out loud. Not releasing her but turning and keeping her just as she was in his arms, he strode across the room. Falling down on the bed, he took her weight on top of him so that she was cushioned. "Umm, wonderful. I like you on top of me." With a quick tug he pulled the damp towel from her body. "This is better."

"Isn't it?"

His eyes went over her in passionate assessment. "Have I told you how much I love your pink nipples, darling?"

"About a thousand times, but feel free to express yourself." Happily Pan blotted everything from her mind but Silver.

Like children they began to love wrestle, each trying to inflame and please the other more.

"My love." Silver buried his face between her breasts, his blood pounding through his veins, his mouth loving every inch of skin there before moving upward to minister to her neck, ears and hair. Her face was not forgotten as those warm, searching lips adored her eyes, nose and mouth.

When their lips came together, Pan dug her nails into his shoulder, holding him to her, her fingers probing the smooth muscles, eager to know every inch of him as she felt him shudder against her.

"God, I love it when you do that to me," Silver said huskily against her. "You drive me crazy, wife."

It awed and excited Pan immeasurably when he told her that. No one had ever been as open with her as Silver. Not another person had ever expressed love to her in such a way. If there were still small barriers between them, they didn't manifest themselves in their lovemaking.

All at once the many fears intruded in her passion. Had she killed her uncle? She really didn't know, nor had she ever known. Protesting her innocence had been automatic because she was unable to conceive of killing the man who had been both father and mentor to her . . . but she couldn't remember anything after she'd entered his study that evening. Had her uncle been asleep then? Could she have bludgeoned him while he slept, as had been intimated? She really didn't know, but the fear that such a thing could have happened had driven her away once, and she felt like running again.

"Hey, when did you get away from me? I must be losing my touch." He laughed lightly, but his insides churned in frustration at her sudden withdrawal. Though it irked and annoyed him a great deal, he'd not asked Pan why she seemed to travel away from him at odd times. More than once it had happened while they were making love, and he'd gritted his teeth and forced her attention back to him. The restraint surprised him, because it was more in character for him to demand to know what she was thinking and why she had been able to turn off her feelings that way. But something held him back from saying anything. He especially didn't want any candid references from her about Sydney's sexual performance, and though he wanted to know all about her life, he was loath to have her discuss the man she'd lived with before she met him.

"Oh, I don't think you're losing your touch, husband." Pan's arms tightened on his neck. "You make me melt."

Silver laughed thickly, her words acting like a sexual spur. "And you've shot me down in flames, lady mine."

"Isn't that what spouses are supposed to do?" Pan asked in giddy joy.

"Yes, it is." Silver put his fears behind him and concentrated on bringing her to the brink of fulfillment, his own body shuddering with joy when her caresses intensified. He felt his control disintegrate as her small hands took hold of him and caused a sexual explosion that shook him apart. He knew with abject certainty that Pan held him in thrall for all time. The acceptance of that made him turn her toward him, though both were still panting slightly from their wondrous exertions. "Tell me, my sweet, what were you thinking of when you had that dreamy, faraway look on your face before?"

"You, of course."

And he knew she lied. Angry trepidation rose like a flood in him.

CHAPTER NINE

Pan noticed her husband's restraint at the breakfast table the next morning, though he responded readily to her whenever she spoke to him and he was pleasant and relaxed to his family. But she knew better. Whatever it was that was bottled up inside him, he was seething about it.

Hodgkins came into the morning room with more coffee and went to Silver's side and whispered to him.

Silver rose to his feet. "Excuse me. Ladder is calling from New York. Crisis, I suppose." He smiled at Pan but didn't round the table to kiss her as was his custom when he left the room. He saw the flash of uncertainty and hurt in her eyes, but he didn't go to her.

"Minicrisis, more like," the Commodore grumbled, putting a bit of strawberry preserves on a triangle of toast and handing it to his wife. "He just wants to know what's going on," he announced to the table, slathering more jam on a full slice of toast and biting into it with a sigh of satisfaction. Then he looked at his daughter-in-law. "He's mighty fond of you, like the rest of us."

"Thank you, sir." Pan blinked back tears at his words, feeling morose that her husband was being cool with her after the night of lovemaking that they had just shared. Men! Damn them!

"Well, my dear, our strategy today is to go for the

throat." The Commodore wiped his hands on the linen napkin and glared at his daughter and son-in-law, who chuckled, then changed the sounds to coughs. "And so I told our lawyers. I don't want you in court beyond today, and they had better know I mean business."

"Sterling, you mustn't interfere with Pan's counselors," Felice pointed out gently, winking at Pan and noting the wan smile in return. Something was out of whack with her son and his bride. Oh well, they were bound to sort things out, they loved each other so much.

Pan felt rather disoriented and removed from the court proceedings when they began later in the morning. She was aware only of Silver seated directly behind her. Once or twice when the other lawyer was hammering away at her, pointing his finger at her as she sat next to Wilson Carpenter and the other lawyers hired by Galen's, she'd felt the slight pressure of his fingers on her shoulder, reassuring her.

Finally the testimony was done and the judge adjourned the courtroom. "This court will reconvene on Thursday. At that time I will give a ruling on whether there is sufficient evidence to warrant an indictment."

Pan stood silently with the others but she wanted to scream at the judge that she was tired of waiting, that she had been hanging by her thumbs for too long, that she couldn't have harmed a man whom she'd loved so much.

"Pan? Wait a minute. There is something we must discuss with the lawyers." Silver turned her to face him and saw the blind pain in her gaze. He pulled her into his embrace. "It's all right. I'll take you home, then I'll come back and talk to the lawyers. There's no need for you to stay." Silver looked over his shoulder and snapped something at one of the lawyers, who nodded and smiled sympathetically at Pan.

"I'm being stupid, I know." Pan couldn't seem to control her footing. Even with Silver's arm around her waist, she kept stumbling. She was blind to the world around her. Panic that had no basis seemed to rise in her throat and choke her. Running seemed the only alternative.

"Silver. Wait." One of the lawyers by the name of Newsome came down the steps after them. "Could we get you to come back here to Wilson Carpenter's office? There are things we should discuss. Ideally your wife should—"

"No!" Silver's face contorted with anger. "I'm taking her home. After I have her settled I'll come back, but she won't be with me. She needs rest." Silver had not stopped moving toward his car, and though media people were trying to speak to them, their private detectives managed to keep most of them at bay.

"Okay, okay." Newsome put both hands up in front of him, palms outward. "We'll wait for you." Newsome turned and fought his way through the phalanx of reporters, his "no comment" ringing in the air after each question.

Once they were in the car, Silver wasted no time in pulling away and flooring the accelerator. He hit the steering wheel with the flat of his hand and muttered a curse.

Pan turned her head without lifting it from the cushioned rest of the seat back. "What's wrong?"

"I just remembered that my mother and sister are going to visit an old aunt who lives near Carmel, so you'll be in the house alone. I won't go back. I'll call Wilson and tell him I'm not coming."

"Don't be silly. Dex will be home, not to mention

Hodgkins and Maria. I won't need anything anyway. I'm just going to climb between the sheets and take a nap."

Silver shot her a quick look. "Don't arouse me."

"Silver." Pan chuckled.

"I'm serious. Thinking of you between silk sheets makes my body temp shoot through the roof."

"I can't believe you ordered silk sheets for our bed here."

"How can you say that? You know how wonderful you look on the ones we have at the apartment in New York. Why would I deny myself the pleasure of looking at you on them here?"

"Crazy man." Pan sighed, feeling measurably calmer as they gibed at one another in a familiar humorous way. Pan was well aware that Silver was trying to distract her. She sank lower in her seat, her head pressed back against the soft leather, her eyes on her husband. "Aren't you even curious to try satin sheets?" she chided him, chuckling.

"How unobservant of you, wife! Didn't you look in our linen closet? There are satin sheets in a gorgeous shade of violet to match your eyes. Just wait until we slide around on those. God, I've got to get that picture out of my mind. It wouldn't be to my credit if I went late to a meeting with your lawyers."

Silver could have bitten off the end of his tongue when he saw her eyes cloud over again. "Listen to me, my stout-hearted bride: I don't like it when you have a defeatist attitude. I won't leave you at all unless you promise me that you'll think positively. Wilson Carpenter was very encouraged today." Silver took hold of her hand. "We're winning, love. I'm not a lawyer but I felt the vibrations there today. All the raving rhetoric from the other side of the aisle isn't going to wash. There are too many experts advising Wilson, and we're going to win because there is no real concrete case against you."

Pan nodded, feeling the familiar fighting response deep inside her. This certainly was not the worst time in her life. She had Silver with her now. Last time she had been alone, and running had been her only option. Not so now! Pan Drexel Galen wasn't running or hiding! She was going to fight.

"Good. I felt your hand squeeze mine, love. You're going to be the strong woman you've always been. I can feel it."

"Yes, I am, but a great deal of my courage comes from you, Silver, darling."

The car veered when his head shot her way, his mouth slightly ajar, his eyes wide.

"Whoops, it's a good thing we're not too far from the house." Pan laughed at him, moving closer to him as he tugged gently on her hand.

"I can't help myself when you call me darling," he told her hoarsely.

"I'm sorry." She chuckled.

"No you're not, brat, but tonight when we get into bed, you had better be rested."

"I will be." Deliberately she loosened her hand from his grip and scored his palm with one fingernail. "I hope you'll be ready."

"Damnit, Pan, when did you become Circe?"

"The moment you found me in the men's room, I think."

Silver threw his head back and laughed and parked the car with a flourish in front of the five-story house on the San Francisco street.

"I see you've remembered to cramp your wheels to the

240

curb," Pan told him when he came around to help her from the car.

"I learn fast." Silver bent and kissed her nose as she stood beside him on the sidewalk.

"No need for you to see me into the house. You'd better hurry back or you'll be late for the meeting."

Silver shot out his wrist and frowned at his watch. "I have time to see you to our bedroom. I want to make sure you're safe."

Pan grinned at his mulish look when she stopped him at the front door. "No. I'll be fine; there should be lots of people inside. Now get back there and meet with my lawyers." She leaned up and kissed his mouth. "I need you to fight for me."

He hesitated for a second, then nodded. "I will. You can bet on that, love. Promise me you'll go right to bed."

"Promise."

Silver wrapped her in his arms and began kissing her over and over again.

"Stop now," Pan told him breathlessly.

"I have to, or I'll be following you to bed." Silver sighed and released her, pushing her through the door, then running back down the steps to the wrought iron gate. There he paused and looked back and saw her waving at him through the beveled glass of the front door. He threw her a kiss and got into the car and fired it up. He paused before he pulled away, caught by a whirlpool of emotions that told him to go back into the house, sweep her up in his arms and take her to the mountains, or the desert, or out on the ocean where he could be alone with her. Damnit, he was a complete fool about his wife!

Pan walked from the small outer foyer into the main part of the house. Hodgkins hurried from the back of the house, smiling at her. "I'm sorry, Miss Trisha. I wasn't sure anyone was at the door. Earlier I thought I heard someone come in, but when I came out here no one was waiting. It makes me question my hearing, Miss Trisha."

"There was no need for you to stir yourself, Hodgkins, when I have a key."

Hodgkins lips tightened, as though he didn't quite approve of what she said, but then he smiled at her. "Could I get Maria to fix you something light, miss?"

"No, I think I'm just going to lie down. Is Dexter here?"

"He might have gone out again, miss." Hodgkins frowned. "He seemed to be preoccupied when he came down from his room."

"I'm sure that Mr. Dexter is a very busy man."

"Yes, but I think it's good for all of us that you've come back, miss." He smiled at Pan. "Perhaps I could get you something to drink, Miss Trisha."

"Thank you, no, Hodgkins." Pan felt a sudden weariness as she made her way up to the suite she shared with Silver. She was grateful that she didn't have to face her sister-in-law and Silver's mother. As fond as she was of the two of them, what she needed at the moment was quiet and rest.

Stripping down to her bra and panties, she then climbed between the sheets. Myriad visions of the courtroom and the happenings of the last several days danced behind her eyes as she dozed off.

Pan struggled up from sleep feeling an indescribable panic. She was smothering, unable to breathe. All at once she felt a stinging pain in her arm. Even as she fought to open her eyes to find the enemy, she dropped down a drug-induced well, trying to call out but finding her mouth paralyzed.

Dexter paced his room, his brain in turmoil. Why hadn't Silver asked him to stay with the others and confer with the lawyers? Was there something he suspected? Where the hell did he get off, suspecting him of anything?

Dexter sat on his bed, leaning forward with his head in his hands. His world was spinning off its axis. Nothing was going right. No matter what he tried he couldn't seem to bring it all together. Damn, why had things exploded in his face? He had every right to be in this house and in Drexel's.

He rose and went to the window. When he looked down and saw the old limousine that had belonged to his uncle but was seldom used by his father beginning to pull away from the front of the house, he stared, puzzled. "Who the hell is driving that old bus?"

After a minute he turned away with a restless and clammy feeling, all at sea, hoping a shower would get him into a better frame of mind.

Later, dressed in a sports shirt and summer slacks, he ambled downstairs to the kitchen, hungry as usual. The cook was happy to provide him with fruit and a sandwich, and he was working his way through this fare when Hodgkins walked into the kitchen, yawning. He had obviously been napping, as he sometimes did on quiet afternoons.

Dexter swallowed a bite of apple and stared at the older man. "I thought I just saw you drive away in the old limo, Hodgkins."

Hodgkins blinked at Dexter. "What? Oh no, sir, you must have made a mistake. The auto is still in the alley garage. I worked on it this morning." Hodgkins referred to the huge three-car two-story garage that was at the foot of the property and opened onto an alley in the back.

It was rarely used by the family anymore, since the one car the family used was kept in the garage under the house.

"Sorry, Hodgkins, I don't mean to jump at you."

Hodgkins smiled at the man he'd known since boyhood.

Still restless, Dexter returned to his own room and changed into sweats and running shoes, hoping to file down the sharp edge to his nerves by exercising. He wandered outside, ready to begin the jogging he hoped would clear his head and bring his life into focus a bit more. Maybe when he could clarify his own goals, he could then talk to his cousin Trisha and they could come to some sort of agreement about how Drexel's should be run in the future. More and more he had begun to believe that the best road open to him was to be up front with Trisha, to let her know that he might have been the person who struck his father because he had been drunk that night and had little memory of the incident. More than once he and his father had had flaming arguments.

He stopped right in the middle of the thoroughfare he was crossing. No! Damnit, he couldn't have struck his father, drunk or sober. It had never entered his mind to do that. It was Alan Winston and Maeve who said he could have done it. And they were wrong!

The angry blaring of horns brought him sheepishly out of his reverie. He waved at the autos in apology, then continued on his way, running the events of that painful evening around his brain.

Working up a lather didn't seem to dissipate the ghosts that haunted him, so he cut his run in half by taking a shortcut that brought him along the back of the property to the alley.

Using his passkey, which fit all the outside doors on

the estate, he opened the old two-story garage. Shutting it behind him, he locked it again and picked his way across the floor, which was clean and swept. When he happened to put his hand on the engine of the limousine that had belonged to his uncle and had been used by his father on formal occasions, he drew back quickly.

"Ow." Dexter pulled his hand back from the hood of the car, blowing on his burned fingers. "What the hell . . ." He grumbled about Hodgkins all the way back to the house. He banged in the back door and startled the cook, who smiled at him indulgently. "Sorry, Maria, I'm in a hurry to get some cool water on my hand."

"Oh? What has happened?"

Hodgkins came into the kitchen at that moment and walked over to the sink, clucking at the red mark. "You must be careful of matches and things like that, Master Dexter."

"Damn, it wasn't a match, though it burns like one. It was the hood on the old limousine. When you put it back after driving it, I think you should have thrown a bucket of cold water on the hood."

"It couldn't have been that, sir. I wasn't driving it and I never do because it does have a tendency to overheat. I was going to ask Miss Trisha if she would sell it to an antique car dealer because I rarely use it now, just keep it cleaned and polished."

"Must have; the hood was hot."

"No, sir, the car was not used today," Hodgkins told Dexter firmly.

"Well, check it yourself," Dexter told the older man testily. "I tell you it was hot." Dexter was about to leave the kitchen when he turned back. "Did Miss Trisha waken yet?"

Both retainers shook their heads.

245

Dexter went up the stairway and was about to turn toward the wing where he and the guests stayed when something made him go along the hall toward the master suite in the wing where Trish and Silver stayed. He rapped at the door once and waited. "Trish? It's Dexter. Are you awake? Trish." He rapped harder. On impulse he grasped the door handle and turned, pushing it open.

He squinted into the dimness of the room. It was such a large room he couldn't tell if she was in the bed or in the bathroom that led off the bedroom. "Trish? Answer me, will you?" Irritation overrode his main fear that Silver would break his body into matchsticks for entering their bedroom when Trish was sleeping, and he strode into the room. "I don't want to bother you, I just want to discuss something with—" Dexter hesitated, his glance taking in the open bathroom door with no lights on in the room and the mussed clothes on the empty bed. "Trish? Where are you?" Going closer, he turned on the light. Dexter noticed that her shoes were still near the bed. He felt the sheets. They were cold.

Retracing his steps out of the room, he closed the door behind him and went back downstairs to question Hodgkins about Trish, even though the retainer had evinced no knowledge of her just a short time ago. As he reached the front foyer and was about to turn toward the kitchen, the front door opened and the Galens entered—the Commodore, his wife, daughter, son-in-law and son Braden.

"Hello." Dexter wasn't on sure footing with Silver's family, though they were always polite to him.

"My daughter-in-law still sleeping? She was a bit under the weather, don't you know?"

"Ah, Commodore, I don't know where Trish is. She—" As Dex was speaking, the door opened again and this time it was Silver. Dex noticed how he stared at his

246

family in turn, then looked at Dex before his glance flew up the stairs toward his suite of rooms.

"What's up?" Silver questioned tersely, barely nodding to his family in greeting.

"Pan's cousin says she isn't in your suite," the Commodore stated.

"Dex?" Silver's voice dropped a few decibels.

Dexter shrugged, feeling all eyes on him. "I went up there to talk to her. I knocked a few times, then went in . . ." Dexter faltered at the hot look in Silver's eyes. "But she wasn't there. No one was."

Silver went up the stairs two at a time. Braden took one look at his brother, then said that he would talk to Hodgkins and the cook.

"I don't like this, Sterling," Felice told her husband while he patted her hand and assured her that everything would be fine.

"I'll check in the library, sir. Why don't you take the two women into the sitting room. I'm sure we'll all be joining you soon," Ben told his father-in-law, gesturing with his head for Dex to join the women. Ben felt an unnamed dread, his skin prickling, not waiting until the others moved before he shot down the hall toward the large, book-lined room.

"Good idea," the Commodore said gruffly, his eyes shooting up the stairs as his older son came bounding down them. "Find her?"

Silver shook his head.

"Ben's checking the library, Silver. Don't worry. She'll be fine." The Commodore gripped his son's shoulder, his heart wrenching with compassion when he saw how rigidly in check his son was keeping himself. His father knew that it wouldn't take much for his son to explode in a rage at the world and at whatever force was keeping him from his beloved wife.

Ben came into the room slightly out of breath, his eyes going at once to his brother-in-law before he gave a negative shake of his head.

Braden returned a few moments later from the servants' area of the house. "Hodgkins said that she returned home about two hours ago, that she didn't eat anything and she seemed very tired—"

All eyes went to Silver when they heard the expletives issuing from his mouth.

"Hodgkins also said that he was pretty sure she hadn't come downstairs again and that no one had come to the door since Pan arrived home." Braden shrugged. "I suppose he meant that no one had called to see Pan."

When all of them were seated, though alert and restless, Silver paced the Oriental carpet, frowning. "Then where is she? What happened to her?" His head shot up and he stared at Pan's cousin. "Is there a secret room where she would go? Someplace you went as children?"

"That must be it," the Commodore boomed, palpable relief in his voice, until Dex shook his head.

Dexter stared at the man whose staccato question had bounced off the wall like rivets fired into steel. "The only place we had like that was the old gazebo in the middle of the yard. It was quite a way from the house and we could play there, make noise and not disturb anyone. My stepmother had it removed years ago." Dexter sat back in his chair for a moment, frowning. "Ah, Silver, I don't know if it means anything . . ."

"Go on. Tell me whatever it is. Braden, you call the detectives and get them in on this, fast. I'm not going to fool around. Commodore, call your boyos."

"I'll use the phone in the library."

248

"Hurry, son," the Commodore urged.

The two men hurried across the room, the Commodore going to the extension in the corner, Braden sprinting out the door to the hall.

Silver's gaze fixed on Dexter once more. "What were you saying?"

"Well, before I went up to your wing to speak to Trish, quite a while before, actually, I went up to take a shower." Dexter saw an exasperated frown gathering on Silver's face and hurried his words. "When I looked out the window a while later I spotted what I thought was the old town car that had belonged to Trisha's father and that my dad used a time or two—"

"Make your point," Silver said brusquely.

"Sterling, do give him a chance," Felice said quietly.

Silver's lips tightened but he gave a quick nod, then gestured with his hand to Dexter to continue.

"I hadn't seen the car out in years but I didn't pay too much attention, even when Hodgkins told me that the car had not been used." Dexter took a quick breath, noting with relief that Silver's mother had put her hand on her son's arm to restrain him. "Anyway, I went jogging, but halfway through I decided it wasn't doing me any good, so I took a shortcut back that took me to our alley. Using my house key, I let myself into the garage because the property is all fenced and electronically patrolled, and if I tried to get in without using the key I would have set off mega number of alarms. When I was passing the car I stumbled and put my hand on the hood. I burned my hand, it was so hot. Now that old car couldn't have gone far because it does have a tendency to overheat and sometimes stall, but clearly, the engine had been running recently."

Silver ground his teeth. "So you're saying that some-one used the car to take my wife off this property?"

Dexter shrugged. "I don't know if I'm saying that, but it is funny that the car should be used so secretively."

"Yes, it is," Sasha said quietly. "I think something is not right, Silver."

"You've got that right," her brother said grimly. He looked at his brother-in-law. "I want you to question the help once more, Ben." His teeth clicked together as an-other thought intruded. "If Pan isn't at that hearing to-morrow, the judge could rule against her. Despite the fact that there is no evidence to hold her, he could think that her absence is some sort of contempt or fear, and he could judge against her and remand her over for trial." Silver stalked up and down the room. "Damnit, I know she wouldn't have left this house without telling me." He stared at his mother, his eyes tortured. "She isn't totally well yet."

"You mustn't worry, dear. She's fine. I know it."

Silver stared at Dexter again. "Where did you say that old touring car was kept?"

"In the old garage at the foot of the property, quite a way from the house, actually. Shall I show you?"

Silver nodded, then looked at his sister. "Man the phones, will you, Sasha?"

"Of course."

"Let's go, Dexter."

Dexter hurried behind the taller man, the stiff set of his shoulders telegraphing the urgency of the situation. Dex-ter had a strange hollow feeling in the pit of his stomach, as though he were in the epicenter of a hurricane, as though the storm was put on hold for a moment before turning its fury on them.

The minute Silver was out of doors he broke into a run, covering the long stretch of property in short order.

"What a hell of a place to put a garage!" he muttered to Dexter, who huffed up behind him. "It's a damned country mile from the house."

"They used to do that in the old days, when everybody had chauffeurs on property like this. This is practically one of the original estates in San Francisco."

Silver looked around him, not really seeing anything. "Choice piece."

"Yes. My father was approached time after time to sell it, but he wanted to keep Trish's legacy intact."

"Let's look at that car, shall we?" Silver smelled the fuel as soon as he entered the garage, and he knew without touching the now-cool hood that the car had been used. Staring around him, he tried to calm himself and get vibrations from the car, from the garage, from anything that would telegraph some information to him. "Where does that door lead?"

"That's to a stairway to the second-floor apartment. It hasn't been used in years, not since we had a chauffeur . . . then sometimes Alan used it, but he hasn't for a while now."

Silver walked toward the door and opened it. The stairway sent a message quivering through him. This was not an unused area. "Someone has cleaned this lately." Silver felt a prickling awareness, and he looked over his shoulder at Dexter. "You say that no one has used this place?"

"Right." Dexter saw the suspicious look on Silver's face. "Hey, I'm not lying to you."

"Aren't you? Come over here and look at these stairs. There isn't a cobweb anywhere." Not waiting for him, Silver turned and climbed the stairs, turning the handle

251

at the top of the steps, noting that there was no rusty squeak but a well-oiled hinge swung the door inward. Bracing himself, Silver stayed where he was, looking into what must have been the living room of the apartment. It was clean, with good furnishings.

Dexter looked over Silver's shoulder, dumbfounded, but when he would have spoken, Silver gestured him to silence.

Silver's spine was beaded with cold perspiration, much the same way as he'd been just before a race began, with engine racing, blood pumping. Before he stepped into the room, he turned and looked at Dexter, then put his mouth to his ear. "Get help."

No. Dex formed the words silently. *I'm not leaving you.*

Silver was caught in lacerated amusement. With a terse nod of his head, he swung back and stepped into the living room, looking all around him before moving into the center of the area. Taking a deep breath, he moved toward the kitchenette, checking every cranny.

The bathroom was the first door he opened. The tile and appliances were clean and shiny.

Then he opened another door, the handle turning easily to show a small room with a bed in it, not as well cared for as the bathroom or the main room.

The last door wouldn't open. Silver tried a second time to turn the handle; then he put his hands on the door and pushed. Locked! Gesturing to Dexter to step back, he also reversed himself a few steps, then raised his right leg, kicking out in the karate fashion he'd learned from a Vietnamese. With a splintering crash the door gave, splitting in the middle and hanging from one hinge.

Silver didn't move into the darkened room until his eyes adjusted to the dimness. He noted the window shades that had been drawn over the sill, the pulls fastened to a hook so that there would be no chance of them snapping up again. There was a dresser with a mirror over it that reflected the bed . . . Silver froze, feeling Dex bump into his back. Though Silver hadn't been able to see over the foot of the old-fashioned mahogany bed, he could make out the outline of a form on it. Even as he watched, he heard a muffled groan. In a flash he realized that whoever was on that bed was tied and gagged.

Flinging himself at the bed, he lifted the person and looked into his wife's face. "Christ! Pan, darling." Even as he lifted her in his arms and pulled the gag from her mouth, he could sense that she was only semiconscious, that she had a temperature and that she was possibly drugged.

"Oh God, oh God," Dexter murmured, untying her feet with difficulty and rubbing the reddened marks on her ankles. "Who did this? These ropes were like a tourniquet on her." When he couldn't get the ropes off her arms, he took out a pocketknife and severed them.

"Dex, get on the phone and get the emergency squad. She's been heavily sedated. Damn their souls to hell! She could have died here, unattended." Rage and agony tore through him as he held her limp form in his lap. "Damnit, Dex, hurry."

"I'm dialing." Dex looked at the anguished man sitting on the bed. "What if we hadn't come down here? She could have smothered on that gag or . . ." Dex's voice trailed at the look of hell in Silver's eyes. "This is an emergency! Send an ambulance—"

Silver didn't hear the rest of Dex's conversation. He carried Pan into the bathroom, kicked off his shoes, then stepped with her, both of them clothed, into the shower, holding her to him while he regulated the water to cool but not cold, keeping her face sheltered against him so that she wouldn't choke.

When she began to cough as a semblance of consciousness intruded on her somnolent state, Silver turned off the water. "Darling? Pan, wake up. It's Silver."

"Sil . . . ver." Pan's head lolled on his shoulder as she tried to open her eyes and focus on him. "Wet."

"Yes," Silver whispered, his voice a mix of amusement and relief. "Trust you to hit on the obvious." He wrapped her in a towel, looking out into the bedroom and ascertaining that Dex must have gone into the living room.

Pan felt herself lifted and carried, but she was too groggy to do more than grunt when her clothes were stripped from her and her husband began drying her body.

When Silver heard the bedroom door open, he shielded his wife's nude body with his own. "Dex? Call up to the house and get some dry clothing for her, and make it fast. Get something for me, too, because I'm going to the hospital with her."

"Right. I'll go and get it myself after I talk to your father."

Silver barely nodded, all his attention on his wife. When she was dry he returned to the bathroom, rummaging through the drawers until he found a selection of emollients. He chose the one that had never been opened, then went back to her and began applying it in soothing strokes.

"Silver?" Again her eyes opened and she stared at him. "I was frightened."

"You're safe now, love, and I'll never let you out of my sight again."

"Good." Pan's eyes fluttered shut.

All at once the silence was broken by a cluster of voices demanding to know where they were.

Shortly after that an ambulance came up the alley and the attendants hurried up the stairs to get Pan.

"Someone tell me who brought my daughter-in-law here," the Commodore boomed, angry red slashing his face, his gray hair quivering in fury. "I'll have heads for this, damn them to hell," the older man muttered as the stretcher carrying Pan passed his wife and him.

"Oh, Sterling, she does look so white." Felice bit her lip, clutching her husband's arm.

"I won't stand for it," fumed her husband.

"Neither will I, Father," Silver promised quietly. "Ben, take them all back to the house. I'll call you from the hospital." Silver looked at Dex's stricken face as he watched Pan being taken out of the apartment. "I owe you, man. I won't forget it."

Ben and the Commodore clapped Dex on the back, then Dex followed them back to the house, his brain churning with what had happened to his cousin.

"Don't berate me. You should have seen to it that she was attended."

"I? You are the one who should have watched her."

"I had a close enough call with Hodgkins without risking him coming up to the apartment and catching me there. Now she's coming home from the hospital today and we won't have another shot at her, you can bet the rent on that. Her husband will be careful as hell."

"But Silver, I can't imagine why you want to have such a gathering. Even your parents are puzzled." Pan looked at her husband and felt her mouth go dry as he walked out of the bathroom without a stitch of clothing

255

on. His body scars paled in the natural beauty of the man. "My, you are one hunk, Silver Galen." Pan started to laugh when she saw his neck redden. "Have I embarrassed you?"

"Just pleased the hell out of me, that's all. I want you to love me as much as I love you."

Pan's breath caught in her throat. "That's a very provocative statement, husband." She couldn't seem to clear the huskiness from her throat.

"Come here." He held out his arms, his heart thudding against his breast when she glided into them. "You smell so nice. I love that robe you're wearing."

"I'm sure you do, since you picked it out."

"Oh. Is that one of the ones I got you for the hospital?"

"Yes. I was the only patient who was there overnight who had five silk robes delivered to her room." She leaned up and kissed his nose, glad that the harshness that had been in his eyes since she'd been abducted was gradually disappearing. Pan had never seen Silver quite like that. He had turned granite hard before her eyes and developed a killing look that did not belong to the man she knew, the one who cherished her and treated her so gently. The latent savage in Silver had sometimes coursed just below the surface in their lovemaking, though he was unfailingly sweet with her, but Pan had never seen the beast unleashed before, and alarm quivered through her at what she saw. "Come and help me choose a dress for this evening." Pan was trying anything to get that hell-for-leather look from his eyes.

Silver smiled down at her, aware that she was concerned about the way he had been acting, but there was just so much he could hide. He was on a mission, and nothing and no one would come between him and his goal. "No need to help you choose something. I called Charine and had her send out something new." He touched her cheek with a finger that trembled slightly. "I wanted something to complement your eyes."

Pan reached up and took hold of the hand held to her face. "I'm truly fine, Silver. You know that."

"I know that I almost lost you." The words pushed through his lips like missiles.

"But you must put that behind you. I have."

"Oh? Is that why you whimper in the night unless I'm holding you in my arms?"

Pan felt her smile slip a little. "That's just because I'm so possessive of you. I get angry when I can't hold you. That's something I'll have to change or you'll never get to work."

"Don't change. Be as possessive as you like. If need be I'll do my work with you on my lap."

Pan burst out laughing. "Picture the board meetings."

Silver bent over her, his body tenting hers. "I don't give a damn about anything or anyone but you—and I will never forget what was done to you."

Pan felt a shiver of fear at the hatred in his eyes. "Don't. Don't dwell on that. It will come between us, perhaps smother what we have together."

"Nothing can come between us, my love, because I won't let it." Silver lifted her up his body, his mouth feathering over her face and neck.

Pan clung to him, not able to wipe away the specter that hung over them. She wished with all her heart that he could rid himself of his obsession, because she had a strong feeling that it could mar their love, no matter how strongly Silver voiced his opinion against such a contingency.

Silver let her slide down his body again. "Come with

257

me and I'll show you your new dress." He frowned for a moment. "Though it looks like it might be too revealing and it isn't violet."

"You'd think a nun's habit showed too much of me," Pan shot back, chuckling when he grimaced and nodded.

He opened his closet and pushed aside his suits so that he could unzip a garment bag with Charine's name scrolled on it in gold. "Do you like it?"

Pan stared at the froth of French voile draped over his arm, the coral hue perfect for her coloring. "It's lovely. Grecian drape, isn't it?"

"Beats me. Charine said it would be perfect on you." Silver shrugged. "But then you look wonderful in everything . . . and nothing."

For a moment Pan saw a flash of his old devil-may-care look. She cast herself at him, rocking him back on his heels for a moment. "Never mind the dress. Love me, Silver Galen, love me."

Silver flung the dress toward the chaise longue before lifting her up the front of him again and staring at her. "What is it? Are you ill?"

"Yes. I'm sick to death of you not making love to me, which you haven't done since I came home from the hospital."

Silver laughed lightly, though his eyes still went over her. "Darling, you just came home yesterday."

"And the doctor said I was fine. So?"

Laughing, he swept her up in his arms. "We'll be late for our guests, but who the hell cares. Mother and Sasha will handle everything."

It was Pan who became the aggressor once they were in bed. She pushed her husband back on the bed and began undressing him, cursing when a button became stubborn.

258

"I'm shocked at your language, Mrs. Galen." Silver felt a hot, lazy satisfaction as his wife disrobed him, but even as the sexual power built between them, he was fully aware that she was using her wonderful body to make him forget. Silver wasn't quite sure that she wouldn't be successful.

"You shouldn't be. I've heard worse from you—and stop laughing. You're not easy to undress." All the feelings she had for her husband erupted in Pan. Gratitude, passion, love, humor—all became a vortex of emotion directed at the man who had made such a wonderful life for her. Silver had brought her out of herself, made her whole again. Pan knew that in a thousand lifetimes she would never be able to show him how much he meant to her, so it would just have to be very basic love that she gave him, the foundation of herself. "I love you—so very much," she whispered when they were naked and pressed to each other.

Silver felt a moistness in his eyes at her sweet declaration.

Imitating the many wonderful caresses he had given her, Pan wouldn't let him move. When her mouth moved down his form and she gave Silver the same intimate caresses that he had given her time after time, it surprised and delighted her when he moaned and trembled beneath her on the bed. Her own libido climbed out of sight just because she was loving her husband and could bring him to the heights of sensuous fulfillment.

"Enough." Lifting her up, he swung her under him until he was suspended over her. "You blew me away, lady, took me apart and rebuilt me just now." He grinned at her. "But we've only just begun. I'm going to love you now."

"Good." Pan held him to her, her eyes locked with his. "Do your damnedest, Silver Galen."

"You little devil." Silver stared at her, taken aback. She was new again, another wonderful person that he was soon to meet on a very passionate journey.

All mirth ceased when the powerful force took them and they were welded in the most profound rhythm on the planet. Giving became paramount, so that each one strove more for the other and gained so much in the giving.

Breathing was stilled; nothing moved as they crested the cyclone.

". . . and it is the judgment of this court that there is no evidence linking Mrs. Patricia Galen to the untimely death of her uncle and so there is no reason to bind her over for trial. This hearing is adjourned." Judge Needham banged his gavel.

Silver leaned over the seat to catch hold of his wife and turn her toward him. "Let's go home, lady." He caught her close so that she couldn't see the hard look he exchanged with the detective named Walzer. The issue wasn't settled yet, but it would be.

CHAPTER TEN

Dexter stared at his cousin as she walked into the room on her husband's arm, the coral-color dress giving her eyes a vivid violet sheen, her hair a rioting flame around her head in masses of shining curls.

"I can see you're as taken with your cousin as I am," Braden whispered to the other man. "But I can tell you now that if you're a tad more than friendly, my dear brother will remove your arms and legs."

"I know." Dex smiled at Silver's brother. "He's already threatened to throw me from the Golden Gate Bridge if I've been involved at all in hurting her."

Braden cocked his head, looking from his sister-in-law back to Dex. "And I will help him, I'm afraid." Braden looked sharply at Dex when the other man frowned. "What's wrong?"

"I haven't been the best friend Trisha could have—" Dexter began.

"Good God, will you look at that! I didn't know Silver invited them."

Dex whirled, feeling the blood drain to his shoes as he stared at his stepmother and Alan Winston. "My God, is Silver crazy? Things are starting to go well for Trisha now that she's been cleared of any wrongdoing. Now he's invited the very people who want his wife's company

261

. . . and Slate, their lawyer, is with them." Dex's voice rose in amazement.

"My brother has a reason for everything, that much I know," Braden said slowly, staring at the new arrivals, then looking at his own family as they gazed at the newcomers, plastic smiles of welcome on their faces. "I think this is going to be one fun evening."

"I wish I agreed with you," Dex muttered morosely as other persons he didn't know came through the doorway and were greeted by his cousin and her husband.

"Ladder!" Braden said, laughing. Then he turned to Dex. "Excuse me a moment, will you. That's someone I didn't expect to see."

"Sure." Dex had grown to like Braden, and he'd shown the New Yorker the night life of San Francisco. And it had pleased him when Braden invited him East. Seeing New York might be a good excuse to get out of the city until the fracas died down at Drexel's. Silver had already made some changes, and though Dex's job hadn't been affected, he had no sure feeling that it wouldn't be eventually. Silver was one of the toughest persons he'd ever encountered, and Dex was quite sure that he was capable of chopping anyone or anything that hurt his Pan.

"Well, well, still here? How is it that you've remained, Dexter? Did you beg them?"

"No, Maeve, I didn't. Trish wanted me to stay here." Dexter glared at his stepmother. "How's your job at Drexel's?" When he saw how his stepmother flinched, then reddened, he realized that he had touched on a very tender subject. He felt grim satisfaction that his self-assured stepmother could be shaken by anything or anyone. "What's wrong? Did Silver fire you? I understand he's been doing a bit of that."

"No, he did not," Maeve snapped. "But the changes he made are not good for the company."

As Dexter opened his mouth to retort, Hodgkins came into the room and announced dinner. The meal was a strange amalgam of silence and conversation. The lawyers and the detectives hired by Silver seemed to have the most to say to each other, but the others stared around them, puzzled and frowning, their mouths tight as though afraid of revealing something.

Only Silver seemed to savor the braised tuna steaks with tomato and endive. Now and then he would look down the table and smile serenely at his wife, who was only pushing the food around on her plate.

The Commodore opened and closed his mouth several times, his eyes going from his daughter-in-law to his son, then to his wife, who gave him benign smiles.

It was with a general sense of relief that all rose from the table to take coffee in the sitting room.

"I think this farce has gone on long enough. We agreed to come here because you said that you had important information that pertained to my husband's death. Since there has been nothing said about that, I feel this evening has been a waste of time." Maeve stood just inside the sitting room, staring at Silver.

Voices erupted all around the room in rebuttal or agreement to Maeve's remarks, but Silver rose from where he had been sitting close to Pan on a settee, his hands upraised, palms outward. "Please, please, everyone be assured that I will do what I said, but since revealing some new evidence we have might spark a little trouble, I've taken the precaution of inviting some of the San Francisco police as guests."

Heads swiveled as he gestured at two of the guests, who stood and smiled at everyone.

"So if you'll take a seat, Mrs. Drexel."

"I will, Mr. Galen, but if I think this charade is a fool's game, I am going to leave."

"I'll keep that in mind. Let's get on with this." Silver looked at his wife. "Darling, I don't want to upset you in any way, but you told me that the evening of your uncle's death you were out with friends, and this was corroborated by them at the time of the initial investigation." At Pan's wary nod of her head, Silver smiled at her, then turned back to Dexter. "And you had come home before Pan, hadn't you?" At Dexter's nod, Silver continued. "But you and your father had a—fearful row." Silver consulted a paper he'd picked up from a side table.

"Because of my drinking and things, yes."

"Then you left the house?"

"No, I think I must have passed out—or something, because—"

"Because later when you came to, your stepmother and her friend were standing over you and they told you that your cousin had killed your father—"

"And that's true. Trisha was lying on the floor with the paperweight next to her," Maeve pointed out, sitting straight in her chair.

"Ah, but there were no fingerprints on the paperweight —none, not even Henry Drexel's, the man who owned the object."

"Alan and I both heard my husband tell his niece not to come back to the house; neither did he want her working at Drexel's."

Silver whirled to face the woman, his teeth bared. "Isn't the truth that he didn't want her to have to face what was going on in his home? Weren't you carrying on with this man while your husband was alive and weren't you doing it in this house?" Silver pointed to Alan Win-

264

ston, who jumped to his feet in protest. Silver ignored him and kept talking. "Wasn't your husband going to divorce you and name Alan Winston as corespondent in the case?"

"How dare you speak to me like that? I will not stay here and listen to this—this vilification."

"I think you will, Mrs. Drexel." Silver went to the stereo system in the wall of the sitting room. Turning, he brandished a disc. "I'm going to play this for everyone, but I think we should go to the library where the crime—"

"Crime? Damn you, Galen, what the hell do you think you're doing here?" Alan Winston had jumped to his feet again, his face mottled from anger. "Your damned Perry Mason melodrama has come to an end."

Ladder stepped next to the man and took his arm. "I don't want to use force, sir, but you will go into the study and you will listen to the disc."

Every person in the room stood as though on some silent signal, and all eyes were on Silver as he went to his wife, helped her from her chair and led her from the room.

"Silver?"

"It's all right, Pan. Trust me."

The library was smaller than the sitting room, but chairs had been arranged in a sort of semicircle so that there was space in front of the huge desk.

After seating his wife, Silver looked at each guest in turn and nodded to one of the private detectives standing at the door, who closed it, then stood in front of it, arms crossed on his chest. "Let me just say this before I play the disc. The car that struck my wife and could have killed her and my mother has been found . . ." Silver ignored the outraged gasp of his father, fixing his eyes on Alan Winston. "It was leased by you, Mr. Winston."

"I'll kill the bastard," the Commodore roared, surging to his feet and struggling against Braden and Dexter, who had taken hold of his arms to restrain him.

"What? What the hell is this? I don't know anything about the accident your wife had." Winston was chalky-faced but defiant.

"Don't you? It just so happens that there is a warrant out for your arrest that will be served on you before you leave this house, Winston—and you should be glad the police are handling this, because if they weren't here, I would tear your heart out," Silver told him in satin tones.

"And I tell you I know nothing about the accident except what I read in the newspapers." Winston stared stonily at Silver. "I give you my word on that."

Silver laughed softly. "You'd swear to anything to save your hide."

"You are going too far, Mr. Galen." Maeve glared at Silver before turning to her lawyer, who sat next to her. "Lawrence, do something."

Slate jumped to his feet. "You have no need to answer anything, Alan. And you, Mr. Galen, are traveling on the dangerous ground of defamation of character, and don't think we won't press charges when this fiasco of yours draws to a close."

"Feel free to press any charge you like, Slate. Just remember that I won't allow my wife to be harassed any longer. She will have what belongs to her. I promise you that." Silver's words hung in the air like a bona fide threat.

Someone swallowed, and it was like a pistol crack in the quiet room.

Silver turned and went to the desk, opening the top drawer and pressing a button.

"That's to release the hidden drawer. My uncle showed me that," Pan said in low, measured tones. "How did you find it, Silver?"

"I didn't. One of the men I had go over this room with a fine-tooth comb found it. He's an expert and still it took him days to discover it. Your father and uncle were secretive men."

Pan nodded. "I don't think anyone else knew about that."

"And I'm sure you're right." Silver leaned down out of sight of the others, the slight scraping of wood against wood telegraphing the opening of a drawer. In minutes a voice was speaking.

"That's Father!" Dexter said, surprised anguish in his voice.

"And I will not have the Drexel Holding Company split or taken away from my niece. My son is well provided for in my will. My wife will get a minimal amount, since she and Winston have been skimming from the company. Therefore I do not feel they need any more from me—"

"That's a lie." Maeve jumped to her feet. "My husband didn't want his niece in the company. He knew that I'd do well. I don't know how you managed to fake his voice, but that disc is a lie." Maeve's arm shot out, pointing at the desk.

"And I maintain that you slipped away from your supposed 'banquet' that night, that you came home and heard your husband making that disc, that you stood outside that door listening to it, and that you went into the room. What did he do then? Press a button, like this?" Silver moved his leg, and the voice droning on the

267

speaker system ceased. "You must have gone crazy trying to locate that recording of his voice."

"Your fabric of lies won't protect your wife, Mr. Galen. I intend to get a court order to stop you—" Maeve's voice rose, her hands closing into fists.

"Oh? Do you think you can?"

"Of course we can." Lawrence Slate shook his finger at Silver. "Alan, you needn't say any more. Maeve, let's go. We can leave."

"No, you can't, not until I'm through." Silver's soft voice went around the room like a boomerang.

Maeve looked at the guarded door, then she shrugged and sat down, as did the other two.

"You argued with your husband, Mrs. Drexel. And I think you lost your cool with him because he told you that you were through, that he wanted you out. Is that when you picked up the paperweight and struck him as he sat at his desk? The medical examiner's report states that he was struck as he sat, that if it had been an intruder there would have been signs of struggle, but there were none."

"I never said it was an intruder. I said it was my niece who killed him," Maeve stated coldly.

"That's true. You did say that."

"So if it wasn't your wife who did it, it must have been Dexter. He was drunk when he came in. No doubt he lied about seeing Trisha on the floor. No doubt he struck her when she came into the room shortly after he had killed his father in a drunken rage." Maeve's voice was measured and cool. Each remark she made was punctuated with a nod, as though all the puzzle pieces were coming together.

"Why didn't my wife see Dex when she came into the room?"

268

"Because no doubt he hid behind the door when she approached, then when she entered he struck her and placed the paperweight at her hand as she lay on the floor."

"First wiping the fingerprints from the paperweight?"

"Yes."

"You describe what happened fairly well, Mrs. Drexel," Silver said calmly, leaning back against the desk.

"Because you did it, not me." Dexter leapt to his feet. "I wouldn't have killed my father, drunk or sober." He shook his head rapidly. "I was a fool to believe you, to think that anything you said about Trish could be true." His face twisted with grief and bitterness. "Maybe I always knew you did it; maybe I hid it from myself because it was easier than facing the truth. Even with all the facts in front of me, it was easier to believe an intruder did it and allow you to make veiled accusations against my cousin." Dex's fist smacked against the palm of his other hand. "In a way I'm guilty because I didn't stop you right away. Damn you, Maeve, you killed my father!" The pain-filled cry went around the room, freezing everyone in place.

"And you're the only one who had access to the keys to my car," Alan muttered dazedly. "Did you hit those women?" Alan stared at her as though she were a stranger.

"Shut up, you Judas," Maeve snapped.

"Why? Why, for Christ's sake? Why do anything like that? There was no need to kill the poor bastard. We were taking money out of that company. He knew it but he didn't stop us—" Alan felt the cold sweat break out on his body as Maeve's eyes glittered over him. This was a part of her he'd never known; neither had he realized what she was capable of doing to achieve her goal. "Maeve . . . darling . . ."

"He was going to cut me out of everything I'd worked for, damn you." The words slipped from between Maeve's half-closed lips like snakes. "No one was going to steal that from me." She looked around her. "This is my home. It's my company. He had no right, and that's what I told him." Maeve's eyes glazed over in hot and cold fury. "Henry, I've worked too hard. My social life depends on Drexel's. You're not giving it all to a half-fledged girl who doesn't really care about it. No! It isn't hers! It's mine, damn you, it's mine!" Maeve's hand swept up and down in a chopping motion, hitting the back of the chair in front of her with a resounding crack as Ben, who had been sitting there, rose to his feet to face her with grim pity.

Ben took hold of her forearms, shaking her gently, his face ashen. "It's all right, Maeve, it's all right," he told her in a soothing voice.

"Drexel's is mine!" Maeve yelled over and over as the two detectives took hold of her on either side and led her from the room.

Alan looked after her, both he and Slate on their feet. Then he looked at Silver. "I'd like to go with her and take Slate. She'll need representation."

"Of course. Go ahead." Silver raised his hand. "Winston, you'll have to answer charges that will be made by Drexel's about your fiscal habits. And you're fired." Silver's teeth bared in a feral smile. "There will also be the charge of kidnapping, since the police tell me that the finger points at you and Maeve."

"Say nothing, Alan," Slate interjected.

"I understand." Alan swallowed, looking at Pan. "I'm

270

sorry about all this, but I did think you were involved in your uncle's death."

Pan nodded, watching as they left the room. Then she went to her cousin, who was seated in his chair, his head forward in his hands. "Dex? Don't blame yourself. Please. I don't, and neither would your father. He loved you."

Dex lifted a tear-stained face. "If I had had half your guts maybe none of this would ever have happened."

"Hindsight isn't wisdom, Dex, so don't embrace it. Rather face the present and future and get a handle on both. It took my husband to teach me that. You'll have a good life here, running the business for me when I'm in New York. Right?"

"You'd trust me with the business after this mess?"

"Of course. Uncle Henry would have chosen you. You know the business as well as anyone, and we can build and expand it with the help of the Galen people. It will be the best news chain in the world."

Dex gave her a half-smile. "Yeah. I guess you could do almost anything you set your mind to, as long as you had that husband of yours riding shotgun."

Pan laughed and hugged her cousin. "Isn't he one tough cookie?"

"There's nobody tougher."

When Pan felt hands lifting her, she knew it was Silver and she turned to kiss him. "Thank you, husband." Then she looked past him to the family, all watching her anxiously. "And thanks to you, Galens. What a family I have!" She included Ladder in her smile.

"Of course you do, my dear. How could you doubt it?" the Commodore asked her gruffly, holding out his arms to her and hugging her tightly when she moved into them. "I'm just glad this damnable charade is over."

"Amen to that, darling." Felice came up to them, kissing her daughter-in-law. "Now maybe you'll take me sightseeing in San Francisco," she said to her husband. "I have an urge to spend some of your money."

"You'll put me in the poorhouse yet, Felice." The Commodore tried to scowl at his wife, but he couldn't quite mask his pleasure in his spouse.

"I think Silver should entertain all of us for the next week with rounds of partying and general debauchery," Braden chimed in.

"You'll have a day of celebrating, friend. Then it's back to the salt mines for you," Ladder announced, sprawling indolently in a chair, his eyes going from one to the other of the Galens.

"Slave driver," Braden teased.

"Regular Simon Legree, ain't he, Braden?" the Commodore chortled.

"Don't say *ain't,* darling." Felice smiled at her younger son when he nodded sharply to his father.

"I say that we all enjoy a couple of days here before we return to New York," Silver ventured, his arm around his wife, but looking at the lawyers who hovered close to the family, Wilson Carpenter in low-voiced conversation with Ben. "I don't think there's any need for my wife to be involved in the investigation right at the moment, is there?"

"Ah, Silver," Ben interrupted before the others could respond. "Wilson says he feels that I could act for Pan in most of the proceedings in the business, and he could also apprise me of what is happening with Mrs. Drexel. That way Pan needn't worry about anything out here except visiting and overseeing the business."

"And Dex can help you, too, Ben." Pan spoke before her husband.

272

"Right." Ben smiled at her, then glanced at Dexter and nodded. "We'll work it out."

Pan took a deep breath and looked around the room, biting her lip for a moment, feeling her uncle's presence like a hand on her shoulder. "Yes, we will." She turned to look at her husband, the sheen of tears in her eyes. "Thanks to a man called Silver. How my uncle would have enjoyed you."

"Yes, he would have." Dex rose and put his arm around Pan, kissing her cheek. "And how pleased he'd be with you."

"And you." Pan hugged her cousin. "Is anyone else hungry besides me?"

The stay in San Francisco was enjoyable, and one of the best parts for Pan was when she accompanied her husband and her cousin into the Drexel main office building to meet the staff.

Pan could sense the subtle vibrations directed at her husband, and she knew that there had been changes engineered by him already. She masked the smile as she saw the many females eyeing him with appreciation and realized that she would be flaming mad if her husband weren't showing complete attention to her. With vinegary amusement she accepted that her life was so closely entwined with her husband's that nothing could separate them. So much for her theory that she could go it alone; that she could ever have had an affair with him and been able to walk away after a period of time. He'd dropped a net over her, and even if she desired to go free—which she didn't—she doubted if it would be possible. Silver was a magnet to her.

"You seem preoccupied. I think you've hurt Dex's feelings that you haven't been as enthusiastic as you should be about the changes."

Pan stared up at her husband. "Your changes, you mean. Are you hurt that I didn't make appropriate remarks?"

Silver cocked his head. "A little. I'm always showing off for you, you know."

Pan chuckled. "You are not."

Silver nodded. "Yes, I am. I didn't like it at first, but I've learned to accept that you're so important to me that I have to do mighty deeds to impress you."

"Fool."

"About you I am."

Pan felt an absurd desire to preen, to climb to the top of the Drexel Building and shout to the populace below that Silver Galen loved her, that he wanted to show off for her, that he belonged to her and nothing would ever change that.

For the rest of the tour through the main office, Pan paid close attention, asking questions and contributing to the conversation. When she saw how delighted Dex was, she was glad that she made the effort.

On the night before they were to leave for New York, Silver was down in the sitting room, fixing himself an Irish whiskey on the rocks, thinking about the change that had been wrought in his wife in just the few short days since Maeve had been taken away and charged with the death of her husband. When he heard a sound behind him he turned. Dex was standing there solemnly. "Good evening. Can I fix you one?"

"I'll have seltzer water with a twist of lemon, please. I haven't touched the hard stuff since my father died." Dex paused as he approached Silver. "That's the first time I could mention my father and not feel guilt and shame."

"Good. You made your mistakes and you've learned from them. A man has to do that and keep on going."

Dex took the glass with the effervescent liquid and sipped. "Thanks to you. I love the work now, and though I think the changes you made were good, I have a few of my own to put before the board. When Ben comes out next month, I'm going to hash them over with him."

Silver grinned. "You sound pretty sure of yourself."

"I am."

"Good. Ah, that's my wife's step on the stairs, I think." Silver was about to put down his glass and go to meet her when Dex stopped him with a hand on his arm. Silver looked at him inquiringly.

"She's happier than she's ever been in her life . . . and you did that too. Thank you for that. Patricia Ann Belmont Drexel Galen is the very best person I've ever known."

"We agree on that." Silver's smile widened as his wife stood in the doorway. "Beautiful women should always make an entrance, my darling."

Pan chuckled, feeling sensuous and beautiful because Silver loved her. "I am getting so conceited."

Dex grinned at his cousin. "At the risk of getting killed by your husband, I have to tell you that you look wonderful."

Silver turned, about to say something, when Hodgkins came to the door of the sitting room. "Yes, Hodgkins, what is it?"

"Mr. Winston, sir." The butler's face was pinched in disapproval. Since Maeve and Winston had left the household, the old retainers had been brought back, and Hodgkins had felt some of the old warmth in the house again. He didn't want Mr. Winston back in the place disrupting things.

275

"Winston? What's he doing here?" Dexter slammed his drink down on the portable bar, sloshing some of the liquid over the surface.

"Dex. Take it easy," Silver admonished, then he gestured to Hodgkins. "Show him in here, please." He went to his wife, placing his arm at her waist and facing the door.

When Winston stood in the doorway, glancing from one to the other, his twisted smile took note of their unsmiling faces. "Don't worry—I won't be staying long. I want to make a deal. In order to pay for Maeve's legal fees I would like to sell some of her stock in Drexel's. Are you interested in buying?"

"I might be," Silver said coolly. "How much?"

Winston stated a figure that made Dex gasp and Pan stiffen in Silver's arms.

Silver didn't blink when he counteroffered. "And that's it. There won't be any more deals. If you don't like the offer you can sell the shares elsewhere."

"You could find yourself in a bind if an unsavory group purchased the block."

"And you could find yourself hauled in front of the SEC if you begin mixing it up with a criminal element, Winston. And I wouldn't hesitate to have any sale you conducted investigated."

"Neither would I." Dex faced the man who had tormented him for such a long time.

Winston looked at Silver and Dex, his features hardening. "Stay out of this, Drexel."

"I'm afraid he can't." Pan spoke for the first time. "He will be the executive vice president at Drexel's, answerable to me and the board."

Winston's lip curled. "I accept your price, Galen. Slate

276

will be in touch with your lawyers. Pardon me if I don't linger." Winston whirled out of the room and was gone.

"I think he really loves my stepaunt," Pan murmured.

"They deserve each other," Dex responded.

Silver shrugged and looked at his wife. "My sweet, I'm very hungry. Shall we dine?"

Bermuda was very warm, but the Atlantic breeze made it bearable.

Their months together had changed both Pan and Silver. She had been with him when he had finally gone into the hospital for the very delicate reconstructive surgery on his face. Pan had been so nervous that she hadn't been able to go home, and not all the Galens' coaxing could get her away from the hospital.

"Darling, go home with Mother and Father," Silver had told her drowsily, barely able to form words, he was so heavily bandaged.

"No! The nurses said that I could stay in your hospital suite and I'm going to do that. Once you get out of intensive care we'll be together."

"Why not come out to our house, child?" the Commodore suggested.

Pan shook her head vigorously. "No. I won't leave him." How could she have explained to anyone that she couldn't be separated from Silver. Her recurring nightmare was that he could be taken from her. He was all of life to her.

The days passed quickly in the hospital, and Silver was soon home with a very good prognosis. Pan tried not to cling to him, but it was such a joy to have him home again that she couldn't be around him without touching him.

Despite all Pan's urgings that he rest, Silver was soon

back at work, but only after promising her they would take a vacation in Bermuda very soon.

Now they were on the beautiful island . . . and alone.

They had snorkeled around the coral ledge about a hundred yards from shore, and Pan had been entranced with the undersea life that thrived there. But now instead of Silver being fussy about her well-being, she was the one doing the hovering.

"Pan, sweetheart, we haven't been in the water that long," Silver told her, grinning at her when she frowned at him.

"Do you hate the way I'm treating you, Silver?" she asked him as they walked out of the ocean arm-in-arm.

He sighed, lying back on the white sand. "I should tell you I hate it, but I don't. If I could I'd cuddle up in your lap." Silver grimaced at her when she giggled.

"Just like a baby."

"Yes."

Pan lowered herself next to him under the umbrella propped behind them. Though Silver's face was no longer bandaged, it was still very sensitive and sunning was forbidden to him. It had taken all Silver's coaxing to get the doctor to relent on swimming, but even as she looked at his features, Pan could tell that the scars were disappearing, that the operation was a success. Sometimes she felt shy with the very good-looking man who was appearing before her eyes as more and more of the scar tissue disappeared.

"What are you thinking?" Silver looked up at her as she leaned over him, her feather touch outlining the scar on his chest that had become a thin red line rather than the puckered two-inch-wide flaw it had once been.

"Oh, I was thinking that you're getting even better-looking than you were and that I will have to fight off the women with a club to keep you."

"And will you do that?" Silver whispered.

Pan saw the flash of uncertainty that was quickly masked by his sardonic smile. She realized that even though she'd told him she loved him many times, he was still aware that she had held back a bit of herself from him. It wasn't until everything had been settled in California that she'd felt that she could try to show him how deeply committed to him she was. "Oh, yes, I would beat them off with a whip and a chair if need be, my darling husband. You're mine and I mean to keep you, come hell or high water."

Silver laughed, delighted with her response, his body and mind feeling a giddy lightness at her words. "You'll never have any trouble keeping me, my sweet one. I'm yours. I would do anything to keep you."

"Anything?" Pan saw his eyes narrow, as though he would probe her mind with those navy blue eyes of his.

Silver nodded.

"Good." Pan settled herself on his chest. "Then I want a baby."

Silver surged to a sitting position, his hand convulsing on her. "No! It's too soon. It could be dangerous for you."

Pan put her index finger on his lips. "Shh, silly, we've been together almost a year."

"I know exactly how long you've been in my life."

"Well, then, what's the problem? The doctor said I wasn't to have a baby for a year. She didn't say anything about me getting pregnant in that year."

"Damnit, Pan, I don't want to risk your health."

"I, sir, am as healthy as a horse and we both know it."

She kissed him on the throat. "Let me have your child, Silver Galen."

"Well, you damn well will never have anyone else's."

Pan stared up at him as he held her cradled in his arms, her hands stealing up around his neck. "Wouldn't you love to see what we could produce, Silver?" Pan saw the smile break through his serious mien, and she felt a dart of hope. She had figured trying to convince him of this would take time and a great deal of underhanded persuasion. Kissing his chin, she fluttered her eyelashes at him. "Could I try convincing you?"

"Little devil." Silver's head swooped down and he kissed her with fierce gentleness.

Pan sighed with contentment, knowing that her husband would soon be carrying her into the spacious, pink-cotton-candy-color mansion overlooking Gunpowder Bay. Once in that wonderful canopied bed, he would make wild, sweet love to her.

EPILOGUE

New York was once more basking in a warm early April. People crowded the streets, glancing at the cloudless blue sky above them and glad to be alive on such a perfect spring day.

Pan had arrived home from the hospital that morning, and though her husband protested, she held court in the living room of their apartment so that she could show off the twins—a boy and a girl—to the family.

"Fine names," the Commodore told Pan gruffly, leaning down to chuck little Felice Henrietta Galen under the chin while his wife held and cooed to Sterling Drexel Galen, whom his father had dubbed Drex "because no child of mine will be a junior."

"Thank you, sir. I'm very happy."

"And so you should be. We all are, especially that son of mine, even though he was like a madman when you were in labor."

Pan chuckled, feeling buoyant and carefree after so many months of feeling unwieldy and elephantlike. "He was very good, Commodore, really he was, even if he did have a tendency to bark orders at everyone, including the doctor."

"Bound to do that," the Commodore rumbled.

"Doesn't think anyone can take care of you except himself." The Commodore inclined his head toward Ladder, who was leaning down so that he could talk baby talk to the infant held by Felice Galen. "I never thought I'd see the day when that man would become a fool."

"Dexter's worse. Silver said he was making faces at the twins through the glass enclosure in the hospital."

"Can't understand what gets into some men." The Commodore leaned over Felice Henrietta. "Is'm Grandpa's biggest girl. Ah, sweetums."

Pan bit back a laugh, looking around the room with a deep sigh. It was so good to be home! She caught her husband's eye and smiled.

Later that night when everyone had gone and they were alone in the king-size bed that was their very own private kingdom, Silver held her, his mouth against her ear. "It was the longest hours of my life when you were in the hospital. I was so lonely for you."

"Me too." Pan sighed, pushing her face into his neck. "I love our new house on the island, but I'll hate to leave the apartment."

"Who says we're leaving it? We'll come in at least once a week and spend the night here alone. How does that sound?"

"Like heaven."

"It has been heaven with you, my Pan, from the very first moment I saw you."

Pan leaned back and put both hands on either side of his face so she could look into his eyes in the light of the moon coming in the window. "For me too. It has been an adventure, a happiness that I never dreamed could exist on this planet. I love you and fear nothing because a man called Silver came into my life. Thank you, my darling man."

"You're welcome, my love. Now close your eyes; I'll hold you while you sleep."